NEED

Books by Todd Gregory

EVERY FRAT BOY WANTS IT

GAMES FRAT BOYS PLAY

NEED

Published by Kensington Publishing Corporation

NEED

TODD GREGORY

KENSINGTON BOOKS
www.kensingtonbooks.com

KENSINGTON BOOKS are published by

Kensington Publishing Corp.
119 West 40th Street
New York, NY 10018

All Kensington titles, imprints, and distributed lines are available at special quantity discounts for bulk purchases for sales promotion, premiums, fund-raising, and educational or institutional use.

Special book excerpts or customized printings can also be created to fit specific needs. For details, write or phone the office of the Kensington Special Sales Manager: Kensington Publishing Corp., 119 West 40th Street, New York, NY 10018. Attn. Special Sales Department. Phone: 1-800-221-2647.

Kensington and the K logo Reg. U.S. Pat. & TM Off.

ISBN-13: 978-0-7582-6715-3
ISBN-10: 0-7582-6715-0

First Kensington Trade Paperback Printing: November 2012
10 9 8 7 6 5 4 3 2 1
Printed in the United States of America

Acknowledgments

I wrote this novel in a number of different locations—not just my beloved New Orleans, but in hotels in places as varied as Nassau, Long Island, and Orlando, Florida; as well as at the homes of dear friends in places like Fort Lauderdale and Pembroke, Massachusetts. Thanks to everyone for their hospitality.

I would be extremely remiss if I didn't thank everyone at Kensington Publishing, but most especially my wonderful editor, John Scognamiglio. John has wanted me to write a vampire novel set in my hometown for years, and now I've finally gone ahead and done it. I hope it isn't too disappointing.

Everyone else at Kensington—copy editor, publicity, cover design, book design, etc.—is the acme of professionalism, and has made every book an absolute pleasure to work on.

Anyone who writes a vampire novel set in New Orleans must pay homage to the two great writers who made the city synonymous with vampires: Anne Rice and Poppy Z. Brite. I'd also like to thank both of them for the hours of reading pleasure they've given me, as well as for being incredibly gracious and kind and giving writers themselves.

I also owe a special debt of gratitude to Todd Perley and his husband, Ben—for letting me set this book in their house, Manderley.

I love and adore my co-workers, who make every day at the office fun rather than drudgery: Josh Fegley, Mark Drake,

Sarah Ramteke, Matt Valletta, Brandon Benson, Alex Leigh, Robin Pearce, and Nick Parr. Still here in the office in spirit are Allison Vertovec, Martin Strickland, Daniella Rivera, Eric Knudsen, Jon Pennycuff, Tanner Menard, and Ked Dixon. Miss you all.

Oh, and my favorite nasty girl, Meghan Davidson. I really miss you, dear heart.

NEED

CHAPTER 1

The damp air was thick with the scent of blood.

It had been days since I had last fed, and the desire was gnawing at my insides. *I've waited too long,* I thought as I looked around Jackson Square for a promising human. A wave of nausea washed over me as the dull ache from inside pushed every other thought from my head. The wave passed, leaving me feeling more than a little weak. *That's not a good sign. I'd better be getting on with it—if I wait any longer, I might not be strong enough,* I thought as my head began to clear. I was sitting on one of the benches between the wrought-iron fence and the massive gray stone of St. Louis Cathedral. I stood up, and my knees almost buckled under my weight.

Definitely not good.

My eyes focused on a young man walking a bicycle past the front of the cathedral. He was talking on a cell phone. His face was animated and flushed beneath the black mustache and goatee. There was a scattering of pimples over his pale face and dark circles beneath his round, bloodshot eyes. He was wearing a black T-shirt that read *Who Dat Say They Gonna Beat Dem Saints* in gold letters. The shirt hung loosely over his slender frame. His ratty old paint-spattered jeans were cut off at the knees and were so big his sharp hip bones barely seemed to be holding them up. There was a tattoo of Tweety Bird on his right calf and one of Marvin the Martian on the left. There was a bleeding sacred heart tattooed on the inside of his right forearm. His hair was dark and dirty-looking, combed to a peak in the center of his head. He seemed extremely agitated as he pushed his bicycle, his agitation seeming to grow with every step he took.

He stopped directly in front of an anemic-looking young woman who was putting her violin into a battered black case. He stopped for a moment, letting out an enormous sigh as the young woman picked up her violin case. She nodded at him and walked away. He turned his head and watched her go, a smirk dancing across his thin lips. He started walking again, talking into his phone.

I could smell his blood. I could almost hear his beating heart.

I could see the pulsing vein in his neck, beckoning me forward.

The sun was setting, and the lights around Jackson Square were starting to come on. The tarot card readers were folding up their tables, ready to disappear into the night. The band playing in front of the cathedral was putting their instruments away. The artists who hung their work on the iron fence around the park were long gone, as were the living statues. The square, teeming with life just a short hour earlier, was emptying of people, and the setting sun was taking the warmth with it as it slowly disappeared in the west. The cold breeze coming from the river ruffled my hair a bit as I watched the young man with the bicycle. He started wheeling the bicycle forward again, still talking on the phone. He reached the concrete ramp leading up to Chartres Street. He stopped just as he reached the street, and I focused my hearing as he became more agitated. *"What do you want me to say? You're just being a bitch, and anything I say you're just going to turn around on me."*

I felt the burning inside.

Desire was turning into need.

I knew it was best to satisfy the desire before it became need. I could feel the knots of pain from deprivation forming behind each of my temples and knew it was almost too late. I shouldn't have let it go this long, but I wanted to test my limits, see how long I could put off the hunger.

The first lesson I'd been taught was to always satiate the hunger while it was still desire, to never *ever* let it become need. It had been drilled into me over and over again, time after time. I'd been taught to feed daily, which would keep the hunger under control and keep me out of danger. Better to take small drinks every day, small drinks that left the donor a little dizzy for just a moment, than to wait and gorge on blood. When desire becomes need, vampires might not be able to stop drinking until the human is nothing more than a bloodless husk.

Need was dangerous. Need led a vampire to take risks he wouldn't take ordinarily. And risks could lead to exposure, to a painful death.

I could hear Jean-Paul, my maker, inside my head. *Why do you always want to take such risks? Why do you insist on always putting us all in danger? Why did I ever turn you?*

I never listened to him. And now I was beginning to regret it as my head swam and the predator inside of me began taking control of my mind.

My insides ached, gnawing at me. All around me I could hear heartbeats pounding, everywhere around me a buffet of blood calling to me.

I had waited too long. I gulped, trying to control the rising beast.

I would follow him and drink as soon as it was safe.

He started walking again, and I began following him, focusing on the curve of his buttocks in his jeans. The T-shirt was a little too short, riding up on his back so I could see the dimples in his lower back just above the swell of his ass. He was more slender than I liked, but it didn't matter since I wasn't going to fuck him. I was just going to pierce his neck for a moment and drink from his veins until the desire faded and I returned to my normal state.

You haven't been normal in over two years, a voice whispered inside my head.

I ignored it as I always did.

He crossed St. Ann Street and continued on his way up Chartres, still talking on the phone, completely oblivious to everything and everyone around him. There weren't many people about on Chartres Street as darkness continued to fall on the Quarter, and the moon rose in the deep purple sky. I felt power surging through my body with each step I took. Darkness is the vampire's friend, making us even more powerful, stronger. My eyes adjusted to the darkness, and everything became sharper, clearer. It had taken me a while to get used to the strength of my night vision and how different things seemed after the sun had vanished. My prey glowed in the night, and I could see the vein in his neck pulsing and pounding. I started walking faster, figuring I could catch up to him and pull him into one of the many shadowed doorways. Anyone passing by would assume we were simply enjoying a public display of affection—and the groans of pleasure he would emit as I drained off some of his blood would give further proof to the lie.

The blood scent was so strong I could almost taste it, the need rising in me again—the painful gnawing inside, the blurring in my mind as the predator struggled to take control. My knees buckled momentarily, and I knew I had to catch him soon—

"Cord?"

I froze, stopped walking.

"My God, it *is* you." A hand grabbed my arm from behind and spun me around. "I—I thought you were *dead*, man."

"Let me go," I growled, the need beginning to push everything else out of my mind. I was dangerously close to losing control.

"No way, man!" My old roommate from Beta Kappa, Jared Holcomb, was smiling at me. His entire face lit up with the smile the way it always had. His thick blond hair was longer than I remembered it being, and his muscles were thicker, stronger. He was wearing a tight pair of low-rise jeans and a tight blue shirt that hugged his torso. "Where have you been? My God . . . I'm so glad to see you!"

Always feed before the desire becomes need, Jean-Paul lectured inside my head again. *When it becomes need, you cannot control yourself and you will take risks you usually wouldn't. You put yourself at risk. You put all of us at risk. Is that what you want? You want us all hunted down and killed? Will that make you happy, Cord?*

His voice faded and all of my conscious thought became consumed with the need.

It was too late.

The guy with the bicycle was completely forgotten.

Jared's vein beckoned me forward. I could smell his blood, rich with iron and protein.

And I lost what little control was left.

I grabbed Jared with both hands and pulled him into an unlit doorway, wrapping my arms around him and pressing my body up against his. He made a shocked noise as he slammed back up against the door. He squirmed a bit before I sank my teeth into his neck and started drinking.

He stopped resisting, and his body melted against mine.

I could feel my cock hardening. I could feel his own hardening against mine as he began to moan as the delicious warm blood filled my mouth from the little wounds I'd made, as his precious life force entered my body. It was delicious, so satisfying, and I wanted to drink forever from him, I didn't want to stop until—

But as the need was quenched, I knew I needed to stop.

I'd have to find someone else later, drink a little more, but I didn't want to leave him unconscious in the doorway. The last thing I needed was for him to wind up in an emergency room somewhere.

I pulled my head back, wiping at my mouth, gasping.

Jared remained leaning against the door, his breath coming in shallow gulps. His eyes were half closed, and blood was dribbling down his neck from the holes I'd left in his throat. I took a few steps back and checked the street. There was no one nearby, no one closer than Jackson Square a half block away.

"Fuck," I muttered under my breath. I'd gotten lucky. I shook my head, furious at myself. What if he hadn't been alone? What if someone had come walking along at just the right moment or a police car had come around the corner at St. Ann just as I grabbed him?

When desire becomes need, a vampire forgets everything but the blood. He makes mistakes, takes risks he shouldn't—and frequently gets caught. It must never become need, else you risk everything. Most vampires are caught—and killed—when they've gone too long without feeding. Don't let that happen to you.

I must have been crazy to let it go so long—especially when there were always people about in the Quarter to feed on. What had I been thinking?

You weren't thinking; that's the problem, I scolded myself.

Seeing how long you could go? That's madness, and a one-way ticket to death.

I shook my head again and pricked my right index finger with one of my teeth, then rubbed my blood over the two little holes to heal them the way Jean-Paul had shown me.

The holes didn't close the way they usually did.

Nothing at all happened.

I stared at the wounds. It couldn't be. They *always* healed.

What had I done wrong?

I could feel the panic rising in me as I rubbed more of my blood over the punctures. I heard myself muttering, "Come on, come on, come on," over and over again, but the wounds weren't healing the way they were supposed to, the way they always did. Instead, Jared's blood continued to seep slowly out through them, dribbling down his neck and staining his shirt. The pale blue was turning dark just below the collar, where the running blood came into contact with the tightly fitting cotton. His nipples were erect, and all of his weight rested against the wall. He looked like he was about to fall over, like he couldn't walk and his legs wouldn't support his weight.

I didn't drink that much, I thought, smiling sheepishly at an elderly couple as they walked past us. I shrugged. "My friend's had a little too much," I said apologetically. Their eyes narrowed and they looked away in disgust as they walked a little faster.

Jared opened his eyes a little wider, but they were still half closed. Other than the bleeding neck, he looked like so many other young college boys who drank more than they should in the Quarter. His eyes weren't focused and looked a little too cloudy to me. "What"—he swallowed, his throat working, the Adam's apple bobbing up and down—"wha...happened? Cord? I feel...I feel funny."

I couldn't just leave him there, with his neck bleeding and his shirt getting darker with wetness every passing second. Something was wrong, something was seriously wrong, and I had to get away as quickly as I could—but I couldn't just leave him there.

Modern society might not believe in vampires, but when the police found him—and he would most certainly wind up in the hands of the police—they wouldn't believe for a minute that he'd been attacked by a vampire, but those wounds in his neck? How would they explain them?

I couldn't take the risk he would remember seeing me and mention me to the cops.

And since Cord Logan had died in a fire two years earlier on Lundi Gras, that was a can of worms best left unopened.

I put his left arm around my shoulders and placed his head down on my neck. At least the wounds were hidden that way, and in the growing darkness maybe no one would notice the bloody shirt. "Come on, buddy, you need to walk with me," I whispered to him. "We've got to get you out of here. Can you walk?"

His head tilted back for a moment and his face lit up with a crazy grin. His eyes were still a little glassy, but he just looked drunk, thank the heavens. "Cord, buddy." His voice sounded raspy. "I knew you weren't dead. I tole them all you weren't dead." He shook his head, which seemed almost a little too heavy for his neck. "I tole them I'd know if you were dead, buddy, and no one believed me." He sounded aggrieved, and for a brief moment I felt tears swimming in my eyes.

He'd been like a brother to me, in so many ways.

I wiped at the wetness in my eyes. "Come on, it's just a couple of blocks." I smiled into his eyes, willing him to start walking. "Use me for support if you can't stand up, okay? It'll be like that mixer with the Kappas, remember?"

"Okay, buddy," he replied, and laughed. "Stupid Kappa *bitches*."

A wave of emotion washed over me. That was what he'd always called them, and for a brief moment I remembered the days we'd shared a room at the Beta Kappa house at Ole Miss. The laughs we shared together, the joy in friendship and the bond of brotherhood, and the innocence of two boys growing from teenagers into men together.

It seemed like a million years ago.

I took a deep breath and started walking him along the sidewalk. Most of his two hundred or so pounds rested on me. Had I still been just a mortal, there was no way I could have supported him, and we both would have fallen to the ground. But I was no longer mortal, and while I had not matured into my full strength as a vampire—Jean-Paul said it would take another fifty or so mortal years for that to happen—I was a lot stronger than the twenty-year-old college student I'd been when I'd been turned. We shuffled our way through Jackson Square and past the Presbytere. No one was really paying any attention to us. It was an all too common sight in the French Quarter—Jared looked like every other young man who'd had too much to drink and needed to be helped back to his hotel. We turned and headed down the narrow alley between the Presbytere and the cathedral. The alley was empty and silent other than our footsteps against the stone. Even though I was stronger, I was still having trouble drawing breath by the time we reached Royal Street. We headed up Orleans, past the crowds on Bourbon and the dancing hand grenade in front of Tropical Isle, and before I knew it, I was helping him up the steps of Jean-Paul's house between Dauphine and Burgundy Streets. I put the key in the lock and helped him into the house, setting him down on the couch in the double parlor just inside the front door.

As I turned to shut and lock the door, I stared at the ruins of the little Creole cottage directly across the street. It was still in the process of being rebuilt after the fire. It was there that Jean-Paul had rescued me from the witch Sebastian and brought my dying body back across the street to this house. It was on that very couch where Jared now lay that Jean-Paul had opened the vein in his arm and had me drink his blood, the blood that finished transforming me into the creature I am now, something no longer quite human. I shut the door and drew the curtains shut with a shiver, flipping the light switch. The overhead chandelier came to life, casting strange shadows into every corner of the enormous room.

I knelt beside Jared. His eyes were now fully closed and his breathing was shallow and labored. His skin felt cold, looked slightly bluish, and I pressed my fingers against his wrist. His heart was beating, but not strongly. The wounds on his neck had stopped bleeding yet still were open and angry. I put my hand to my mouth in order to open another wound in a finger, but stopped.

Think about it, Cord. You must be doing something wrong. You've done this before a thousand times and it always, always works. What's different about this time?

But no matter how much I thought about it, as hard as I tried to remember, there was simply nothing else I could remember doing differently that I wasn't doing now. It was very simple, really—you merely opened a wound and rubbed some of your blood over the mortal's wounds. Within seconds, those wounds would close just as your own would.

I shook my head and punctured my thumb.

I pressed my thumb over his wounds, rubbed gently, and pulled my thumb away. Even as the wound in my thumb closed, the wounds in Jared's neck remained clearly visible.

I took a deep breath and tried not to panic.

Jared opened his eyes again and smiled weakly. "Cord, buddy. I knew you weren't dead." He reached with a cool hand and touched the side of my face. "I just knew. Everyone said you were dead—they had a funeral and everything—but I knew." His face clouded with confusion. "But how... I don't understand..."

"Shhhh," I whispered, pressing my index finger against his cold lips. My mind was racing as I tried to figure out what to do.

This was precisely why Jean-Paul had forbidden me to return to New Orleans. He was right again, as usual. *Yes, I know you're not from there, but you do know people who are, and they all think you're dead. You cannot risk going back there. What are you going to do if one of them sees you? How are you going to explain being alive? There is no explanation, Cord, and you will have to kill them.*

And even though Jared had been one of my best friends, one of my fraternity brothers, I knew if Jean-Paul knew what was happening here, he would order me to kill Jared without a second thought. Kill him, and make sure the body was never found.

If you don't kill him, you risk exposing yourself. And everyone else in the vampire world—is that what you want, Cord? To prove to them that vampires DO exist? They would hunt us all down and kill us. It's either him or us, Cord. You know what you have to do... and don't worry. People disappear in New Orleans all the time.

"I feel funny," Jared said, shifting around on the couch. His eyes opened even farther. They weren't as glassy and unfocused as they had been earlier; that at least was a step in the right direction.

Maybe he would recover normally.

I placed my fingers back on his wrist. His pulse felt stronger.

The wounds on his neck were scabbing over.

Well, that's better—scabbing over means they are healing, but it's still not normal. My blood should have healed the damned things! What's wrong? Maybe Jared somehow is different than other humans?

But that doesn't make any sense. Humans are humans; their blood types might be different, but ultimately they are all the same. Vampiric blood could heal them, in small doses, without converting them. It has always been this way, and surely Jean-Paul would have told me there were some humans whose bodies reacted differently than the rest of them.

Or he knew and just didn't tell me for some reason. But why wouldn't he? It didn't make sense. But none of this made sense.

"Kiss me," Jared whispered, smiling at me. His eyes glittered in the light from the chandelier.

"What?" I stared at him. "You can't be serious." My heart began beating faster, in spite of myself.

"I want you," he whispered. His smile grew wider, his white, perfectly straight teeth glistening. "I've always wanted you, Cord. Always. You never noticed, but I always did."

I gulped. In the three years at Ole Miss I'd known Jared, I'd never once gotten the slightest inkling he was gay, or even the slightest bit curious. We'd pledged together, shared a room at the house, and become as close as brothers. Almost from the moment we met during Rush Week, we clicked. Our personalities just seemed to mesh together. He was like the brother I'd never had. There wasn't anything I couldn't tell him, and vice versa. Jared had confided in me about everything, from his darkest desires to his biggest fears. Jared was the only person in the house I'd come out to—and he'd been supportive, even going with me to Memphis to a gay bar. It had been Jared's idea to stay with his parents for Mardi Gras, and his idea to help me break away from the other fraternity brothers who'd also come down so I could go to the gay bars and, in his words, "get my gay on."

Obviously, neither of us had any way of knowing the trip would result in my becoming a vampire—well, Jared just thought I'd been killed, burned to death in the fire.

I'd always been attracted to Jared but never considered acting on it—no matter how drunk or high either one of us might have been. He was one of the most beautiful boys I'd ever met in my life.

And in the two years since I'd seen him, he'd somehow managed to become even sexier than he had been.

And it was very tempting. How many times had I fantasized this very moment? How many times had I jacked off, imagining how it would feel to press my lips against his, to run my hands down his chest, or how his cock would taste in my mouth? He was beautiful; he always had been. The first time I'd seen him at fraternity rush I'd wanted him. All of my high school crushes were forgotten the moment I laid eyes on Jared, with his lean muscles and hard bubble butt. I used to watch him sleep in our room—he always slept on his stomach with that phenomenal ass up, so perfectly formed under the white cotton underwear he always wore. Sometimes it rode up a bit, revealing the smooth white skin with almost invisible golden hairs. He also had never had a problem with walking around in front of me in just his under-wear or even nude. I'd always appreciated that fearlessness, that degree of comfort with me and my sexuality. Sometimes I wondered if he wanted me to try something, if he wanted me to make the first move, if the comfort I so appreciated was, in truth, an invitation.

But I'd never touched him, never tried anything at all—no matter how much I wanted to. Because I couldn't be sure, and the last thing I wanted was to offend him. He was the only friend I trusted with my truth—and I wasn't willing to throw that away on the slight chance he'd welcome an overture from me.

"Jared—"

"I mean it." He licked his lips. "I was too much of a coward to ever do anything before, Cord. I've always wanted you. That time we went to the bar in Memphis . . . I wanted to kiss you that night. It broke my heart when you died, Cord. And now you're alive. I'm not going to miss this chance. I've been sorry ever since you died that I never had the courage to do anything with you." He smiled again. "But now you aren't dead." He reached out and touched my hair. "Somehow, I knew you weren't. I knew that wasn't you in that house. I knew it. I knew I'd know if you were really dead."

Tears filled my eyes. Oh, how I'd longed to hear those words from him! How I'd longed to kiss him, to put my arms around him, to put my mouth on his cock, to let him fill me up with his. But this didn't feel right; it was wrong, like somehow my biting him and sucking his blood had done this to him—was making him think and react in a way that wasn't natural to him.

But his wounds hadn't healed, either. That wasn't natural, either.

He reached up and kissed me.

It felt like an electrical current ran through my body.

Not even kissing Jean-Paul had felt like this.

I felt my cock growing hard inside my jeans, and as Jared's tongue slipped in between my lips and inside my mouth, I could see he was getting hard, too. I reached down and caressed the thick hardness beneath the denim, and he moaned, never removing his tongue from inside my mouth. He began stroking my chest with his hands, pulling and tweaking at my erect and sensitive nipples, and I pushed him back down on the couch, climbing on top of him, our hips beginning to move back and forth as we ground our crotches against each other.

I pulled my mouth away from his lips. He smiled up at me. "I love you, Cord," he breathed. "I always have."

Jean-Paul never said that to me. Not once, no matter how badly I wanted him to.

I wanted to believe him.

I wanted him more than I ever had before. Yet, despite the animalistic need driving me, threatening to take control of my mind and body, I couldn't shake the feeling that something was wrong. This somehow wasn't right, and there was still time to stop this before it went any further—

His hands came up, caressing my hardness through my pants, and pleasure shot through my body. His touch was gentle and sensual, and my rising desire pushed all other thoughts out of my mind.

I reached down and undid my pants, freeing my cock. He smiled up at me and licked his thumb. He started running it over the head of my cock.

"Ooooooh," I moaned. It felt incredible.

I pushed my pants down as he kept rubbing away. Unable to stand it anymore, I grabbed the front of his pants and pulled, the riveted buttons holding his fly closed popping and flying away. I got to my knees and yanked his pants down, freeing his long, beautiful cock. As I yanked, I heard the denim tearing and once they were free, I tossed them aside like the torn rags they now were. I reached for the bottle of lube that was always sitting on the side table, and squirted some onto his erection.

"I want to be inside you," he breathed as I mounted him, spreading my butt cheeks and lowering myself on top of his cock.

The pressure against my anus was sharp and painful; then my muscles relaxed and I slid down, feeling his urgency filling me. I gasped and moaned as I continued to slide, settling down onto him when I felt his thick balls pressing against my cheeks.

His entire body began to tremble, his eyes closing partway as I started moving up and down. He tried to push up into me as I went upward, but I held his hips down with my hands. He struggled against my strength at first, to no avail. I was much stronger than he—he had no idea of how strong, nor did I want him to find out. I was still not completely used to how much power my muscles now contained, and I was afraid if we started struggling, I might accidentally hurt him.

"Your ass is amazing," he whispered, tugging on my nipples and sending even more electricity through my body. "It feels so good—please don't stop."

I smiled. The pleasure was so intense I couldn't stop even if I'd wanted to. I reached down and stroked his chest, and his entire body convulsed, bucking upward. The thrusts were strong, intense, and it felt as though I were being split in two.

I cried out, my head going back as he continued driving up into me. My entire mind was being consumed with the pleasure from his cock, which felt as though it were burning inside of me. No one had ever fucked me this way, not Jean-Paul, not any of the others in our little fraternity of vampires. The passion, the power—my eyes began to lose focus, and everything in front of me seemed to be seared with white, and I was vaguely aware that he was forcing me backward, never stopping with the thrusting, not once relenting, and the pleasure, my God, the pleasure, and I was on my back and he was on top of me, and in the mirror behind him I could see his powerful back, the fleur-de-lis tattoo on his right shoulder blade, his beautiful round white ass clenching and unclenching as he drove into me, as though he were trying to get his cock so deep inside me it might never come out, and I wanted him inside me, I wanted to feel his entire body consumed inside of mine, and I wanted the thrusting and driving to never stop. . . .

And his lips were at my own throat, moving from the base of my chin to the hollow where my neck met my chest, his tongue darting out and dancing against my skin.

And it went on, the pleasure building inside of me until I could barely stand it any longer—

And his head went back and he screamed as his body went rigid, and I could feel him squirting inside of me, his body convulsing and racking with the pleasure with each spurt—

And my own splashed out of me, raining onto my chest and my face and into my hair.

He convulsed a few more times before collapsing on top of me, his energy spent.

I lay there panting for a moment or two, enjoying his weight and warmth on top of me.

His breathing became more shallow and even, and I gently pushed him aside, feeling his softening penis slide out of me. I slid out from underneath him and gently rolled him over onto his back, staring at his beauty as he lay there in the soft glow of moonlight coming through the stained glass just above the front door of the house.

The wounds on his neck had reopened, and blood was oozing from them again.

I grabbed a towel and wiped myself off, then bit the tip of my index finger. I rubbed it over the wounds, but once again, the wounds in his neck did not close.

But the hole in my finger did.

I don't understand. It has always worked. What is wrong? What is so different about this time that the wounds will not close?

He started murmuring in his sleep, tossing a bit on the couch.

I walked over to the front windows and opened the red velvet curtains a bit, looking at the house across the street—the house where I'd almost died, a victim of the desires of the mixed race witch, Sebastian, and his thirst to combine the power of the vampire with that of his own witchcraft. I closed my eyes and remembered being tied to the bed while Sebastian violated my body and went through the mysterious ritual I had not understood until Jean-Paul and the others had come to my rescue. I remembered the feeling of dying, of my body going cold as Jean-Paul wrapped me in a blanket and carried me out of the house and back across the street, and the metallic taste of his blood as he fed me in order to save me.

I tried to remember if my own initial wounds from him had closed that first night he had fed from me, that night when I'd run into him and his friends at Oz while the madness of Carnival raged in the streets of the French Quarter.

Perhaps I'd taken too much from him. Maybe that was why the wounds wouldn't heal. Jean-Paul and the others always warned me about taking too much—but they never said why.

I started to turn away from the window when something flickered in one of the windows across the street. I spun my head back, but whatever it had been was no longer there.

Now you're imagining things. There's no one there. The house isn't habitable yet.

Jared moaned in his sleep, and I walked back over to the couch. I knelt beside him and marveled again at just how beautiful he was.

I had never let him know about my secret desire for him. Never, and I had always been so careful around him. And he'd always, *always*, been very clear about his own sexuality. If he'd even been the slightest bit curious, he would have told me. And there were any number of times we'd been wasted together, stumbling back to the room together with our arms around each other, and nothing had happened.

Then why did he . . . It doesn't make any sense. Was a connection of some sort forged between us when I took his blood? His life force? There's so much I still don't know about all of this. Jean-Paul was right—I should have stayed in Palm Springs with him and the others.

I reached over and stroked his brow. He shifted again, and his eyes opened. I recoiled—they were no longer blue, but rather brown.

He smiled at me. "Sebastian does not rest, Cord."

My hand froze on his forehead. "You don't know that, Jared. You couldn't possibly know that." *How does he even know about Sebastian in the first place? And what is wrong with his eyes?*

His eyes closed and he moaned. When they reopened, they were clearly blue. I must have imagined what I'd seen. Besides, it didn't make any sense. Eyes couldn't change color like that, could they?

"I don't feel so good," he barely whispered as I started stroking his forehead again. "What . . . what have you done to me, Cord?" He shifted again on the couch. "So cold, so very, very cold."

I allowed my other hand to come up and press on the jugular vein in his throat. The heartbeat was weak and faint.

I've killed him.

I felt tears rising in my eyes.

I raised my wrist to my mouth and bit into the artery there. As my blood began to flow over my skin, I lowered my wrist to his mouth.

I heard Jean-Paul's voice in my head. *You are too young to this life to create another such as ourselves. Your heart isn't strong enough yet, so you must never ever try to turn a human until such time as I tell you that you can.*

But he would die unless . . .

"Drink," I whispered, parting his lips and allowing my blood to run onto his tongue.

Jared's eyes opened at the first taste of my blood, and color began to return to his cheeks. He closed his mouth around the holes in my wrist and began to suckle.

I closed my eyes and allowed my head to fall backward.

Whatever the risks, I had to take them.

CHAPTER 2

I gasped in pleasure as his lips closed even more tightly over my wrist.

At first, there was simply a little bit of suction against my skin that made the hair on my arms stand up. It felt like nothing more than a simple kiss, Jared's lips pressing against the inside of my wrist as foreplay. He was hesitant at first, but when my blood began to flow, it awakened a need inside him—a need I knew all too well, the desire to consume as much as he possibly could, to drown in it. His eyes closed and a low growling moan vibrated in his throat as his mouth worked. His tongue lapped against my skin, teasing me, and I closed my own eyes as the intensity of an extraordinary pleasure washed over me from head to toe. Every nerve ending in my body tingled, goose bumps covering every inch of my skin as my cock began stirring to life again. My nipples were hard and sensitive.

I lost myself in the pleasure.

This pleasure was even more seductive than feeding from the warm neck of a beautiful young man.

I had no memory of Jean-Paul feeding from me during that Mardi Gras. It seemed so long ago, but it had been only a couple of years. A little more than two years since I ceased to be human, since I walked away from my life, my family, and my closet. There had been many pleasures in the time since—but nothing like this. This was addictive, dangerous.

No wonder humans stopped resisting when we began to feed from them.

If this was how it felt to have someone drink from you, it was a wonder they didn't line up to feed us.

It also was a wonder there weren't more vampires walking the planet.

Another wave of ecstasy radiated from my self-inflicted wounds as his mouth began working on me, the heat spreading up my arm to my shoulder and into my brain. It felt like I was catching on fire. The burning sensation traveled through my body with each breath I took—and the air itself seemed intoxicating. A ball of fire moved up and down, back and forth through my body. A thousand little pins and needles were piercing my flesh, and I heard myself gasping, gulping in more air that seemed somehow thicker, richer, taking me higher than I'd ever felt before.

I went up onto my toes as each beat of my heart pumped another spurt of my dark blood into his mouth, and I felt his tongue licking at my skin so he wouldn't miss a drop of it, as it nurtured him, changed him, turned him from what he once was into what he was going to be, into what I was. I tried to resist the pleasure, to remain in control of my mind, heart, and body—but it was too much for me. I wasn't strong enough, physically or mentally, and I doubted anyone would have been. I was experiencing pleasure in its purest form, an animalistic pleasure that spoke to my atavistic core, until I finally surrendered to its insistent demand for obedience. There was no way I could resist, no way I could stop even had I wanted to.

So I stopped resisting the pleasure, the sheer joy of how

it felt to have him feeding from me, drinking from my veins, and allowed it to take me, consume me, and I heard the moan come from deep inside me and explode out through my mouth.

I brought my free hand up to touch my hard nipple and an electrical current went through me. My body shook, convulsed, and trembled. I couldn't catch my breath and simply gasped air.

I felt like we were connecting in some primal, instinctual way that felt so right, like our souls were mating and coming together, like I was becoming him and he was becoming me, and together we were becoming something else completely.

But even though my mind was so deeply lost in animalistic pleasure, there was still a sense that there was something important that I couldn't grasp, something I'd missed earlier, but before I could try to focus, the pleasure electrified me again. My entire body went stiff as his mouth's grip on my wrist somehow became even tighter, and I gave in to it again, let myself go, and hoped that I would remember when it was over.

The only thing that mattered now was the pleasure.

My other hand brushed against his forehead, which was hot and damp with sweat. I opened my eyes and saw the rivulets of sweat pouring down the side of his face. His hair was wet and slick, and his eyes also opened, locking on mine, and I almost lost myself in the beautiful deep blue of his eyes.

It was like drowning.

I love you so much, Cord. Thank you for this. We'll be together forever, always together, just the two of us, and I will love you forever.

And again a thought danced through my head—*this is wrong*—but it was gone in an instant as he brought one of his strong hands up to my crotch, his thumb teasing the head of my cock, until a drop of precum leaked out, and he kept rubbing his thumb over it, toying with the slit, and I didn't want him to ever stop.

Ever.

I wanted to feel this ecstasy forever.

Our shadows danced across the ceiling as my eyes half closed. The light of the chandelier flickered briefly, as though there was some kind of power surge. I moaned again, an involuntary sound of pleasure as my head went back and my blurred vision tried to focus on the ceiling.

I could feel my cock getting even larger as my blood pumped into it, growing long and hard and strong with every beat of my heart, an urgent need for release radiating from my balls, which were beginning to ache.

And still his thumb rubbed over the head.

I almost whimpered.

I'd never felt such pleasure before. I'd never felt anything like this before. This was better than getting fucked, getting my cock sucked, or fucking someone. My years with Jean-Paul and his fraternity had taught me sexual delights I'd never dreamed possible, even in my wildest dreams and fantasies back when I was in my fraternity closet back at Ole Miss looking at gay porn on my laptop late at night in my room. They taught me positions and activities that made my eyes roll back into my head and forced animalistic howls to escape from my throat as they drove me nearly insane with the unimaginable pleasures they'd spent centuries seeking out, learning, and perfecting. Almost every night it had been something new as they initiated me into the world of vampiric desire and pleasure, each night instructing me in a carnal knowledge that left me spent and exhausted and panting on the bed or the floor or the mat or hanging from whatever device I'd been attached to.

But all of those nights combined were nothing compared to how this felt.

I wanted Jared to keep sucking my blood forever and to never, ever be sated. I wanted his need for my blood to be as powerful as my need for him to take it from me. I wanted him to never remove his mouth from my arm—to always be there on his knees before me in supplication, need, and desire, as my blood changed his into something else, transformed his beautiful body, turned him from being merely human into something ever so much more than he ever dreamed possible.

I felt like I was transforming from a vampire into a god, because I was feeling the joy of creation.

This must be what God had felt like when he created life, the universe, the planets, the sun and the moon and paradise, the animals and birds and trees and plants. How had God stopped, if the story I'd been taught from childhood, had been drilled into my head, was in fact the truth?

If this was creation, the rush God must have felt on each of those six days must have made him drunk.

No wonder he'd rested on the seventh day, collapsing onto his couch, spent and exhausted and panting from the exquisite pleasure and pain of creation.

Had it been like this for Jean-Paul when he created me, when he took me from my old human life and made me what I am now?

Dear God.

There was no drug or intoxicant that compared to this.

During my years with Jean-Paul, I had tried everything he'd given to me—Ecstasy, cocaine, marijuana, crystal meth—stimulants whose addictive properties we vampires were immune to, but these drugs still altered our states of consciousness. Jean-Paul claimed we felt them even more intensely than humans could, as we experienced everything with a much higher degree of intensity than they did—which made me pity them all the more. Wasn't it sad enough their bodies aged, withered, and died, but they couldn't even experience pleasure as intensely as a vampire?

It hardly seemed fair. . . .

Ecstasy was my favorite of them all, of course—the joy of warmth glowing from within, of feeling beautiful and wanting to touch and be touched, of feeling music wash over my body and get inside my very soul until I was one with the beat, with the lyrics, with the emotion, of dancing in a crowd of incredibly beautiful men until the sun came up, of feeling like the night could, should, would, last forever.

But this . . . this was *better* than Ecstasy.

This was a pleasure I would never tire of, a pleasure I wanted to go on forever.

This pleasure was seductive, addictive.

Both of his strong hands came up, grabbing hold of my arm so tightly he almost pulled me down on top of him. I closed my eyes and somehow regained my balance as yet another shudder of joy wracked through my body and my brain—pushing every thought out of my head other than how incredibly magnificent his lips felt against my skin, and I could hear the thundering beat of my heart.

I could feel pressure building inside of my balls.

I started bouncing up onto my toes.

I opened my eyes as my breath started coming in gasps.

I opened my mouth to say *I love you*, but I couldn't get the words out around my panting breaths.

I smiled hesitantly down at him, and our eyes met.

What I saw in his eyes in that moment sent a chill through me.

His eyes were *different*.

Jared had always had dark blue eyes—but the eyes that

were looking up at me, full of lust and desire, were brown with golden flecks.

I hadn't imagined it that first time.

What the hell?

I'd seen eyes like that before—

Sebastian.

But he was *dead.* . . .

Another wave of pleasure pushed everything out of my mind.

He'd said Sebastian was still alive.

But that wasn't possible.

My mind flashed back to that horrible night.

I was tied to the bed, completely helpless and at the mercy of a crazy man, a man who was not just a man but was also a witch and was working a powerful spell on me, a spell with an evil purpose. He was a beautiful man, such a beautiful man . . . and then Sebastian began sucking my cock—remember? Remember how that felt? I remembered the feeling of another consciousness inside of my head, filling my thoughts, almost as though determined to take over my mind and my body while Sebastian worked his magic on me. I was helpless and at his mercy; there was nothing I could do. I was tied, spread-eagle, each wrist and ankle to a different post of the bed, and I called for help, and help finally came before it was too late, before Sebastian could drain my body of its blood entirely, the blood that was already starting to change from whatever it was that Jean-Paul had done to me the previous night. Sebastian was going to kill me and drink my blood. Jean-Paul had taken some of my blood, but he'd given me his vampire blood to drink in return, and that had started to change me. All day long the sun had bothered my skin and hurt my eyes, and a connection had been forged between our minds, and it was that connection—the connection of our commingled blood—that allowed us to communicate in our minds together. Sebastian wanted to combine the power of a witch with that of a vampire and it could not be allowed . . . so all of them, the entire fraternity of vampires headed by Jean-Paul, they came to my rescue and murdered Sebastian, burned the house down with his body and that of another inside, gave out the story that I'd somehow died in the fire—I don't know how they worked the dental records and so forth; all I knew was there was another corpse in the house with Sebastian's and it was positively identified as me and I was dead—free to live my life as a vampire, free to escape from my old life and begin anew.

I opened my eyes with a start.

There was that feeling again, inside of my mind.

Someone—some *thing*—was trying to get inside of me.

And it wasn't Jean-Paul this time. I knew how Jean-Paul felt, recognized the feeling when his mind entered mine. We'd connected many times over the past few years—and it was a comforting feeling when his mind joined with mine, whether it was across a crowded dance floor while music blared from speakers or on an airplane as we traveled to yet another of the endless circuit parties we always seemed to be going to.

This was someone else—and despite the pleasure still radiating from where his lips were locked onto my wrist, the heat was burning out and turning cold.

I looked down into Jared's eyes—the eyes that weren't Jared's. The corners of his lips curved up into a smile even as he maintained their pressure on my wrist. One of his hands let go of me, sliding down and closing again around my hard cock. He began stroking me slowly, his hand moving back and forth slowly, and my eyes closed again.

How does he know to do that?

The thought flashed through the pleasure before disappearing into the ecstasy.

There's a lot about me you don't know, Cord.

He was ... he was *inside* my head.

But the voice . . . it didn't sound like Jared's.

And the thought that had danced in and out of my head came rushing back.

Whenever you feed from a human, you see into their mind. But when I'd fed from Jared, his mind had been closed to mine.

That was what was wrong.

And perhaps that was why the wounds wouldn't heal.

Something was *wrong* with Jared.

How does he know how to pleasure another man? He's a straight boy.

You weren't so concerned about that when I was fucking your ass, Cord. You didn't give a shit that I was straight as long as your tight hole was riding my big cock. Isn't that right? So now you care? I bet if my big thick cock was pounding your tight little ass, you wouldn't care anymore, right? Why question it? Why not just enjoy the ride, little vampire?

I forced my eyes open and looked down at him again.

His eyes were now closed, the sucking becoming even more urgent as I noticed his own erection, a clear drop of liquid glistening at the slit. He was moaning, a deep guttural sound from deep within himself.

I could hear Jean-Paul's voice: *The conversion doesn't change the basic core of who you are as a person; becoming a vampire will not make a good person evil, nor an evil person good. Vampiric blood brings with it great power—power that many humans could not handle. Have you heard that power corrupts and that absolute power corrupts absolutely? Many have allowed the new power to corrupt their soul, turn them into something evil—but the seed was there all along. Likewise, I was a lover of men when I was human, with no interest in women. Over the centuries, I have taken women as lovers—but that was more from boredom, a need for something different. And yes, there are male vampires who were repulsed by the thought of loving another male when they were human who, out of ennui or curiosity, have taken male lovers. But the blood itself will not make someone change something so basic as their sexual orientation.*

I bit my lower lip and pushed Jared away from my wrist. His eyes opened as he fell backward against the couch.

They were blue again.

Had I imagined the whole thing?

It was possible. The ecstasy—

I felt dizzy. He had taken too much of my blood; the pleasure had distracted me. I was too drained. I felt weak . . . my mind . . .

He smiled up at me, my blood smeared all over his lips, his chin, his teeth reddened with it. He tilted his head to one side as he wiped the blood from his chin with his right hand before licking it off. There was something almost predatory in the smile, in his eyes as he kept looking at me. "I want more," he purred, getting to his feet. His erection slapped against his stomach. He put his left hand on it. "I want more of your blood, Cord." He took a step toward me. "I want to fuck you some more. I want—"

I shook my head and took another step backward. The red holes in his neck looked even angrier than before. "You need to rest, Jared," I managed to say, relieved that somehow my voice didn't quiver or break. I folded my arms. The wounds in my wrist were closing. I licked the smeared blood from my forearm; when I looked again, my wounds had completely healed.

So why won't the holes in Jared's neck heal? Even now that he has ingested my blood? What the hell is wrong?

"I want—"

"No," I cut him off firmly. "You drank my blood, Jared. You don't know what that means, what that's going to do to you. Trust me, you need to rest."

"I didn't ask for it." He smirked at me as he sat down on

the divan, leaning back against the arm. The muscles in his torso flexed as he shifted, and I noticed that his tan skin was getting lighter. The blue veins that had crisscrossed his muscles were even more prominent than they had been. He was changing before my eyes.

And I didn't know how to handle any of it.

I'd made a terrible mistake.

A horrible mistake—and it was too late to fix it.

Other than killing him, there was nothing else I could think of to do.

What had I done?

"Why don't you lie down in here?" I somehow managed to keep my voice level as I walked across the room to the big double pockets doors. I pulled them open, revealing the small guest bedroom. I turned and smiled at him. "This bed is much more comfortable than that couch."

"I am rather tired," he said, masking a yawn with his hand. He stood up and stretched, the muscles in his stomach rippling as he raised his arms over his head and arched his back slightly. "I think I will sleep for a bit." He went through the doorway, sitting on the edge of the double bed. "Are you sure you don't want to lie down with me?" He patted the mattress next to him, his right eye closing in a wink. In the moonlight coming through the window, his body looked like carved marble. He pouted as he slowly reclined until his naked form was stretched out completely. "Please?" He placed his hands behind his head, his latissimus muscles flaring out and turning his armpits into deep, hairy craters.

"I'm not tired," I replied, trying to keep my eyes on his. I didn't trust myself to look at his body—the temptation might be too much for me. "You go ahead and get some rest. I'll join you in a little while, I promise." I stepped closer to him and kissed his cheek. His skin felt cold against my lips.

He closed his eyes, and within moments his breathing became even. His mouth fell open, and he snored. Inside his mouth, I could see that his canine teeth were longer, more pointed.

The conversion was already starting.

I stepped over the threshold back into the living room and slid the doors closed behind me. I closed my eyes and leaned back against the door. Scooter, the striped orange cat I'd adopted since my arrival in New Orleans, wound around my legs and howled at me.

What have I done?

I couldn't remember my own conversion and had never witnessed another one. I had no idea what to expect, or if something was required of me.

Calm down.

Needing some fresh air, I walked through the big double parlor and kitchen to the French doors leading to the back gallery. I stepped out into the cool air of early evening, drinking in the smell of the night jasmine and bougainvillea, which covered the fence separating the property next door from the back courtyard. I took some deep breaths and sat down at the small wrought-iron table on the mossy paving stones, then looked up at the sky. It was covered with fast-moving clouds, stained pink as they reflected the garish neon lights of the French Quarter back down at me.

Again, I heard Jean-Paul's voice in my head: *You're such a foolish boy, aren't you? You think you know everything there is to know, don't you? Then go, and go with my blessing. I'm tired of arguing with you! You make me feel every day of my years, so go, leave us—but when you get yourself into trouble, don't come crying for my help. Do you understand me? Because you won't get it—I am through with you. Through.*

Jean-Paul simply hadn't understood me, wasn't even interested in trying to, for that matter, and that was the bottom line, why I had to leave him and the others.

He'd been either unwilling or unable to recognize the truth that was staring him in the face, for reasons of his own.

I'd loved him, but he hadn't loved me back.

He cared for me, yes, but he didn't love me.

Once I finally recognized that, I couldn't stay with him any longer.

After that Mardi Gras when he'd converted me, we'd left for Miami—all of us. Cord Logan died in that fire, and it was in Miami I got my new identity—driver's license, birth certificate, passport, Social Security number, credit cards, and a bank account.

Cord Logan was dead and buried.

And it was Cord Forrest's time to live.

I didn't miss the old me in the least—the fraternity boy from Alabama who was afraid of who he was, who he was meant to be. The boy expected to go back to Fayette County with a teaching degree, get married, and live in the rural area, go to services at White's Chapel and raise his children to be devout members of the Church of Christ. My parents had already picked out the place where my house would be built, just down the blacktop county road from theirs, in the midst of what had been a cow pasture when my father was a child and now was simply an empty field going back to nature.

I'd escaped the shackles of my old life by accepting Jean-Paul's offer to become a vampire and was now free to live the life I'd always wanted, the one I had dreamed of while lying awake in my bed at the fraternity house in Oxford while Jared snored in the other bed.

Jean-Paul's vampire blood had kicked open my closet door and brought me out into a world I'd never dreamed existed.

Not having to hide my sexuality any longer was a gift I'd forever be grateful to Jean-Paul for giving me, no matter what happened between the two of us. And there were so many willing men out there—beautiful men with thick muscles and firm asses who were willing to expose their throat to me, just as they worshipped my body and told me I was beautiful.

Jean-Paul and the rest of our vampire fraternity showed me a life that exceeded my wildest dreams. Finally freed from the confining chains of the closet, my eyes wide open with awe and wonder, I shed my old skin and basked in the sun for the first time in my life. I was surrounded by beautiful men, who wanted nothing more than to give me pleasure, to worship my body and be worshiped in return. I was introduced to expensive clothing and designer drugs that intensified pleasure to a point I could have never imagined. I danced every night to thumping music as my mind swirled in clouds of ecstasy and heretofore unimagined joys. There were no limits on the credit cards, and I came out of the expensive stores of South Beach with bags and bags filled with more clothing than I could ever possibly wear, clothes that fit and flattered my body. I discovered a fondness for Dolce & Gabbana underwear, for shirts of silk and satin, for tight-fitting pants that hung low on my hips. I strolled along the beach in the bright sunshine, in swimsuits that were little more than strings and pouches, laughing with delight when the eyes of some intensely beautiful stranger met mine with lust and desire reflected in them. The warm green water of the Gulf Stream washed over me when I danced into the gentle waves kissing the white sand of the shore.

And when I needed rest, I simply cuddled into Jean-Paul's strong, muscular arms and woke up with him pressing his lips to my neck, his hand on my cock, and we made love gently and passionately.

I was in love, floating on a cloud of joy, warm and secure in myself for the first time in my life.

I'm not exactly sure when I began to suspect the truth about Jean-Paul.

There were five others in our little group, living in the beautiful house on Ocean Drive on South Beach in Miami. The house itself was not the place one would think a group of vampires would inhabit; it was white and full of windows to let in the sun. There was a gorgeous pool within the tall stone fence, and a hot tub. I sometimes wondered where the money came from to pay for everything—the house, the parties Jean-Paul threw on a fairly regular basis—but whenever I questioned anyone, I was simply dismissed or the subject was changed. "Don't worry your pretty little head," was all Jean-Paul would say, kissing the tip of my nose. "That isn't for you to concern yourself with."

The other vampires in our little group were all sexy creatures, with gorgeous bodies and handsome faces. There was Clint, who looked like he was in his early forties, with a head shaved down to the gleaming scalp and the most amazing blue eyes. Clint was the first one of the group I'd met during that fateful Mardi Gras—I'd run into him on Bourbon Street at the corner of St. Ann, where I'd been standing in the middle of the street trying to decide whether to go into Oz or the Pub. He'd been wearing no shirt or underwear beneath his faded low-rise jeans, and I'd been attracted to his hairy, thickly muscled torso. It was Clint who'd taken me by the hand and led me into Oz and onto the dance floor, where I'd first laid eyes on Jean-Paul.

And I'd pretty much been a part of the little group ever since.

But I'd felt closer to Clint than to any of the others outside of Jean-Paul—that night when I'd gone back to the house on Orleans Street with them, it was Clint and Jean-Paul I'd had sex with in a mind-blowing three-way, one that made me know there was no question about my sexual preference, no way I could even pretend to be sexually attracted to women ever again. Clint sometimes joined Jean-Paul and I in the massive bed in the master bedroom of the sun-drenched manse, and sometimes I caught him looking at me in a pensive way I couldn't quite comprehend. But I knew I could always count on Clint for anything.

Perhaps three months had passed since my conversion and we'd arrived in South Beach. There was yet another party going on in the house, and I was bored, sipping a glass of red wine and walking around the pool in my red bikini. It was early evening, and the sun was beginning to set. Tiki torches around the pool had been lit, and a thin sheen of sweat covered my skin as I smiled and muttered inanities at beautiful young men with exceptional bodies, ignoring the obvious invitations in their eyes as they looked over my body. The music was blaring, and a sweating group of men in thongs and bikinis were dancing on the other side of the pool, their slick skin glowing in the torchlight. I hadn't seen Jean-Paul in what seemed like hours, and I was wishing I were anywhere but there when Clint came up behind me and cupped my ass in his big hands. I spun around and smiled at him. "Having fun?" I asked, gesturing with the wineglass at the dancers.

Clint shrugged. He was wearing a metallic-blue bikini barely containing the bulge in the front. "Every once in a while I get bored with all of this," he said, taking my hand and leading me back into a dark secluded corner. He pulled me to him, rubbing his bulge against mine and pulling me into a deep kiss. His hands drifted down to my ass, and he pulled me even tighter against him, and his tongue went into my mouth as my back arched a little bit.

He was a great kisser.

I could taste blood in his mouth, a hot metallic taste.

"You've fed," I whispered in his ear.

"And now I want to fuck you," he whispered. He slid a finger into my ass, and I moaned. The taste of blood, the feel of his damp skin, and the pressure of his finger as it toyed with my asshole were driving me mad with desire.

But before I could lose myself in pleasure, out of the corner of my eye I noticed another couple.

The boy getting fucked was about my age, maybe a little younger. He was Latino—dark cinnamon skin, black hair, and lean and muscular. His bright yellow bikini was down around his knees, and he was getting ridden very hard from behind. His eyes were closed, and he was moaning, pulling on his own nipples with his hands. He was up on his toes, two big strong hands grasping his waist to keep him from pitching forward from the power of the thrusts. He was so beautiful that I couldn't help but smile.

And then I saw the man fucking him was Jean-Paul.

I couldn't believe it.

I gasped.

Clint turned and looked. He gave me a sad look. "You didn't think Jean-Paul was going to be faithful, did you?" He nuzzled my neck.

I tried to pull away from him, but Clint was too strong for me. "I thought he loved me," I said, knowing as I said the words how pathetic they sounded. I didn't expect Clint to understand. Yes, Jean-Paul and I had sex with the others in our little fraternity—sometimes with more than one at a time—but this Latino boy was a *human*.

And watching as Jean-Paul rode this boy, I remembered that night they'd found me at Oz and led me back to the house on Orleans Street—when *I* had still been a human. I knew then the sad truth—that I wasn't special, after all.

What had drawn Jean-Paul to me that night?

He looked over at me, and our eyes locked. A slight smile played at the corner of his lips.

And I was inside his mind for just a flash of time.

And I knew.

It had been the heartbeat, the pulsing of my fresh human blood through my veins, and my youth.

I stifled a sob.

He didn't love me. He was simply attracted to young humans.

But he didn't just drink from me—he allowed me to drink from him that very night. He'd decided then and there that he wanted to convert me, to take me away from New Orleans and the old human life I'd been leading. That had to mean something, didn't it?

I clung to that thought as I watched the man I loved fuck another young human.

I stopped resisting Clint but didn't react either as he slid my bikini down my legs and lifted me up, closing his arms around me, and I could feel his thickness probing between my cheeks.

And as he entered me, I kept watching Jean-Paul and the Latino. I moaned and gave myself to the pleasure but never closed my eyes. Even as Clint pounded away at me, the intensity and violence of his movements growing with each inward stroke, I didn't—*couldn't*—take my eyes off them. Even as Clint toyed with my nipples, kissed my throat, moving faster and more intent on achieving his final pleasure, I kept watching them.

Jean-Paul reached his climax at the same time as the boy, both of them shuddering and moaning so loudly I was surprised the entire party couldn't hear them over the music.

I watched as Jean-Paul spun the boy around and kissed

him, the moonlight shining on the boy's perfectly shaped round ass, the thin triangle of lighter skin at the bottom of his back, just above the curve of his cheeks.

I couldn't blame Jean-Paul for wanting him—he was indeed quite beautiful.

But I could blame him for having him.

And for the first time since I became a vampire, I felt the dark pull of hatred filling my heart.

And when Clint was finished, I kissed him on the cheek, pulled up my bikini, and disappeared back into the crowd of dancers. I accepted a hit of Ecstasy from someone and lost myself for the rest of the night in the music.

I stared up at the pink clouds over New Orleans. That was the night everything changed for me—everything about Jean-Paul, about being a vampire, about my new life and world.

The others noticed—I've never been great at hiding my feelings. I withdrew from all of them, refusing to talk about my sadness. I knew how to block Jean-Paul from reading my thoughts, and every so often, I saw him looking at me with confusion in his eyes. I simply smiled back at him and every morning returned to his bed. I continued as before, occasionally slipping out at night onto the crowded sidewalks of Ocean Boulevard to find someone's luscious neck to feed from.

And then one night, maybe three weeks later, I saw the Latino boy again.

A blinding rage rushed through me when I saw him walk out of the Dolce & Gabbana store with a large bag. He was wearing khaki shorts that reached past his knees and a black tank top that hugged his lean torso. He was yakking away on a cell phone, and in that moment I wanted nothing more than to see him dead and writhing at my feet.

The feeling was so strong I could see it as clearly as if it had actually happened.

Make him suffer, a voice whispered inside of my head. *Make him pay for daring to love Jean-Paul.*

I tried to resist—it wasn't a good idea.

I crossed the street and followed a few steps behind him, listening to him talk on his phone, completely oblivious to everyone and everything around him, unaware that death was not even a yard behind him.

The person on the other end of the phone was obviously a close friend, perhaps a lover—I couldn't determine which from the way he spoke to him. His voice would lower into a husky, lusty whisper one moment before rising into a joyful shout of laughter.

Poor, stupid, pretty little Latino muscle boy who had only a few hours left of life to him.

I followed him all the way to his apartment. It was a white building, without a doorman or any kind of security. He took the elevator up to the fourth floor, and then I took the stairs. I could smell him—he was inside apartment 4-B.

I didn't hesitate, even for a second. I knocked.

"Yes?" He opened the door, his big white teeth showing in a gorgeous smile. Dimples deepened into his tanned cheeks, and he'd removed the shirt. His torso was smooth and hairless, his pectoral muscles perfectly shaped, his nipples large and a dusky shade of purple. Muscles bulged in his stomach, and his navel was tantalizing. I could feel my cock growing hard inside my own shorts, and I knew that I was going to fuck him. I could see in his dark brown eyes his own interest, his desire for me. His shorts hung low off his narrow hips, and I could see stubble from where he'd shaved his pubic hair just above the waist of the shorts. There was a nice bulge in the front of the shorts, and one of his hands absently brushed against it as he stood there smiling back at me.

"Hi," I said after a moment, unsure what to do now that he was right there in front of me. I could see the vein in his neck, beckoning to me. It was pulsing with each beat of his heart—which I could almost hear.

It would have been so easy to just feed from him, push him back into his apartment and sink my teeth into his neck, draining him until his heart ceased to beat and leave him there to be found.

But as I looked into his soulful brown eyes, I realized killing the boy would solve nothing. It wasn't his fault Jean-Paul had found him attractive, had seduced him at the party—Jean-Paul probably never bothered to learn his name. Jean-Paul wouldn't know the boy had died, would never know that I had killed him in a fit of insane jealousy he would consider unseemly for a vampire.

He stood there looking at me expectantly.

"We met the other night," I went on smoothly, "at the party on Ocean Drive. I'm Cord, remember?"

He looked puzzled. "I don't remember you, I'm sorry." The smile flashed again. "I must have been some kind of wasted, huh?" He barked out a laugh. "Where are my manners? Come in." He shut the door behind me. "Would you like something to drink?" He held out his hand. "My name is Luis, Cord. I'm sorry." His voice had a sort of accent, a lilt to it that was rather seductive. "I honestly don't remember you, but the whole night was kind of a blur for me. But I must have given you my address—and I'm really glad that I did."

The apartment was beautifully furnished, as was the community spread out beyond the wall of glass. One wall was covered with framed posters of the young Latino—one was an ad I recognized for Calvin Klein underwear, another for a swimsuit company whose name I couldn't recall.

A catalog was sitting on the coffee table with the address label up. LUIS PALENZUELA. "I think we were all pretty wasted, Luis." I laughed.

He sat down next to me. I could smell his cologne—ck one. I could hear his heartbeat, smell the slight odor under his arms. He crossed his legs, his left leg brushing against mine softly. He smiled at me. "You're very handsome, Cord."

I returned his smile and traced his cheek with my right hand. He closed his eyes and leaned in for a kiss.

I left him an hour later, the wounds on his neck already healed into what could pass for small hickeys. I started whistling as I walked back to the house on Ocean.

A few days later, we left Miami and started going to circuit parties all over the country. Jean-Paul always became restless after a few days in any city, and I lost myself in the haze of parties and drugs and bodies. Montreal, Toronto, Palm Springs, Philadelphia, New York, San Francisco, Los Angeles—the next two years passed in a blur of airports and suitcases, hotels and rental condos.

But things were never the same again between us after that party, after I saw Jean-Paul with Luis. His interest in me didn't abate, but his eye wandered. And each time I saw him with another beautiful young human, a knife twisted in my heart.

And each time, I cared a little less than the time before.

The bells of St. Louis Cathedral began ringing, startling me out of the memories and returning me to the present.

I stood up and started pacing. I wasn't dizzy anymore, but I needed to replace the blood I'd let Jared have. I felt hollow and empty, and the craving was there again, getting stronger with each passing moment.

I had to feed again—and I couldn't make the mistake of waiting again.

I cursed myself as a fool again. Why had I been so stupid?

I went inside.

I pulled my clothes back on, and glanced over at the bed where he lay.

He was sound asleep—would it be okay to leave him? I didn't know. It might be yet another huge mistake.

It was a risk, but I couldn't think of anything else to do with him.

I had to feed again—and soon.

I couldn't let the desire turn to need again.

Shaking my head, I slipped out the front door into the warm New Orleans night.

CHAPTER 3

New Orleans is a dark city of dancing shadows after the sun goes down.

I stumbled as I stepped out onto the front stoop of the house, locking the door behind me. I felt a little dizzy, and another wave of nausea forced me to lean back against the house. It wasn't a good sign, I realized as I waited for my body to shake it off. It meant that my blood loss was even greater than I originally had thought—and I didn't have nearly as much time as I had anticipated to feed and replace the blood I'd given Jared.

You've really done it this time, idiot, I cursed myself as I took some deep breaths to steady my nerves. *This is precisely the situation that caused this whole fucking mess in the first place.*

Of course, beating myself up over it wasn't going to change, or solve, anything.

I sat down on the top step and took another, deeper breath. I could hear the music and noise of Bourbon Street just a block and a half away. I could smell the intoxicating scent of human blood. I rubbed my hands over my eyes and glanced across the street at the house where I'd almost died.

Had I really seen someone in the window earlier, or had it been my imagination?

I shook my head. *You're just imagining things—you've got Sebastian on your mind. Jared's eyes couldn't have changed color, and you didn't see anything in the window. It's some kind of post-traumatic stress thing, triggered by being back in New Orleans and being on your own for the first time in your life—or else it's just your imagination working overtime, that's all. You've fucked up, Cord, and you know you're going to have to call Jean-Paul for help.*

Which, of course, was the last thing in the world I wanted to do—and wouldn't do until I'd exhausted every other possibility.

And once I'd replenished, I could undoubtedly think of some options.

The nausea passed and I opened my eyes. I felt better. I probably had at least a few hours before the desire became need again, and surely I could find someone to quench my thirst long before—

Before you fuck up again.

I shook my head and stood up. I breathed in deeply. I could hear the crazy woman who lived in the carriage house next door screaming. I rolled my eyes. She was smoking crack again—my heightened senses could smell it—and sure enough, the man she lived with started screaming back at her. Every night, like clockwork, they'd get high and start their little sideshow. It was annoying to say the least, and when I was trying to relax in my own courtyard or watch something mindless on TV in the living room, it was incredibly distracting. Several times, I'd considered putting them out of my misery.

Crack-laced blood, though, tasted terrible, like it was rotting, and I didn't like the effect it had on me.

Then again, I didn't have to drink their blood to kill them.

But that wouldn't be a smart thing to do, I reminded myself. *Vampires don't kill. That brings attention to us, and—*

"Whatever," I said out loud.

Someone was coming—I could smell their blood. It was two people, a man and a woman, and they were almost to the corner at Burgundy. Young, from the scent. I could almost taste it, it was so strong. They both were wearing perfumes from Calvin Klein—Obsession, maybe. It barely masked the stale sweat under his arms and inside his shoes. I could also smell their pheromones—they were terribly attracted to each other and certainly at some point in the evening ahead he would be mounting her.

I turned my head to the right and watched for them. A few moments later, they came around the corner. I looked back in the other direction toward Bourbon Street. Orleans Street was deserted from my stoop all the way to where the fool in the hand grenade costume was dancing on the corner, trying to get people to go inside the Tropical Isle Bar for one of those lethal green drinks. A car drove through the intersection at Dauphine—a United cab with several women in the backseat. I looked toward the young couple. Cars were rushing by on Rampart Street a block and a half in the other direction.

The only people on Orleans Street all the way back up to Rampart were this couple and me, standing on my stoop.

There were no witnesses, no one anywhere to hear or see anything.

They were perhaps in their early twenties; she was a petite young woman who probably didn't weigh a hundred pounds soaking wet and needed heels to top five feet. She was wearing a denim miniskirt that barely covered her, her tan, shapely legs teetering on heels so high her back had to hurt. She was wearing a spaghetti strap top with no bra—I could see her nipples through the thin cotton top. Her light brown hair was streaked with blond. He towered above her at well over six feet and over two hundred pounds. His long sandy blond hair tumbled out from beneath the backward LSU baseball cap on top of his head. He was wearing an oversized white LSU football jersey with the gold and purple stripes on the shoulder. His jeans were baggy, faded, and torn at the knees. His arm was draped loosely but proprietarily over her thin shoulders. They nodded at me as they walked past me—both were carrying the large green plastic cups in the shape of a hand grenade with a long handle.

They weren't drunk, but they were well on their way. I could smell the alcohol seeping through their pores, and the sweet smell of marijuana hung around them. They'd left Bourbon Street to smoke a joint in their car, I surmised, and now were on their way back to have another drink.

It would almost be too easy to feed from them.

I started down the steps after them but stopped myself. I wasn't strong enough to handle them both—I'd given too much of my blood to Jared. I cursed myself again for a fool. I could handle only one person, and I needed darkness and seclusion to manage even that.

I listened for Jared, and heard his shallow snoring.

But I could smell the couple's blood, could hear the pounding of their hearts, and could feel the desire growing within my chest. There was still time, I reasoned, but I needed to hurry.

As I watched the couple hurriedly walk toward the lights and noise of Bourbon Street, out of the corner of my eye I thought I again saw movement in the windows across the street.

I stared through the darkness. The pink clouds had cleared,

exposing the velvety bluish black of the night sky and the sparkling of hundreds of stars. The sliver of a moon hung, barely casting any light. *It's amazing,* I reflected for perhaps the thousandth time, *how dark New Orleans gets at night.*

Miami was always so bright you could hardly see the stars at night.

The light from the streetlamps barely penetrated the darkness, and the dampness of the air created a hazy halo around the glowing lights.

Had I really seen something? Had something actually moved in the window, or was I just imagining things?

I swallowed and walked across the street.

Vampires have much more powerful night vision than humans. The first time I'd experienced it, it had kind of freaked me out. That first night after my conversion, when Jean-Paul took me out to feed from the house on Orleans, was forever burned into my memory. It was Ash Wednesday, and the sun had already set. It had rained all day, so the streets and sidewalks were slick and wet. Water dripped from the overhang as I stepped out onto the steps. A cold wind was blowing from the direction of the river, and Bourbon Street sounded muted. But despite the gray fog and the darkness, I was stunned at how vividly I could see. The thick fog was simply like a veil of gauze, and the glowing streetlights seemed to dance with vibrant, living light. I stood there, with the water dripping onto the side of my face, enrapt, looking first one way, then another, unable to fathom and comprehend how amazingly beautiful everything seemed.

"Come with me, my dear." Jean-Paul had smiled at me and taken my hand. When I reached the bottom step, he leaned over and kissed me on the cheek. "You have all eternity to see the beauty of the world. Come on, it's time for you to feed." He led me down to the corner of Dauphine Street, and we turned left. My tongue kept feeling the incredibly sharp points on my incisors, and I could hear a lot of hearts beating ahead of us. He led me to a bar called Good Friends. There had been only a few people there, besides a cute blond bartender who couldn't have been much older than I was. Jean-Paul ordered us each a glass of absinthe, which he taught me how to sip while he decided which of the few other patrons would be perfect for me to take my first drink of human blood from.

My preference would have been the bartender. He was so beautiful, with his blond hair and golden skin, with his perky little butt inside his black shorts.

But Jean-Paul finally settled on a dusky man in his midthirties, who kept looking at us over the rim of his glass of vodka and soda. He got up and joined us, introducing himself as Matt. He said he was from Iowa—Des Moines, to be exact—and came down for Mardi Gras every year. He was tired, worn out from the five days of excess that had preceded Ash Wednesday, but he wasn't leaving until the next morning. His leg kept brushing against mine under the bar, and I could smell his desire for me—he also desired Jean-Paul but didn't think the odds of a three-way were in his favor.

Eventually, the three of us walked out of the bar. It had started raining again, and I shivered. Dauphine Street was filling with water, and rivers of it were cascading from roofs and balconies. The wind had also picked up, and it had gotten even grayer outside.

Jean-Paul nodded to me, and I allowed Matt to kiss me. He tasted of vodka, lime, and tonic water. I could smell the alcohol his body was trying to expel through his pores. I put my arms around him and closed my eyes. I could hear his pounding heartbeat, and in the gloom the big blue vein in his neck almost seemed to glow. He gasped when I sank my teeth into it, and as his blood gushed into my mouth, I could hear his thoughts.

"Oh my God, that feels so good. How on earth did I get so lucky two sexy studs going back to my hotel room with me this young one my God he is so gorgeous and that ass I can't wait to taste it put my finger inside of it and the older one, his arms and chest, I want him to fuck me. I bet he can put me through the headboard—

And then I heard Jean-Paul's voice inside my head: *"Don't take too much, my little one. This was just a test, for you to get used to it. Now it's time to stop."*

I pulled my mouth back from Matt's neck, and in my head I saw myself biting my thumb, rubbing my blood over the wounds on his neck. I looked at Jean-Paul, who smiled back at me and nodded. I bit my thumb and rubbed my blood over the holes. Matt's eyes were still closed, and he was swaying back and forth. I watched as the holes closed, leaving only what looked like two small hickeys.

"Go back to your room and sleep," Jean-Paul said softly, "and dream of a beautiful young man and a muscular older one joining you—and when you wake in the morning, you will take with you a beautiful memory of the three of us together."

Matt nodded and, as I watched in amazement, turned away from us and ran across the street in the pouring rain, running away from us toward Canal Street.

"And now you've had your first taste," Jean-Paul whispered into my ear, "and tomorrow we leave New Orleans for good. It's too dangerous for you to be here."

I didn't know what he meant by that, but at that point I would have done anything he told me to do. I simply nodded and returned with him to the house.

Back in those days, when all Jean-Paul had to do was

snap his fingers and I would leap, I thought, shaking my head. I started to cross the street but waited for a blue Honda to drive past.

I climbed onto the porch and pressed my face against the glass of the window where I thought I'd seen something. I could clearly see the shapes of boxes and sawhorses through the gloom, but there was nothing moving, nothing else except the usual debris of a construction site abandoned for the night.

It must have been just my imagination. Again.

I took a deep breath and started walking toward Bourbon Street. Several blocks ahead of me, Orleans Street came to a dead end where it met Royal Street. On the other side of Royal was the iron fence enclosing the yard behind St. Louis Cathedral. The shadow of Christ's statue loomed over the back of the building. It always gave me a chill whenever I saw it. His arms were spread, and there was something almost predatory about the shadow on the gray slate. Jared had once called the statue "drag queen Jesus," which had made me laugh, and I remembered that every time I saw the shadow at night or walked past it in the daylight.

That memory always made me smile. No one had ever been able to make me laugh as hard as Jared could.

And look how you repaid him for everything he's ever done for you.

I swallowed and pushed that thought out of my mind.

The first thing you need to do is stop feeling guilty, Jean-Paul had lectured me, so many times I knew the words by heart. *Let go of that nonsensical Christian bullshit your parents brainwashed you with. Doesn't your current existence prove that their precious Bible is nothing but a collection of fairy tales put together millennia ago by ignorant desert nomads?*

He'd been right, of course. But it wasn't that easy to shake off what you'd always been raised to believe.

Then again, I'd also been raised to believe my sexuality was an abomination and I was going to spend eternity burning in hell.

Bourbon Street was crowded, as it always was on a Friday night when there was a convention or two in the city. When I reached the corner, I stood there for a moment, taking it all in. The people were of all shapes, ages, races, and sizes. Their smells, the thumping of their hearts, the buzzing of many voices talking at the same time, the clip-clop of horses carrying mounted policemen, and the astonishing beauty of their humanity overwhelmed me a bit, as it always did whenever I encountered a crowd. I allowed myself to get lost in the overstimulation of my senses for a moment, closing my eyes and letting it all wash over me—smell, sound, and taste.

My reverie was interrupted when someone brushed against me, muttering, "Sorry."

I opened my eyes, smiling as the woman weaved her way up Bourbon Street. I forced my mind to start filtering the overload to something manageable. The massive Bourbon Orleans Hotel across the street had the doors to the two side-by-side bars on its first floor wide open. The one on the left, Napoleon's Itch, was a gay bar and was blasting diva disco music. There was a Lucky Dog vendor on the opposite corner from me, in his red-and-white-striped shirt. He was handing a pair of foot-longs covered in chili, cheese, and onions to a couple of sexy straight boys in their midtwenties who looked like they'd been drinking for a while. A gaggle of young women wearing tight T-shirts and denim miniskirts checked them out as they walked past, carrying forty-eight-ounce Styrofoam cups full of daiquiris. "Hotel California" was blaring from a bar to my right, a few doors down from the corner. I dodged around the dancing hand grenade and could see the couple who'd passed me getting new drinks inside. I smiled and nodded at the hand grenade but didn't go inside. A loud whoop across the street made me look in that direction, and I saw a group of college-aged boys standing in a circle while one of them chugged a beer in the center.

He was wearing a Beta Kappa shirt, and I froze for a moment.

There are Beta Kappa chapters at LSU and Tulane and Southern Mississippi, I reminded myself. *They don't have to be from Ole Miss, and besides, you don't recognize any of them.*

I stood behind a man wearing a sandwich board advertising BIG ASS BEERS $4 while I searched their faces.

No, I didn't recognize any of them.

That would have sucked, I thought as I started walking toward the corner at St. Ann and Bourbon. *Bad enough I already ran into Jared today—and look how that turned out.* But I pushed that negative thought out of my head. No sense in worrying about what to do with him until I'd fed and was back at 100 percent.

"The gay bars are all down around the corner at St. Ann and Bourbon," Jared had told me at that Mardi Gras a million years ago. "You can't miss them—they have rainbow flags and everything. That's where you need to go."

Jared had *always* been a good friend to me. I felt a lump forming in my throat but took a deep breath and forced it back down.

Jared and I had been pledge brothers. We'd met during Rush Week. It was hard not to notice him—he was so damned good-looking; you had to be blind not to notice him. One of the brothers—I think it was Clark Newton, but I'm not sure—was explaining to me what a "great idea it was for pledges to go ahead and move into the house" when

I saw Jared standing on the other side of yard. He was wearing a blue suit with a yellow shirt and a red tie, and was
smiling at the two brothers talking to him. He had a name
tag outlined in red stuck to his jacket, which meant he was
a prospective, and I couldn't take my eyes off him. Clark or
whoever it was ceased to exist in that moment, and all I
could do was stare at this gorgeous young man.

I'd had a crush on Bobby Stovall since the sixth grade,
but Bobby was not in this guy's class.

Not even remotely.

Somehow, I managed to get up my nerve to introduce
myself to him, and he was so nice and funny. We ended up
spending pretty much the whole night hanging out. The
next night, we met in front of the Beta Kappa house. We
went around to some of the other houses, but neither one of
us cared for any of the others. Within two hours, we were
back at Beta Kappa, and the next night we both took bids.

We moved into the house over the weekend. I was really
glad to get out of the dorms—my roommate was overweight
and smelled bad, apparently allergic to soap, water, and de-
odorant.

My parents hadn't approved of my joining Beta Kappa—
they didn't approve of anything that remotely sounded fun.
I was incredibly naïve when I went to Ole Miss. All I really
knew of life, of the world, was my little corner of redneck
Fayette County in northeastern Alabama, where everyone's
lives revolved around church. We were Church of Christ
(pronounced as one word: *churchachrist*), which took great
pride in being the only denomination of Christianity that
worshipped Christ correctly. Anyone who worshipped differently was a blasphemous sinner with a one-way ticket
straight to hell. The Church hated everyone who wasn't
white and straight—and women must be subservient.

Growing up in that environment made me feel like I'd already died and gone straight to hell.

I'd always been more interested in boys than girls—and was convinced I was the only one in Fayette County (if not the world) who felt that way.

I'd chosen Ole Miss instead of the University of Alabama as a means of escaping Fayette County. University of Alabama was in Tuscaloosa, a mere forty-minute drive from my parents' house, and I thought that was way too close for comfort. Ole Miss was far enough away that they couldn't just drop in unannounced or intrude on my life, but not so far away they couldn't be talked into letting me go there— and at that, it was a long, hard-fought battle.

I was confident once I'd gotten away from them I'd be able to break away from the life they'd already mapped out for me. I didn't want to go back to Fayette County and teach at the same rural high school where so many of my relatives also taught. I didn't want to get married and have sons to carry on the family name and tradition of football, hunting, and Jesus Christ Our Lord and Savior.

But they tried to hold on. My father called the preacher at the Oxford Church of Christ, to let him know I was coming there, and the Sunday after Rush, that's where I was on Sunday morning, being introduced to other college-age kids and being pressured into joining a college group called Rebels for Christ.

The umbilical cord from Fayette County apparently could stretch all the way to Oxford, Mississippi.

Jared was from New Orleans—a city my parents always dismissed as a city of sin, and that made him even more exotic to me. He understood my need to never go back there, to get away from my family. He gently made it clear to me he was straight and not interested in guys, but in such a way that I knew I could confide in him when I was ready. It was our sophomore year when I felt comfortable enough to tell him the truth. He understood; it didn't make a difference to him, and he helped me keep it hidden from our fraternity brothers.

The closeted existence I was living at Ole Miss was making me miserable. I hated going to visit my family. I hated summer vacations. I hated sitting in the house listening to my parents rant against the "queers" and the "godless liberals" and all the other people of different racial backgrounds who were dragging the country into the toilet.

I didn't understand how my parents, who were so kind and loving and giving, could be so filled with hate at the same time, thinking nothing of making racist jokes, using racist epithets. I didn't understand how they reconciled what Jesus actually said in the New Testament with the vile, repressive hatred preached twice every Sunday at church. I was tired of dodging their questions about girls, of trying to get out of dates with daughters of other people at church. I was tired of the hideous boredom of life in rural Fayette County, where the highlight of every week was sitting in the heat and humidity on the banks of the Sipsey River, swatting mosquitoes while trying to catch catfish.

And the day of reckoning was coming—graduation was a date that seemed to grow closer all the time with an astonishing speed. I was going to have to tell them I wasn't coming back there. Maybe I wouldn't have to tell them about being gay—if I moved far enough away.

The thought had certainly crossed my mind any number of times.

Maybe becoming a vampire and faking my own death was an extreme way of escaping my old life, but I wouldn't go back for anything.

The great irony, of course, was I had simply traded one closet for another.

No one can ever know you're a vampire, Jean-Paul had said, *because humans aren't evolved enough to coexist with beings they can only comprehend through the eyes of fear. They will* kill *you.*

Being a vampire was no different, really, than being gay in rural Alabama.

One fear traded for another.

I shook my head when I reached the corner of Bourbon and St. Ann, trying to push all the memories away. I hadn't thought about any of this shit in years—I'd embraced being a vampire wholeheartedly. This Jared thing was making me remember all of this shit, I told myself. I leaned against the building on the corner and closed my eyes as another wave of nausea passed through me. I needed to feed and soon.

"How you doing, baby? Everything all right?"

I opened my eyes and forced myself to smile at the man standing there, friendly concern all over his face. He wasn't unattractive. He was older, overweight, and was wearing a flannel shirt tucked into a pair of Wranglers. He was holding a big plastic cup full of beer, and a couple of men around the same age wearing the same clothes were standing a few feet behind him. One had a look of impatience written all over his face.

"I'm fine, thank you." I nodded at him, willing him to go away.

"All right." He backed away, the friendly smile never wavering. "You might want to not have another drink for a while."

"I think you're right." I nodded. "I thank you."

He nodded back at me before rejoining his friends. I watched them as they walked across St. Ann to the other side and disappeared around the corner onto Bourbon Street.

You don't know what a close call you just had, buddy, I thought as a beautiful young man walked past me and smiled. He had that thick bluish black hair I'd come to recognize as Cajun—well, French really. (Jean-Paul's hair was that same thickness and color.) He was wearing a tight red collared pullover shirt tucked into a tight pair of jeans—he had a beautifully shaped ass. He crossed Bourbon Street and went into Oz.

It was so much easier to feed inside the gay bars than in their straight counterparts on the eight blocks between St. Ann and Canal in the other direction. The gay bars were never well lit, favoring red or black lights. The dance floors always had flashing strobe lights that distorted everything. There was darkness everywhere inside the gay bars—in corners, bathrooms, and stairwells. And gay men were remarkably easy to lure into those dark patches. Gay men were remarkably trusting—willing to leave a bar with a total stranger whose name they didn't know and go to a place without telling anyone.

Often, they themselves didn't know where they were going with the total stranger.

This made them remarkably easy prey for vampires. Jean-Paul and the others had the ability to hypnotize humans with their eyes and the sheer force of their will. According to them, I was about fifty years away from developing that skill myself.

I was, as they always reminded me, just a *baby* vampire.

But that was fine, really. As long as I could find a dark gay bar, I could always find someone interested enough in my face and body to slip into an unlit corner with and feed from.

I laughed to myself. It was always about having to wait, wasn't it? It was the story of my entire life. I'd waited and waited to escape from Alabama and waited to graduate from

Ole Miss, and then I became a vampire—the irony being that as a vampire, I still had to wait, but now decades rather than years.

The wave of nausea passed, and I walked over to the curb, looking across to the Bourbon Pub. The downstairs shutters were already closed, the velvet rope set out for people to queue up and pay their cover charge. A thickly muscled man stood in the open doorway to Oz directly across the street, his arms folded and sunglasses hiding his eyes. Behind him, I could see the defined legs and Day-Glo bikini of a stripper dancing on the bar. *What the hell*, I thought, making up my mind. I crossed over to Oz, paid my five dollars, and got a hand stamp.

It was still early in the evening for Oz to be crowded, but there was a decent amount of men inside. There were two strippers on the bar—the one I'd seen from across the street in the bright, glowing yellow bikini and one on the opposite side wearing white. The stripper in yellow had shoulder-length blond hair and a lean, smooth body, and he was kneeling, letting someone touch his smooth chest. He smiled at me over the man's head, and his left eye closed in a wink. I walked around to the back side of the bar and caught my breath.

The stripper in white had his back to me. I stared at his broad shoulders and the muscles rippling in his back. He was moving his hips and came around in a dance turn until he was facing me. His head was shaved—so was pretty much his entire body except for a goatee. His chest was heavily muscled, and his abs rippled as he moved his hips back and forth. He smiled and his entire face lit up, dimples deepening in his cheeks. His legs were thickly muscled. And when he turned to move down the bar away from me, I got a good look at one of the most incredibly perfect asses I had ever seen. It was thick and perfectly rounded and solid. The white material of his bikini stretched tightly across the muscles as he walked, flexing and contracting.

I felt myself growing hard inside my jeans.

I wanted to fuck him, bury myself inside those beautiful cheeks and tongue his hole until he screamed. I wanted to hold him down while I shoved my cock deep and hard inside his exceptional body.

And I wanted to taste his blood.

I walked up to the bar and ordered a beer from the shirtless bartender. I headed over to the back corner where the stripper was coaxing some dollar bills from an older couple. He was kneeling on the bar, muscles rippling in those amazing legs, and as one of the men stroked his leg, placing a dollar bill into the waistband of his white bikini, he made eye contact with me over the man's head.

I winked back, not sure he could see me in the gloom.

That was when I felt . . . *something*.

It was strange, and I stopped watching the stripper as I looked around the bar. A shirtless Latino boy carrying several buckets of ice went behind the bar. The other stripper was bouncing his dick inside his yellow bikini for the bemusement of a trio of college girls, who kept squealing and laughing. A guy with tattoos up and down his arms was playing the video poker machine. Five muscular guys were out on the dance floor, their shirts hanging from belt loops as they mindlessly moved their hips to the beat of a song I didn't recognize.

For a brief moment I caught a glimpse of a young woman in the corner by the ATM machine, but as my eyes focused on her, she vanished.

I shook my head and looked around the bar again. I thought I saw her out of the corner of my eye over by the front door, but when I turned my head, she was gone again.

"Looking for someone?" a deep voice purred.

Startled, I turned my head. It was the stripper. Off the bar he was maybe five foot seven, but he was unbelievably sexy. His smile was infectious—he was absolutely adorable. Even with the shaved head, the big smile made him look boyish. I smiled back at him as he got closer to me than he probably needed to for me to be able to hear him. I could smell him—he smelled like a man, like he'd just worked up a sweat in the gym before coming into the club. "I thought I saw someone I know," I replied, allowing my hand to brush against his muscular shoulder. His firm, hard flesh felt hot, and I could almost hear his heart beating.

"You're really pretty," he said, taking one of my hands and placing it on his hard ass. He tilted his head to one side, still smiling, and I could see the carotid artery, pulsing in his neck. I looked around and no one was watching—if anyone was looking in our direction, their eyes were focused on his magnificent ass—so I bent my head and slid my teeth into his vein.

He moaned and moved in closer to me, his big strong hands cupping my ass.

"Oh, that feels good, damn, man," he whispered, going up on his toes and pressing his crotch into mine. His dick was hard, but I didn't care about that.

His blood was delicious, satisfying. I kept drinking, allowing my hands to slide down his muscled torso until I was touching his big round hard butt.

Do you think that's wise? a woman's voice whispered in my head.

His hands gripped my ass tighter and I could feel his throat vibrating as he moaned.

And I could see mountains in the background, in the not so far distance, but they weren't tall mountains, and I knew exactly where we were. Palm Springs. But as I looked around, I didn't recognize the yard, the pool, anything—and then I realized that this wasn't one of my memories but one of the dancer's.

But when I'd fed from Jared, I hadn't seen any of his.

I'd been so blinded by the *need* that I hadn't noticed.

I pulled my mouth away from his neck and quickly nicked my index finger. I rubbed it over the wounds in his neck and they healed, closing until all that was left were two dark spots that could have just been hickeys.

The way Jared's were supposed to but hadn't.

The stripper swayed a bit as he stood there, the smile still on his face. "Dude, that was *intense*," he said, and I noticed that his dick was hard. A wet spot was spreading where the head rested. He swallowed. "My shift is over at two," he went on. His weight shifted from one foot to the other. "I mean, if you wanted to meet me here..." His voice trailed off.

I reached over and tweaked his right nipple, and his head ducked down a bit as his eyes closed and a low moan escaped from his throat. "I'd like that," I said. I meant it when I said it. I could keep Jared locked up in the front room. . . .

"Do you really think that's a good idea?" The same female voice cooed in my ear. *"Isn't it bad enough you've poisoned your fraternity brother? Do you need to compound the error by bringing a stripper back to the house?"*

He said something else, but I didn't hear. I was looking for the woman the voice belonged to—but there was no woman in the bar other than the girls who were still giggling and laughing at the dick-bouncing antics of the other stripper.

Maybe I was just going insane.

"Two, you said?" I said.

He winked and nodded before turning and walking away.

I watched his oh-so-amazing ass as he headed across the dance floor and down the little hallway where the bathrooms were. He opened a door and disappeared behind it.

I took a deep breath and headed for the front door.

I really should check on Jared, I thought as I walked back out into the warm night.

"Do you really think that door will hold him if he wants to get out?" the voice whispered into my ear again.

I bit my lower lip and started walking quickly up Bourbon Street.

Chapter 4

I leaned against the street sign on the corner and closed my eyes. Who was this woman whose voice I kept hearing in my head?

She had to be a vampire—but why couldn't I sense her presence?

I opened my eyes and looked around. There was a group of young men standing across the street on the corner in front of the pub, all holding plastic cups with alcoholic drinks in their hands as they laughed and joked. I looked down toward the corner at Dumaine Street, but other than a heavy-set man with a beard talking on a cell phone just outside of the Clover Grill, Bourbon Street was deserted as far as I could see in that direction. I looked up at the balconies wrapping around the Bourbon Orleans Hotel, just across St. Ann, but there was no one there. The bar on its first floor was blaring a remix of Kylie Minogue's "All the Lovers," but that bar, too, was completely empty.

She had to be nearby, I reasoned. I didn't know how far a distance the vampiric telepathy could work across—the only time Jean-Paul had ever communicated that way with me had been at circuit parties, but I never really knew how far away he was from me in those vast spaces.

And come to think of it, only Jean-Paul had ever talked directly to my mind. None of the others in our fraternity ever had.

I'd always assumed it was a connection the two of us shared, as maker and creation, but maybe I was wrong.

I'd never had any contact with a female vampire. Obviously, I knew they existed, but I'd never encountered one.

For that matter, I'd never encountered a vampire outside of our circle.

Maybe I could sense others only if they'd also been created by Jean-Paul.

I just didn't know.

I scanned the crowd on the other side of St. Ann, on the "straight" side of Bourbon Street. There were plenty of women over there, but none of them were looking at me. None of them were alone—they were either with a man or in groups, laughing and drinking and clearly having a good time. I looked up St. Ann, but again, there wasn't anyone to be seen.

I need to get back to the house, make sure Jared's still okay, I told myself. The stripper's blood had sated my hunger, and I probably shouldn't have left him alone for so long. I'd never witnessed a transition and had no idea what all it entailed.

I'd been incredibly stupid in letting Jared drink from me, infecting him with my blood. I turned and looked back inside the bar. The stripper was moving his hips from side to side on the far side of the bar, his back to me. The cotton of the white bikini clung to that amazing ass, highlighting its extraordinary beauty.

He truly had an exceptional body, but I could see where I'd bitten his neck. And there were no wounds there— nothing to show that just a few moments earlier I'd taken nourishment from him. I hadn't done anything different with him than I had with Jared earlier on the street. So why had the stripper's neck healed, when Jared's had not?

What had I done wrong? What was different about Jared? It didn't make sense.

Maybe I'd made a huge mistake in leaving Jean-Paul and the others to strike out on my own. Clearly, there were a lot of things about being a vampire I didn't know, didn't understand. Maybe I should call Jean-Paul, swallow my pride and go crawling back to him.

And I could see the smug look he'd have on his face, the sneer on his lips, the triumph in his dark eyes as he made me beg to rejoin the fraternity. I could hear his voice saying, *Why should I take you back, baby vampire boy? So you can defy me, go after the young men I drink from and take their lives like Luis in South Beach—*

I shook my head. I'd left Luis alive.

Hadn't I?

Did you leave him alive, boy? Or did you take so much of his blood that he died after you left him?

I took a deep breath. *Stop imagining things,* I lectured myself. *You don't know what will happen if you call Jean-Paul, if you ask him for help.*

"You're a fool," I whispered. "Jean-Paul would never make it easy for you."

I may have known Jean-Paul for only two years, but I knew him well enough to know he wouldn't make it easy for me to go back. He'd want to humiliate me, debase me and break my spirit to ensure that I'd never go against his will again. Even though I loved him, I knew there was a cruel side to him. And wasn't the reason I left because I knew he'd eventually move on from me? He loved young men, didn't he? Didn't he always choose a young man to feed from? Hadn't he'd turned me into what I had become because I was young, so I would stay young forever, trapped in the body of a twenty-year-old, a body that would never age?

Did I really want to go back to that life, watching him feast upon young men, waiting for the day when he finally tired of me completely and turned some other young man into the newest addition to our brotherhood?

No, I would rather die than sit by while that happened. I would far rather be out on my own in the world, even if I didn't know everything that I should, rather than simply wait for the day when he turned my replacement.

I squared my shoulders and walked up Bourbon Street. I was not going to go back to Jean-Paul. I was not going to ask him for help. Whatever was going on here, whatever had gone wrong with Jared, I would have to figure out for myself. I would solve the problem—even if it meant killing him. It had been weakness to let him feed from me— maybe a sense of loneliness, a need for someone to be my companion so I wouldn't have to be so lonely. Those were human emotions, human needs—and I had to remember I was no longer human.

As I walked down the middle of the street, loud music assailed me from both sides. Harsh, grating, slobbering human voices danced on the air as I passed by groups of them in various stages of inebriation. The couple I'd followed was now standing out in front of the Tropical Isle, each holding a long green cylindrical plastic cup filled with liquor. I could smell the alcohol in the air, the sourness of their breath as I walked past them, turning to go up Orleans Street. Their eyes were glassier than they had been when I'd seen them earlier, and my eyes locked with the young man's for a moment—and I could see curiosity in them.

Desire was there, too, even though he obviously had no intention of ever acting on it.

If I weren't in such a hurry to get back to Jared, I might have played with that young man, gotten him to finally open his mind enough to admit that he had an attraction to other men, set him free from the shame he so clearly felt about those desires—a shame I knew only too well.

There was a young woman standing on the corner of Orleans and Dauphine. She was leaning against the street sign, facing toward Bourbon Street. She wasn't what would be considered classically pretty, but she was definitely an attractive woman. Her thick dark hair was braided, and the braids were coiled around her head. There was a purple streak in one of the braids and a red one in another. Her nose was long and crooked, her lips thick and painted a dark red. Everything about her face was pointed—her chin came to a sharp point, her cheekbones stuck out at a sharp angle, even her lips narrowed to points on either side of her mouth. Her eyes were slanted, dark blue with gold flecks. Her lashes were long. She didn't seem to be wearing much makeup. Her neck was long, and she was wearing a black T-shirt with *Who Dat* written in gold across her chest. Her breasts were small but firm. She was wearing a pair of jeans that rode low on her curved hips, and she was maybe five feet four. There was a mole just under the right corner of her mouth. She'd watched me walk up the block and was still watching as I stepped off the curb. I waited for a black-and-white United cab to drive by before starting across Dauphine.

She tossed the cigarette she was smoking into the street as I stepped up onto the curb. I started to walk past her but was aware something about her wasn't quite right.

She wasn't *human*, I realized as I drew nearer to her. She didn't smell human, and her heartbeat . . .

She was a vampire—and I hadn't sensed her until I was within a few feet of her.

That wasn't a good thing.

"Cord."

She said my name before I could think of what I should do or how I was supposed to act. If there was a protocol for what to do when encountering an unknown vampire, I sure as hell didn't know what it was. It had never happened during the entire time I was with Jean-Paul and the others, and it had never occurred to me to ask about it. I had never thought that we were the only vampires in the world, but now, confronted with a strange vampire, I wondered why we never had run into other vampires during our travels. What were the odds of that—and what were the odds that I would run into one on the street in the French Quarter? Whenever it had occurred to me to ask about other vampires, my question was either ignored or I was told to not worry about it. When I was inside the cocoon of our little fraternity, it really hadn't been an issue.

But I wasn't with them anymore, and now here was a strange vampire.

A strange vampire who also knew my name.

I stopped walking and turned to face her. "How do you know my name?" I asked, watching her carefully. I didn't sense any danger from her, but that was hardly reassuring. I hadn't, after all, sensed her.

I cursed Jean-Paul in my head for leaving me so ignorant.

She stepped into the pyramid of light cascading down from a streetlamp. I took a closer look at her face but I'd never seen her before. I wondered if she'd been the one communicating with me, and if she had been following me for some time and I'd simply not noticed.

She smiled at me mirthlessly. "Do you *really* think it's wise to feed from a stripper in a gay bar?" Her voice was mocking and contemptuous. She stepped a little closer to me, raising one of her eyebrows. "Do you want to be caught, baby vampire? Is that what you wish? Do you hate being a vampire so much you want to die?" She moved even closer to me. "If that's your wish, there are easier ways to die— ways where you won't endanger the rest of us." I could feel her breath on my neck, and it made me uncomfortable.

I took a step back. "It was dark and to the others in the bar it looked like we were just hugging each other," I replied in an equally contemptuous tone. "No one noticed anything out of the ordinary, and—"

"You are a fool, and what's more, you don't even know how big of a fool you are." She cut me off, sneering. "Oh, you can be forgiven much because you're young. And there are those who would overlook your stupidities because you are beautiful." She reached out with a cold hand and caressed the side of my face. "And you are quite beautiful, but still, you know nothing." She pinched my cheek, hard, and involuntarily I cried out. "But for all of those who would forgive you, there are many, many more who won't be as forgiving. Are you aware of that? There are those who could destroy you with a mere snap of their fingers and would think nothing of it—they'd forget you a moment after your body turned to ash." She laughed. "Surely you aren't so foolish, so stupid, as to think that you are the only vampire in New Orleans? In Louisiana?" She shook her head. "You don't even have guards up. You poor young baby. Every vampire in Louisiana knows about you—they can sense you. You didn't even sense me or where I was, even after I started talking to you back at Oz, did you?"

"Well, n-no," I stammered, taking another step back. Violence and anger radiated from her body, and I was growing more than a little frightened of her.

"Don't worry, baby vampire, I'm not going to hurt you—no matter how stupid you've acted. That's not why I'm here, although God knows you need some disciplining." She gestured in the direction of the house. "Care to explain what's going on in your house?" Her smile grew wider. "The pretty young muscular man with marks on his neck, with your blood in his system that is slowly but surely converting him into an incredibly weak vampire—one, I might add, who will be easy prey for the others?" She shook her head. "Did you honestly think no other vampire knew what you were doing in that house?"

"I . . . ," I whispered, but couldn't think of what else to say. I felt mortified—worse than Jean-Paul had ever made me feel. "Go to hell," I finally managed to get out, and turned to walk away from her.

"Not so fast." She rolled her eyes dramatically and bared her upper teeth, exposing long, sharp canines. "I'm here to help you, you idiot." She grabbed my arm—her strength was amazing—and spun me around so I was facing her again. She sighed heavily. "I've already put up guards around the house and around you, so the least you could do is show me a little bit of gratitude?" When I didn't answer, she shrugged. "All right, then, manners are clearly not your strong suit. Come on, let's go check out the damage." She started dragging me up the street.

I tried to resist her at first, but she was too strong for me. It was humbling. I'd known the other vampires in our little fraternity were stronger than I was—Jean-Paul could lift me and toss me over his shoulder with little to no effort at all—but to be so much weaker than a woman? Even if she was a vampire . . .

"Don't be such a misogynistic asshole," she growled at me, interrupting my thoughts. "I might be female, but I can tear you to little pieces, understood?"

"I'm sorry," I mumbled.

She sighed. "It's okay. Well, no, it's not okay." She gave me a brittle smile. "You need to work on it. I get it—you were raised that way, but you need to remember women are just as good as men. And when it comes to vampires, gender doesn't matter. It's age that matters and the strength of the heart." She shook her head. "Jean-Paul really didn't teach you a goddamned thing, did he?"

We walked up my front steps. I unlocked the front door, but she pushed me aside and strode across the front room to the locked double doors. She turned and looked at me, placing both of her hands on the faded wood. "Fortunately, not only is he still here, but also he still sleeps. He's restless—which is not a good sign for a conversion—but he sleeps." She crossed her arms and began tapping her right foot. "And fortunately, if anyone else sensed him there besides me, they didn't do anything before I put up the guards." She gave me a sad little look. "You really don't know what I'm talking about, do you?"

I sat down on the couch and glowered back at her. "Yeah, I'm just a complete idiot," I snapped as I kicked off my shoes. "It's a wonder I'm even still alive."

"Truly, you have no idea how right you actually are." She walked over and sat down next to me. "But it really isn't your fault, you know." She nudged me with her elbow. "It's really Jean-Paul's. He was incredibly irresponsible—as always." She shook her head. "And now we have to clean up his mess. As always."

"You know Jean-Paul?"

"You really don't know anything, do you?" She stared at me. "It's really unforgivable. And he let you loose, out from under his protection." She got up and walked over to the front windows and looked out through the curtains. "I understand why he did what he did originally—on an emotional level, that is. But on an intellectual level, and certainly on a political one, it was a huge mistake." She faced me again. "The Council wants you dead, you know." She gestured toward the locked double doors. "And when they find out about that"—she shook her head again—"you're almost certainly going to be executed."

Executed? My head was spinning. "What Council? Why would they want me dead?"

Her voice was sympathetic. "I'm sorry. I forget you don't know. Anything." She sighed. "Jean-Paul was so completely negligent. Criminally so. If anyone should be executed, it's him." Her eyes flashed. "This certainly isn't the first time he's done something so incredibly stupid. It's a pattern with him—and yet, they never do anything other than reprimand him." She crossed the room and sat down next to me again. She cupped my chin in her left hand. "You are a pretty boy, of course, which clearly is why he did what he did with you. It's not your fault, of course, but the Council doesn't care about things like that—their only concern is protecting our kind, and you're a danger." She looked back over her shoulder at the double doors again. "And if you're going to run around letting humans drink your blood—that's just going to make it that much easier for them to authorize your death sentence. You can't just create a new vampire every time you panic, you know." She took a deep breath and held out her hand. "My name is Rachel, and I'm here to help you—whether you want it or not."

I swallowed and took her hand. It was small and cold, but her grip was strong. "Thanks." My head was racing, trying to digest what she'd said and what it meant, what it might mean, for me. "Can you help me with Jared?"

She shook her head. "I don't know. He might have to be destroyed."

I goggled at her, unable to speak.

Destroyed?

"Oh, come on, don't act so shocked. You thought it yourself when you walked out of that bar—that you might have to kill him." She smiled and patted my hand. "You need to learn how to close your mind so that other vampires can't read it."

I nodded, biting my lower lip.

"As for destroying him, I hope it won't come to that, Cord, really I do. But you have to be tried, you know." She moaned and slammed her fist down on the arm of the sofa. "No, of course you don't know." She looked away from me. "The Council is comprised of thirteen vampires. Every continent has a Council, and their word is law over vampires. They don't usually involve themselves in individual affairs." She looked at me. "Jean-Paul never mentioned the Council? Did he ever say anything about the Nightwatchers?"

"The Nightwatchers?" I shook my head. "No, he didn't. What are the Nightwatchers?"

"Of course he didn't." She slammed her fist down again and took a moment to compose herself. "Jean-Paul really is the one who should be destroyed. Or sent back to Europe—let them deal with his stupidities. That's where he belongs, anyway." She smiled at me. "I'm sorry if it seems as though I am taking my anger with Jean-Paul out on you—he just makes me so angry." She sighed again. "All right, let me try to explain this to you."

There was, she explained, a Council of thirteen older vampires on every continent—and it was their job, as assigned by the Nightwatchers ("I'll explain them to you later," she told me), to police the vampires under their jurisdiction and make sure they followed the rules. The rules have been in place for centuries—*millennia*, actually—and their purpose was to protect vampires from exposure. "Because we frighten humans, and it's been the goal of their religions to destroy us from the very beginning." Vampires who break the rules are called before the Council and tried, with no chance of appealing their decisions.

"But what are the rules?" I asked, confused but fascinated at the same time. "How am I supposed to know the rules if no one told me what they are?"

"It's your maker's role to explain everything to you," Rachel replied. "Now do you understand why Jean-Paul makes me so angry?" She ran her hands through her hair. "The first ten years of a vampire's life are crucial. They should never be allowed out of their maker's sight. You're very weak at this point, Cord. You haven't come into your own as a vampire yet. It's no different than expecting a human baby to feed and take care of itself in the first year of its life. You aren't strong enough. You don't have your strength yet. You are easy prey for those who hunt us." She gestured in the direction of the ruined house across the street. "Before you even finished converting, you were easy prey for the witch Sebastian, weren't you? Had Jean-Paul not come to your rescue, Sebastian would have achieved his foul purpose. Vampire blood—even that of a baby like yourself—is powerful. Had Sebastian succeeded, he would have achieved immortality and eventually would have had the strength of a vampire along with the powers of a witch." She shook her head. "And as much as we would like to believe a powerful creature would work for the well-being of the humans, I tend to think he would have been a monster. And we would have had to destroy him." She gave me a terrible smile. "Many vampires could have been killed."

"So why hasn't anything been done about Jean-Paul?" I asked, worried. I was angry with him, yes, but that didn't mean I wanted him dead.

"The Council has been occupied by other things," she replied. "Which is why the Nightwatchers are becoming involved. Which is why I am here."

"Are you a Nightwatcher, whatever that is?" I asked. I thought I heard movement from behind the locked doors.

She heard it, too, and crossed the room so quickly I didn't see her move. One moment she was by the window, the next she was in front of the doors.

She was right. Much as I hated the sound of it, much as I'd resented it when Jean-Paul had called me that, I was a baby. I couldn't move that quickly. I couldn't read minds unless I was connected to the other person's life force. I couldn't fly.

I was more than human, but I was less than vampire.

I got up and gave her a sardonic smile as I turned the key in the lock and rolled the pocket doors open.

Jared was sitting up on the bed, still naked.

"What's going on?" He was disoriented, his voice groggy from sleep. "What's wrong with me?" He looked from me to her and back again. "Cord? You're alive . . ." He shook his head. "I thought you were dead. . . ."

Rachel sat down on the side of the bed and started stroking his head. "It's all right, Jared. You're just feeling a little under the weather is all," she said, the timbre of her voice dropping a bit. She was mesmerizing him—another vampire skill I didn't yet have. I'd seen Jean-Paul and the others use it from time to time, and they always assured me that I'd learn it in time. "Hush, now, you just lie down and go back to sleep, okay? You just need to rest."

He murmured a bit, his eyes drooping, and he slid back down, curling up into a ball on his side. In just a matter of moments, his chest was rising and falling again in the steady breath pattern of sleep.

Rachel stood up and glared at me. She stalked back into the front room. I started to close the pocket doors, but she stopped me. "There's no point," she replied. "If he wants to hear us, the doors won't stop him, nor will the lock hold him if he wants out." She looked grim. "He's converting, but it's much worse than I feared, than I sensed." She shivered and grabbed a pack of Pall Malls out of her purse. She lit one and took a long drag. She blew the smoke out and started pacing. "There's a reason why his wounds won't close," she said, still pacing. "You never should have fed from him."

"I know that," I replied, irritated. "It was a mistake—"

"It's even bigger than you think," she cut me off, flicking ash on the hardwood floor without a care. Jean-Paul would have a stroke if he saw it. "Jesus fucking Christ." She ran her other hand through her hair. "I don't know how to break a curse, or if it's even possible. This is out of my league."

"Curse?" I stood up. "What the hell are you talking about?"

She stopped pacing and ground the cigarette out under her shoe. She turned and faced the front door. "He's almost here, thank heaven." She plopped down into a wingback chair and sprawled across it, swinging her feet over one of the arms. She smiled at me. "This is a lot to take in, I know." Her tone was kind, which was rather a surprise. "I know I've been a bit of a bitch to you, and I'm sorry. I'm worried, is all, but Nigel's almost here and—"

"Nigel?"

"My master."

"Master?"

"You really don't know anything, do you?" She sighed. "My creator. He turned me into a vampire. Jean-Paul is your master."

"I don't know that I like the sound of that."

"That's because you were created by a lazy, indolent idiot who doesn't take his responsibility to his creations seriously," she snapped. "Making a new vampire is a responsibility that shouldn't be taken lightly. Jean-Paul . . . he only makes vampires out of men he wants to fuck, at the risk of sounding crude."

Even though I knew what she said to be true, I still felt the urge to defend him. I fought it down and said nothing.

"I'm sorry, Cord, but it's true," she said softly. "And you know it's true."

I nodded, feeling the sadness and desolation roll over me again like a wave. "I know," I whispered. "It's why I left."

In a blink, she was sitting beside me on the couch, holding my hand in her cold ones. "I know." She kissed the side of my head. "I know it hurts." She swallowed, and stroked the top of my head. "I know how hard it is to cope with such a thing."

Everything I'd been holding inside since I left Palm Springs came rushing out of me in one fell swoop.

I'd been so stupid to think Jean-Paul cared about me. All I had been to him was a piece of ass, a pretty boy one of his coven had seen on the streets of New Orleans and taken to meet the master on the dance floor. He'd seen me, and I'd been a plaything for him, nothing more—someone to introduce to the pleasures of man-on-man sex. Was it my virginity that had struck his fancy or my deeply religious upbringing? All he wanted was a young man—it didn't matter which one—and when he tired of me, when I stopped amusing him, he'd started looking for other young boys. I'd first realized it at the party in Miami, and the pattern had continued after that as we traveled far and wide, to the Black and Blue Ball in Toronto, to Cherries in Washington, DC, and finally Easter in Palm Springs—when I'd finally rebelled. I'd told myself for months that he'd turned *me*, that all he wanted from the others was to fuck them and drink from them, but he'd made me one of them so that I could be with him forever.

Forever didn't last long in Jean-Paul's mind.

"He never told you why he turned you?" she asked me in a whisper. She had her arms around me, my head down on her shoulder as my tears flowed and my body shook with my heartbroken sobs.

"I thought it was to save me because Sebastian had drained me." I wiped at my eyes, smearing blood on my hands. I licked them clean. "But Sebastian wanted my blood *because* I was already turning. I don't remember what happened that first night with Jean-Paul and the others. I don't. But I must have drank from him, right? Why else would Sebastian have wanted me?"

"There's no memory of that night in you." She kept stroking my hair. "The only person who can answer those questions is Jean-Paul, and the Council of Thirteen will want answers from him, I assure you. But first we have to solve the problem of Jared." She sighed. "The easiest thing to do would be to kill him, you know, and dispose of his body. His family and friends can have closure that way—

knowing that he's died, rather than spending the rest of their lives wondering."

"No," I replied. "It's not right. It's not his fault."

There was a knock on the door, and she stood to answer it.

I rose as she answered the door. I watched as she reached up to hug the man standing there, but all I could see was a thick head of white hair as he put his arms around her and returned the hug. He was wearing a seersucker suit, and as I stood, not sure what to do next, his head lifted and I saw his face.

He looked old, older than anyone I'd ever seen before— yet his face was free of lines, his blue eyes bright and alert. The white hair was perfectly combed, parted in the center and falling down to his broad shoulders. The age was more of a sense I got from looking at him than any physical representation. He simply gave off an air of great age, of experience, of having seen the world in all of its ugliness for more centuries than he cared to count. But with that same air, a feeling of great power, strength, and compassion radiated from him—a feeling that calmed me, convincing me that everything would, indeed, work out for the best.

Or at least the way it was supposed to.

He murmured something to Rachel that I couldn't hear, and she nodded as they separated and he entered my house. Underneath the seersucker jacket he wore a salmon-colored silk shirt and a blue-and-white-striped tie knotted firmly at his throat. He was tall—certainly taller than me, most likely well over six feet.

He looked at me with a gentle smile and spread his arms wide. "And you must be Cord."

I nodded and took a hesitant step forward. He beckoned to me with one of his hands, a slight gesture that was almost imperceptible, and I crossed the room and put my arms around him, placing my head down on his chest as his arms went around me.

"We will take care of this, my child," Nigel whispered to me. "There's nothing for you to fear anymore."

CHAPTER 5

I sat up in my bed with a start, my heart pounding in my chest.

I opened my eyes. The light outside the window was fading, which meant the sun was starting to go down. I could hear pigeons cooing.

The dream began fading out of my mind, yet I still felt nervous and unsettled. It had seemed so vivid and real; it had been like living the whole thing all over again.

And it was just as awful this time as it had been when it all actually happened.

In my dream, I'd been back in the house across the street, tied to the bed while Sebastian toyed with my body, laughing as he tormented me and performed his strange rituals. I wrapped my arms around myself and shivered. My cock was still hard from the dream. It had always disturbed me that my dreams about him were so erotic, so arousing—he had wanted to kill me and had almost succeeded.

But I hadn't had the dream in quite some time, either.

Maybe it meant something that it had come back.

I stretched and yawned, my head still foggy from sleep as I tried to shake off the dream. When I'd been human, it had always been hard for me to wake up—and that hadn't changed. Back in our room at Beta Kappa, Jared used to always laugh about how I "could sleep through nuclear war." My mother had always used to say I slept like the dead. While I never felt tired or sleepy, once I lay down in my bed and closed my eyes, sleep came quickly and deeply. And the dreams... when I'd been human, I rarely remembered my dreams. Now my dreams were almost as vivid as reality, and when I woke up, it was sometimes hard to differentiate between what was real and what wasn't, what had just been a dream. My mouth was gummy, the way it always was when I'd fed before sleeping. The light outside continued to fade, and I shifted in the bed, and my leg brushed against another leg.

There was someone else in the bed with me.

I turned and looked at him in the fading light.

It was Jared, all right—so that hadn't been part of my dream. That nightmare was all too real. Last night had really happened, which meant Rachel was somewhere in the house, and everything the old man (Nigel) had told me last night had also been all too real. My dreaming subconscious had not made any of that up.

I swallowed and resisted the urge to scream in frustration.

Jared moaned and shifted in his sleep at my side, turning over so he was facedown on his pillow.

I had placed a blanket over him the night before, but he had wormed his way out from under it at some point after I had climbed into the bed with him. The first rays of the morning light had been working their way through the window as I undressed—sharing this bed with Jared had been Rachel's idea.

Someone has to be there in case he needs someone, she'd said, and the old man had agreed with her. *And since you're responsible for his state . . .* She'd let her voice trail off. She hadn't needed to say anything more, really. I understood.

I was responsible for him now and forever; they'd made that abundantly clear to me. It was an obligation I might never be free of—unless of course he was put to death.

The wool blanket I'd covered him with was lying in a heap on the floor at the foot of the bed. His naked body glistened and glimmered a bit in the fading light.

I slipped out of the bed and pulled my robe on to cover my own nakedness. I looked at Jared's naked, recumbent body—the sexy curve of his ass just below the dimples in his lower back, the broad expanse of his upper back, the mussed hair on his head. He looked beautiful, the way he always had.

I remembered the first time I'd ever seen him—at Preference Dinner the semester we pledged. It was the last night of Rush Week, and all the newly recruited pledges were in our best suits and ties, every hair in place, shaved and scrubbed and clean. The brothers of Beta Kappa took us to a really nice restaurant—the Prime Steakhouse on Jefferson Avenue in Oxford. There were some alumni there, too—the state's attorney general, a bank president from Memphis, and a state senator from the Biloxi area showed up to impress the new pledges with the greatness of Beta Kappa and its rich tradition at the University of Mississippi. The brothers seated us alphabetically at our own table in the banquet room, so naturally I wound up sitting next to this incredibly beautiful boy from New Orleans.

I wanted him from the moment we introduced ourselves and shook hands. I'd seen him during the rush parties, but there were so many good-looking boys going through Rush

at the Beta Kappa house that my mind—and hormones—
were on overload. I'd never been in a room with so many
gorgeous guys before. The brothers were also, for the most
part, really attractive. I knew from the first minute I walked
into the plantation-style house with the big Doric columns
and the wide veranda that this was the fraternity I wanted
to join. I'd decided to go through Rush in the first place because I thought joining a fraternity might actually help
"straighten" me out. (Although why I thought that would
work when playing football, basketball, and baseball at
good old Hubbertville High School hadn't done the trick
was still a mystery to me.) My decision to go Greek was also
helped along by the fact my parents were dead set against
it. My father told me all kinds of horrible stories about what
fraternities were like when he was at Alabama, which only
made me even more determined to get a bid from one of
the houses at Ole Miss. It also amazed me that it never occurred to either him or my mother that if they'd *encouraged*
me to join Beta Kappa, I would most likely have avoided
the place like the plague. But they did offer me a bid, and I
had walked on air all the way back to my dorm.

And when I walked into the banquet room of the restaurant for the preference dinner and saw all the good-looking
boys cleaned and pressed and spiffed up, I wondered if
pledging was such a good idea. Would I be able to keep the
secret of my sexuality surrounded by so much mouth-watering
temptation? How on earth would I be able to use the communal showers without an erection giving me away?

Yet despite my instant crush on Jared, I soon realized I
had nothing to worry about on that score. The way he
flirted with our waitress, a pretty young thing with black
hair and white skin and dimples and an accent thick
enough to cut with a knife, it was pretty obvious he wasn't

gay. And no matter how much I might wish he was, that wasn't going to change him.

But it was impossible not to be fascinated by him. I couldn't take my eyes off him, and I couldn't remember ever meeting someone I so desperately wanted to like me. It wasn't that he was the best-looking guy in the room—he wasn't. He didn't have the best body of all the brothers and pledges. There were two pledges in our class who should have chucked college and run off to New York to be underwear models.

But there was just something about him that drew your eye, made you feel good and comfortable and relaxed. His grin was so infectious that no matter how down in the dumps you were, you *couldn't* help but smile back at him. His blue eyes twinkled—I'd read that description in books before, but never really knew what it meant until I met Jared. He seemed larger than life somehow, like he took up more space than most people did. And I wasn't the only one who felt that way. He wound up being our pledge class president, the brothers voted him the outstanding pledge award, and every semester he was elected to whatever office he ran for. Every girl he met was his for the taking—but part of what made Jared so special was he treated girls with respect. He didn't do the one-night-stand thing—he preferred to have a steady girlfriend, and he never participated in any of the usual frat boy boasting about his sexual expertise.

And he was from New Orleans, a city I'd always wanted to visit—a place that seemed exotic and foreign to me.

We talked and laughed and joked all through the dinner. He showed me a picture of his girlfriend, Josie, who was pledging Kappa Kappa Gamma, and promised to take me to Mardi Gras sometime.

And by the time the meal was over and we headed back to the house with our pledge brothers to tap a keg and get drunk for the first time with the brotherhood, we'd decided to move out of the dorms and share a room in the house.

Jared turned out to be the friend I'd always wanted, had always dreamed of, when I was growing up. There wasn't anything I couldn't tell him—even the gay thing. He was cool with it. His mother's brother was gay and lived in the French Quarter. I knew my secret was safe with him from the homophobic brothers of Beta Kappa. He even encouraged me to drive over to a gay bar in Memphis and went with me the first time, getting us fake IDs and finding the place on the Internet. He encouraged me to talk to a guy who was checking me out, gave me a couple of ones to tip the hot guy dancing on the bar in his underwear, and stayed sober so I could get more courage from alcohol. It was his idea that I go with him to Mardi Gras so I could go visit the gay bars in the Quarter, and he disguised the visit by inviting two other brothers to come with us to New Orleans. Once we were there and out watching parades, he helped me escape from the crowds watching the parades on Canal Street so I could go, as he put it, "get my gay on."

How was he to know I would encounter a pack of gay vampires that first night on my own?

And now it had all come full circle, hadn't it?

I'd repaid his friendship, his kindness, everything he'd done for me by infecting him and forcing him to give up everything that was important to him.

I walked around to his side of the bed and knelt down next to him. He looked so innocent and beautiful in his sleep, with his eyes closed.

I remembered as I looked down at his face how kind his parents had always been to me, his older sister and brother.

On that trip down for Mardi Gras, they'd welcomed me into their beautiful home. Even before that, when they came to Oxford to visit, they'd always treated me like a member of the family. They'd always included me in dinner invitations or on day trips—anything they did I was more than welcome to join them.

Thank you, Mr. and Mrs. Holcomb, for making me feel like I was part of your family. By the way, I've poisoned your son and destroyed his life. You'll never see him again.

I sighed and tucked the blanket around him again. He murmured and rolled over onto his back. His eyes fluttered briefly and subsided again.

I walked down the hallway and brushed my teeth, splashing hot water onto my face and rubbing goo out of the corners of my eyes.

I could smell fresh coffee and headed into the kitchen.

Rachel was sitting at the table, reading the newspaper. Without looking up, she said, "I hope you don't mind I made coffee."

"I'm glad you made yourself at home," I replied a little sarcastically. "Did you sleep well?"

She didn't look up from the paper. "I haven't slept. Someone had to keep watch. How was your rest?"

I poured myself a cup and sat down across from her. "I was hoping last night was a dream." The coffee was incredibly strong. I took a deep breath and set the cup down on the table. "But it wasn't. I really fucked up, didn't I?"

"Spilt milk, Cord, and all that. No sense beating yourself up about it anymore." She waved a hand but still didn't look up at me. "Nigel's doing some research. He'll be back in a while. With any luck he'll figure this all out. He's pretty damned smart, and he's been around forever." Now she looked up and gave me a wry smile. "And I do mean forever. I take it Jared's still sleeping?"

I nodded and took another sip of coffee.

"That's good." She closed the newspaper, folded it, and gave me a look I couldn't decipher. "It's better that he sleep through the entire process." She looked out the window. "With Nigel's blood in him, the conversion should be over by tomorrow night." She sighed. "It's never a good idea to mix the blood of two vampires in someone who's transitioning." She tried to give me a reassuring smile. "But there's nothing we can do about that now. I'm sure it'll be fine."

I looked down at my hands, remembering.

Nigel had examined Jared for almost an hour while Rachel and I sat in the front room in silence. When he finally rejoined us, he looked tired. "I let him drink from me."

"But, Nigel, that's *dangerous*." Rachel's voice had been awed and quiet. "You've always told me—"

"That in a new convert, one must never allow the blood of two vampires to mix, yes, I know. It can cause madness." He sighed and sat down in a wingback chair, his eyes closed. "And the last thing this world needs is another mad vampire." He steepled his fingers in front of his face. "I saw no other option besides destroying him. And I didn't think that fair." He opened his eyes and turned to me. "Then again, turning him in the first place was not fair, was it, Cord?"

I looked away from him. "I didn't think I had a choice."

"You had many choices, Cord." His voice wasn't unkind. "Yet you panicked—a perfectly natural reaction, given the circumstances—and chose the worst possible option of many. But I—and the Council—can't and won't hold you responsible for this. You won't be punished. And if we can fix the damage you've done"—he cleared his throat—"then perhaps Jared will come out of this okay. That's why I gave him my blood, Rachel."

"Your blood is so powerful," she said, her voice barely above a whisper. "Isn't that dangerous?"

He smiled at her. "I gave you my blood. Was it dangerous then?" He turned back to me. "Do not worry, little one, about your mistake. You're just a baby. How were you to know?"

My temper flared, but I bit my tongue and didn't snap at him. Right now, I needed Nigel and Rachel, and I would have to tolerate their condescension until Jared was out of danger. And as soon as he was okay, I was going to throw their asses out of my house and be done with them.

"Ah, that makes you angry, doesn't it?" Nigel laughed softly.

I raised my chin. "I can't imagine anyone likes being referred to as a baby, Nigel."

He nodded. "It is disrespectful, yes, and I apologize. I will try to watch my tongue in the future. Jean-Paul should have never let you out of his sight, and he will have to answer for that to the Council." He shook his head, his long white locks moving. "But he also clearly had no idea that you were cursed."

"You said that before. What do you mean, I'm cursed?" This time I did look up. He was smiling, and the sting of his earlier words was lessened. I sensed that Nigel wasn't cruel, and relaxed. "I don't understand. If you mean being a vampire—"

"You carry a witch's curse, my young friend, from a very, very powerful witch." Nigel closed his eyes and rested his head against the chair. "I sensed it when you first came to New Orleans several days ago. Oh, yes, we knew you were here, and we've been watching you. One never knows in these times whether a vampire is friend or foe—or a rogue." He sounded tired.

"A powerful witch?" I looked from him to Rachel and back again. "Do you mean Sebastian? Am I in danger from this curse?" I felt a chill go down my spine. I really didn't like the sound of this. But a curse...I looked over to the closed double doors. Maybe that was why the wounds in the stripper's neck had closed but Jared's had not.

"We're always in danger," Nigel replied. "Danger from humans, danger from our own kind, danger from other creatures out there that aren't human, that hate us for who and what we are. But there's no need for you to worry about that now. Our primary concerns are lifting the curse from you and taking care of your friend—making sure his transition is safe and pleasant, and he doesn't go insane."

"Is that possible?" I barely breathed the words out. I closed my eyes.

"You know so little, you poor thing," Rachel said. The words were harsh, but her tone was more kind and sympathetic than it had been before. "Seriously, Nigel, Jean-Paul cannot be allowed to get away with this." She slammed her fist down on the table with such force it cracked. "A vampire cannot convert a human and then just leave him to his own devices. It endangers us all."

Nigel rose. He walked over to me and cupped my chin in his hand. "You look tired, my young friend. Perhaps it would be best if you got some rest." He gestured over his shoulder. "Go lie in the bed with your friend—someone needs to watch him anyway. I will go start my research and will return when I am finished, when I have found what I need. Rachel, I want you to stay here and watch over them."

She bowed her head and nodded.

And he swept out the front door.

Once the door shut behind him, she gave me a look. "Go

lie down. Do as he said." She clapped her hands together. "Go."

Meekly, I obeyed, and once my head rested on the pillow and my eyes closed, sleep came. I slept through what was left of the night and most of the next day.

And now, I wanted to know what was going to happen to Jared, just how dangerous was it for him to drink the blood of two different vampires?

"You said that last night," I said. "How dangerous is it?"

"Well, in this case it isn't as dangerous as it would be with two equals." She gave me a look. "No offense, but your blood and your vampire's heart are very weak. A vampire as young and weak as you . . . I know it bothers you to hear this, but you really are just a baby. To give your blood to a human? It would be the same as a human woman giving birth to a child with birth defects."

I made a face. "Great."

"Whether he would have completely converted isn't a guarantee, either. Your blood simply isn't strong enough. He most likely would have died during the process, or he would have been so weak. His fangs might not have fully formed, and then he wouldn't be able to drink." She sighed.

"And if he isn't able to drink . . ."

"He'd either starve to death, or you would have to hunt for him, feed him," she finished for me. "I doubt that you would enjoy being saddled with a weakling like that. And his weakness would be a threat to other vampires. He would be hunted down and destroyed. With Nigel giving Jared his blood, he might have a chance now. Nigel might seem very old to you, but with our kind, that is a sign of strength. Unlike humans, we become stronger the older we are. Nigel is one of the most powerful vampires in the world. The strength of his blood will very likely consume yours, obliterate it and burn it out of his system." She sighed. "The blood... I don't understand how it works. I've only been a vampire for twenty years myself—but vampire blood fights inside a human when they've drunk from two different vampires." She waved her hand. "I should have paid more attention in my biology class, I suppose. That's what causes the madness—the blood fighting inside the convert's system." She closed her eyes and shook her head. "So, Jared's probably not in any danger, really."

"You've only been a vampire for twenty years?" I stared at her. "But your powers... they're so advanced. Jean-Paul told me it would take me almost a hundred human years to come into my own."

"Nigel converted me, Cord." She got up and walked over to the sink. "I drank his blood. Nigel is very old. I don't know how old he is. He will never say. But he was around when they built the pyramids."

I couldn't have heard that right. "You mean, pyramids like in Egyptian pyramids?"

She laughed at the look on my face. "Yes. Like I said, the older the vampire, the stronger and more powerful his heart—and his blood. Jean-Paul is at most four hundred years old, so, yes, it would take about that long for your heart to become strong enough to handle vampiric powers." She waved in the general direction of where Jared was sleeping. "You know how weak you are in comparison to other vampires—imagine how weak *Jared* would be if it was your weak blood that converted him. You really weren't doing him any favors. Someone would have killed him. He would have been too easy of a target to survive long." She shrugged. "Even now, there's no saying what the Council of Thirteen will do when all of this is brought before them."

"The Council won't terminate him, will they?" I hated asking. I was afraid of the answer.

She shrugged. "There's no telling what the Council will do." She walked out the door to the back gallery. She paused. "Your neighbors—are they always as annoying as they were this morning?"

I nodded.

She smiled. "Well, I took care of that little problem. They won't be bothering anyone with their idiotic behavior again." She let out a laugh that curdled my blood. "Seriously, some humans truly don't deserve the gift of life, do they?" The door shut behind her.

I wasn't sure what she meant by that but figured it was better to not ask.

I finished my coffee and got another cup.

Okay, think, I thought. *Nigel said I'm cursed. Well, that's obviously a leftover from Sebastian. He probably died cursing me. But . . .*

It didn't make sense. I hadn't killed him; why curse me?

And Jared . . . I walked back over to the door and looked in. He'd rolled over onto his back and was murmuring in his sleep. He was quite beautiful, and I wondered, for the first time, what his life had been like in the two years since I'd "died."

Guilt is a completely useless emotion. I heard Jean-Paul's voice inside my head again.

I leaned against the door frame.

He'd said that to me on my last night in Palm Springs.

The White Party had been that night, and we'd all worn identical costumes. Clint had thought it would be funny if we'd all gone as angels—sexy angels, of course. Any costumes we ever wore were designed to show off as much of our bodies as we could get away with. We did look amazing in our little white Lycra-blend bikinis, with white leather harnesses holding our wings on, and white boots and wrist-bands. The Ecstasy we took started to hit as we danced in a room full of beautiful men all dressed in white, and Jean-Paul fixated on a muscle boy wearing white jeans and a white Lone Ranger–style mask over his eyes, covered in se-quins and glitter. He had no shirt on—no one at the party seemed to have one—and was dancing by himself, sweat glistening on his darkly tanned hairless torso.

"Stop glaring. Don't pay any attention," Clint whispered in my ear as he slipped behind me and put his arms around my waist, pressing his crotch against my ass. "Let it go, Cord, and have fun."

I wanted to kill the little bitch.

Adrenaline surged through me as I watched the boy and Jean-Paul checking each other out. I rubbed my ass against Clint's crotch, grinding against him as the two of them began dancing together, flirting, touching.

"You and Jean-Paul have all of eternity." Clint nibbled on my earlobe, which he knew always drove me near mad with desire. "So he wants to nail a muscle boy here and there? They'll be moldering in the grave and we'll still be dancing the night away."

I pushed him away from me. "It'll never end, Clint. There will always be another pretty one to catch his eye, won't there? There was before me, and there will always be. Why did he convert me if he didn't want me to be with him?"

Clint folded his arms. "Must you turn everything into a soap opera?" he snapped at me, his eyes narrowed angrily. "Why must you try to ruin everything every time?" He leaned in toward me. "Well, not this time. If you want to be a pouting little bitch, you're not ruining my evening. You think I can't find another pretty little boy to fuck?" He snapped his fingers, and two shirtless, smooth-chested boys seemed to materialize out of the smoke and began touching him. He flicked his hand at me dismissively and turned his attention to the boys.

I stood there for a moment, watching, and finally realized he wasn't kidding.

Clint was done with me.

I knew it was just for the evening—and to be fair, I was behaving childishly. But I didn't care, and it made me angry.

And I wanted to be anywhere but there.

I started pushing my way through the crowd of drugged-out dancing men, smiling at guys who would reach out and touch my ass, my chest, calling me "angel," but I never stopped.

I walked out the doors and into the parking lot.

Now what? I asked myself. *What do I do now? I don't have any money.* And as I stood there, another wave of the Ecstasy began building inside of me.

A man came walking out of the parking lot, heading for the building.

He wasn't wearing anything but a white jock strap and a pair of white boots and a white leather harness with a matching leather cap.

He was about six foot four, with thick muscles and a handsome face.

And I could feel the desire welling inside of me.

Desire and bloodlust.

I could smell his blood.

"Hey." He smiled at me. "You okay, pretty boy?"

I grabbed him. He let out a startled *hey* but big as he was, he was no match for my strength as I forced him down and turned him so the big vein in his neck was exposed to me, and I could feel my cock growing hard as I released my teeth and sank them into his warm skin. It was so warm, and then his blood was flooding my mouth, and it was delicious, and he was moaning as one of his hands grabbed my hard cock and he started playing with it—

And I was pulled off him.

"Are you insane?" Jean-Paul's eyes flashed angrily. "In the fucking *parking lot?* Do you want to be caught, you stupid boy?"

"I'm not a boy!"

"Go home," he said, turning his back to me. He bit his finger and rubbed the blood over the gashes in the man's neck. They healed instantly. "Go inside and have a good time. This never happened," Jean-Paul said to him. He staggered off through the parking lot, looking like nothing more than another inebriated partygoer. Jean-Paul turned back to me.

I wiped the blood from my mouth. "I'm tired of the way you treat me!" I screamed at him.

"Then go," he sneered at me. "Get out of here. Leave here. The sight of you sickens me. I'm done with you. You're on your own."

He turned and went back inside the party.

And I left. I didn't stop running until I was back in New Orleans.

It would have probably been better had I stayed with Jean-Paul.

I went back into the bedroom and started dressing. Jared was still asleep. I touched his forehead—his skin was extremely hot. He mumbled as I finished dressing, and I was at the door when he sat up.

His eyes opened, and they weren't blue—they were brown flecked with gold.

"Sebastian—" His eyes rolled back into his head and he fell back into the bed.

"That's odd," Rachel said from behind me, making me almost jump out of my skin. "Did you call him *Sebastian?*" She shook her head. "Wasn't he the witch—"

"I'm going for a walk," I said, pushing past her and heading for the front door.

"Suit yourself."

I slammed the door behind me.

CHAPTER 6

I stood on my front steps, leaning back against the door as I tried to catch my breath, trying to figure out what was happening to me—and to Jared.

It was a cool night. A chilly breeze was blowing down the street from the direction of the river. I could hear the music and noise from Bourbon Street, and the clouds overhead were that odd pinkish color from the neon lights in the Quarter. Orleans Street was deserted, but there were crowds down at the corner at Bourbon. I wasn't sure where I wanted to go, or even what I was running away from.

Was it just my imagination? Or was Sebastian—or rather his spirit—somehow coming through Jared? Was this all my fault?

I sat down on the top step and buried my face in my hands. The old man had said I was cursed, that Sebastian had somehow cursed me as my brotherhood had killed him. But why was the curse only now rearing its ugly head and affecting my life and the people I fed from?

It isn't affecting everyone you feed from. Remember the stripper at Oz? His wounds healed the way they always did before. It's just Jared. Somehow, if there is a curse, it has something to do with him.

It didn't make sense.

Nothing made sense.

"You really should wait for Nigel to get back," Rachel's voice whispered inside my head as I stood up and leaned against the railing.

"And you really should stay out of my head. You're starting to annoy the crap out of me," I told her. *"And don't you think it's kind of* rude *and invasive to just go inside of someone's head without permission?"*

"You only say that because you can't do it yet."

Much as I hated to admit it, she had me there.

"I knew it!" Somehow she managed to make it sound smug and triumphant. I heard her laugh, and then, *"No worries, baby. I'll teach you not only how to do it but also how to block others."*

I gritted my teeth and started down the steps. I took a deep breath, trying to decide where to walk. I wasn't hungry, so there wasn't a need to go hunting. I had just decided to go down to the levee and watch the river for a while—I always found that to be relaxing—when I heard someone start playing the piano. It took me a few moments to realize the sound was coming from inside the house.

Who else could it be but Rachel? She was the only person inside the house it could have been—Jared couldn't play anything. She played beautifully, and the song was vaguely familiar. I closed my eyes and focused, and after a few moments I recognized the song—"Save the Best for Last." She started singing, and I was amazed to hear that she actually had a beautiful voice, a soft alto that soared over the notes of the piano as she sang. I sat down on the bottom step and listened. There was a poignancy, a longing in her voice that touched me deep inside. Who would have ever guessed that a snarky vampire could not only sing so beautifully but also put so much emotion into a lyric? Her voice was almost heartbreaking, and I found myself thinking about Jean-Paul yet again.

And if I was going to be completely honest with myself, I had to admit that he had broken my heart.

And that, really, was what it had all been about. Me tracking down the hot Latino underwear model in South Beach, having sex and feeding with that guy in the parking lot of the White Party in Palm Springs, all the little fights and bickering and defiance. I'd fallen in love with him and had thought he was in love with me—when the truth was I was nothing more than the latest version of young flesh he wanted to fuck. It was all me, acting out because he didn't love me, and he never had, not even in the beginning. I understood that now. Maybe he wasn't even capable of love the way I felt it, the way I understood it to be. What a fool I had been, thinking that Jean-Paul and I were going to be joined together, a couple for all eternity, walking hand in hand through the centuries together.

I couldn't believe how naïve and stupid I'd been. Jean-Paul and the others had probably laughed at me.

Clint had tried to warn me when I'd seen Jean-Paul fucking the underwear model at the house in South Beach. But instead of being rational and accepting the truth, I'd gotten all emotional, lost control, and basically made a complete fool of myself.

Was it different for humans? I wondered, my head in my hands. All I'd ever wanted was to fall in love and have someone love me back. I never thought that was too much to ask. But maybe it was for vampires—after all, human couples seemed to have trouble making their relationships last, and they didn't have an eternal life span. But I didn't expect to fall in love with a vampire who didn't love me back.

And look where that had gotten me! Alone in New Orleans, paying back the kindness of the human who'd been the best friend I'd ever had by destroying his life completely.

When she finished the song, she started playing another one I didn't recognize but sounded vaguely familiar. I sat there, letting the melancholic notes swirl around me. They seemed to fit my mood perfectly.

Of course it does. She can get inside my mind, I reminded myself bitterly.

She didn't answer this time, so maybe she wasn't listening to my thoughts anymore.

A sound across the street startled me out of my reverie. I opened my eyes and saw someone locking the door of Sebastian's house. The man was wearing a pair of loose-fitting jeans that had slid halfway down his ass—I could see his red underwear—and a sleeveless navy blue T-shirt. It was a really nice ass, actually, and the shoulders were broad and strong, the waist narrow. He put the keys into his pocket and turned to go down the steps.

My breath caught in my throat, and I stifled the involuntary cry that rose in my throat.

It was Sebastian.

But that . . . that wasn't possible, was it?

Sebastian was dead. My brothers had killed him, torched the house, and his remains had been found in the fire. And if I'd learned anything for certain in the last few years, it was that vampires knew how to kill.

But he'd been a witch. Maybe witches were harder to kill; maybe he had cast a spell that had made them think he was dead when he was actually alive.

Then whose body had been in the smoldering ruins?

I swallowed. They'd thought they'd found my body and were wrong about that. It was possible another mistake had been made. . . .

And there was something wrong with me. Nigel thought Sebastian had cursed me. But if he were still alive . . .

Somehow, I managed to get to my feet just as he glanced over at me. He gave me a half-smile and nodded slightly as he started walking down the sidewalk in the direction of the cathedral.

He didn't seem to recognize me.

Confused, not knowing what I should do, I started following him down the street. Crazy thoughts raced through my head.

Hadn't Jared said that Sebastian still lives? Neither Rachel nor Nigel had witnessed the weird way Jared's eyes changed sometimes, had not heard him speak in a voice that was slightly different than his own. It was possible my own guilt over Sebastian's death had caused those odd delusions.

If they actually *were* delusions.

It was possible. Before that Mardi Gras when I met Jean-Paul, I didn't believe vampires existed, and now I was one. Witches certainly existed—I had firsthand experience with them. So, it was possible that somehow Sebastian had also survived that night. He'd ingested some of my blood, believing the power he would derive from vampire blood mixed with his own powers would make him a god. That was why he'd been destroyed, or at least that's what Jean-Paul had said, and I'd had no reason to doubt him.

That was also when I thought he actually loved me, thought I was more to him than a young piece of ass. The only doubt I'd had back then was whether he'd acted more

out of revenge than out of a need to destroy the hybrid creature Sebastian was becoming.

No, I thought as I reached the corner, *it can't be Sebastian.
But I'm not imagining him. This isn't some kind of crazy halluci-
nation. He's right there across the street. I can see him, and he even
kind of walks like Sebastian.*

He weaved his way through the crowds of people at
Bourbon Street and dodged around the Lucky Dog vendor.
I had to hurry to not lose sight of him—his legs were longer
than mine, and for every stride he took, I had to take two.

He turned to his right when he got to the corner at Royal
Street.

I reached the corner just in time to see him unlock a door
in the corner building and disappear through it. I crossed
Orleans Street, dodging around an enormous couple with
incredibly pasty white skin, and stood in front of the door.
There were a number of buzzers on the right side of the
door frame, with just numbers and names neatly printed on
white cards next to them. It was enormously frustrating. I
wanted to slam my fist against the door, but stopped myself
with inches to spare. I smiled at a couple of young women
holding supersized daiquiri cups. They averted their eyes
and walked faster.

This was one of those times when having my full powers
would come in handy.

I could have gotten inside his mind—

I slammed my palm against my forehead in irritation. *Why
didn't you get Rachel to go inside his head, you moron?*

"Maybe I wouldn't have done it after you were so rude to me."
Her voice sounded smug. *"Not so annoying when you need it,
is it?"*

I cried out, startled. The enormous couple with the pasty

skin gave me a strange look and hurriedly crossed the street. *"Don't do that!"* I told her, hoping my irritation was clear in my tone.

"Yes, no worries on that score. Your tone comes across loud and clear, Cord. So sorry about that, didn't mean to make you jump." Her tone, though, made it pretty damned clear to me she wasn't in the least bit sorry. *"Besides, you're right. It's not Sebastian. His death was pretty well documented."* Her tone turned grim. *"It wasn't a pretty death, and the Witches Council wasn't happy about it."*

"Witches Council?" This was the first I'd heard of that.

"There's so much you don't know. Remember, you hadn't heard of the Council of Thirteen before yesterday. Hang on, I'll be there in a moment."

"It really is shameful the way your education has been so thoroughly neglected," she said as she materialized next to me. "Jean-Paul is lucky he isn't called before the Council." She gave me an enormous smile. "He still might be. And if I have anything to do with it . . ." She let her voice trail off as she turned toward the door, putting her left palm against my forehead and her right one on the door. A couple in their forties gave us an odd look as they went past us, and she glared at them. They walked faster.

Her eyes narrowed, her brow furrowed. "That's strange." She dropped her hands and took a few steps back away from me. "I'm not getting anything—there's no image of him in your head, and I get no sense . . ." She rolled her eyes. "Of course." She stepped out into the street and looked up. "Is that him, by any chance?"

I followed the direction her finger was pointing. The building was about five stories high, and on the Orleans Street side there was a rusty and not very secure-looking fire escape. On the Royal Street side, there were several small balconies on each level, with French doors opening out onto them.

A man had stepped out onto one of the balconies on the third floor. He'd removed his shirt, revealing a perfectly smooth, well-defined torso. His skin almost seemed to shine in the light from the streetlamps. His jeans looked to have slipped down another inch or so—it looked like the only thing holding them on in the front was a rather prominent bulge. I nodded, licking my lips. "Yes, that's him. How did you know if you can't—"

"Because I can't read him, either." She smiled. "He isn't wholly human, you know. That's why I can't read him—I can only read humans and other vampires. Nigel would be able to, if he were here." She bit her lower lip and hummed for a moment. "He's definitely a relative of Sebastian's; that's for sure. He's at least part witch." She narrowed her eyes. "But I don't sense any danger from him—and I should." She tapped her forefinger against her temple. "Interesting." She reached over and rang the third buzzer from the bottom. A name card next to it read Q. NARCISSE. She gave me a smug look.

I really am an idiot sometimes. I hadn't even looked at the names.

Up above, I saw the shirtless man turn and walk inside from the balcony. After a few moments, there was a burst of static from the speaker mounted above the buzzers. "Yes?"

The sound of his voice raised hackles on the back of my neck. He sounded just like Sebastian.

"Mr. Narcisse?" Rachel asked smoothly, not missing a beat. "My name is Rachel Dufour, and I'm a special agent with the Federal Bureau of Investigation, working in tandem with the New Orleans Police Department. May we come up? I'd like to ask you some questions about your brother."

She was really an accomplished liar. She sounded completely convincing. I gaped at her, and she winked at me and gave a slight little shrug.

"That's something else you need to work on, Baby Vamp. You need to lose the Christian brainwashing about telling lies. They're a necessary part of life as a vampire in the human's world."

I just nodded, and she gave me a playful punch in the shoulder.

There was a buzzing sound, and Rachel pulled the door open. She gestured for me to go inside. I made a face and walked in. It smelled dead inside—like urine and stale alcohol. There was a rickety-looking staircase a few yards inside the door. The banister didn't look stable, and the stairs were worn, sagging in places, and badly in need of paint. The stairwell wasn't particularly well lit—there was a naked bulb just inside the door, but the bulb at the landing was burned out. About hallway up, the stairs were enveloped in darkness. Of course, that didn't bother me with my nonhuman eyesight, but I didn't understand how the humans stood it. Before I changed, it would have made me incredibly uncomfortable to climb stairs in darkness. I started climbing. At the first landing there was a worn-looking warped door, and I kept going up. The landing on the second floor was well lit with a yellow bulb, and I breathed a slight sigh of relief as I stepped into the warmth of the light.

"You really need to let go of your human superstitions," Rachel said from behind me. "It should be pretty clear to you by now that the dark is your friend, and clearly, the religion you were raised in was wrong about pretty much everything."

I didn't answer her; there wasn't really any point, so I

kept my mouth shut and kept climbing the stairs. Several of them sagged under my weight, and finally I reached the third landing. It was also lit, but there was a white globe over the lightbulb so the light was softer and not quite as harsh as at the lower landing. The door was open, and the man was leaning against the door frame. He smiled at me, and in spite of myself I felt my knees go a little weak.

"Get a grip, idiot," Rachel's voice sneered in my head.

This close, the resemblance to Sebastian was so remarkable it took all of my control not to gasp. His golden-brown skin gleamed in the light like it was lightly oiled, and his reddish gold hair was plastered down to the scalp. His eyes were brown with gold flecks, just as Sebastian's had been, and were wide set on either side of his strong nose. His skin was free of blemishes, and unlike Sebastian, his eyes were warm and friendly. There were other, subtler differences that weren't so obvious at first. There had been a deep dimple in Sebastian's chin—this young man didn't have one. This young man had the same type of frame as Sebastian— wide-shouldered and narrow-hipped, but Q. Narcisse's muscles were thicker and better defined than Sebastian's had been. There were deep crevices between his eight pronounced abdominal muscles. Thick veins lined his forearms, and I could see almost every fiber of muscle in his chest, shoulders, and arms. His neck was also thicker, and he seemed to radiate sexuality in a way Sebastian hadn't. His jeans still hung loosely off his hips, and there was a dark line of dampness just below the waistband of his red underwear—Unico, according to the emblem on the elastic. "You're a cop?" he asked, raising an eyebrow at me.

"I'm a special agent with the FBI, not a cop," Rachel said from behind me. She flashed a badge.

Where the hell did she get that? I wondered.

She went on, "My friend here is not a cop. He's more of a consultant. I brought him with me because he's an expert on the supernatural." Her tone was no-nonsense, I'm-in-charge-here.

I wondered if she'd impersonated a federal agent before.

The young man closed his eyes and barked out a harsh laugh. "You might as well come in, then." He stood aside so we could walk in. He shut the door behind us and crossed his arms. "I knew Sebastian's death was too good to be true."

I glanced over at Rachel. It was a strange thing to say. How could a death be too good to be true?

She gave a little shrug.

The apartment was incredibly neat and tidy. It was really just one large room, with a nook area that served as a galley kitchen. There was another door on the opposite side of the front door, which I assumed was a closet. There was a set of French doors directly opposite to the galley kitchen, leading out to the balcony—which was a lot smaller than it looked from the sidewalk. There was a double bed pushed up against one wall, an armoire, and a flat-screen television mounted on the wall. He unfolded two chairs and gestured for us to have a seat. Once we sat down, he hopped up onto the bed and crossed his legs. Every muscle in his torso rippled as he made himself comfortable.

"So, I'm right? This is about Sebastian?" He leaned back on the bed, and the muscles of his stomach flexed under that gorgeous, smooth golden-brown skin. There was a trail of wiry reddish gold hair running from his navel into the waistband of his underwear. "I've spent my entire adult life distancing myself from him—from my whole damned family—and no matter what I do..." He shook his head. "Sebastian told me once I'd never fully escape. I guess he was right."

"You wanted to escape from your family?" Rachel replied, pulling out a little notepad and pen from her jacket pocket. I was impressed—it was very official-looking. "I'm sorry, Mr. Narcisse. I didn't catch your first name."

"It's Quentin." He leaned forward, sticking his hand out toward me. "You said your name is Rachel, but I didn't catch your supernatural guy's." He flashed a smile at me that made me tingle a bit inside.

"You're acting like a schoolgirl," Rachel's voice mocked inside my head. *"Yes, he's very sexy, but if you're going to go all goofy every time we're around a hot man—"*

"Cord Logan," I said without thinking, cutting her off and instantly wanting to bite off my tongue.

Cord Logan was supposed to be dead—but it didn't matter, really.

He raised an eyebrow. "That name sounds familiar," he replied, offering me his hand.

I took it, almost losing mine inside his grip. His hands were much larger than mine, powerful and strong. His skin was warm but dry. I felt an electrical current flow through my entire body from the skin contact. My cock began to harden inside my pants.

"Can't you keep your mind on the business at hand for a fucking change?" Her voice echoed angrily around the inside of my head. *"If you want to fuck him, worry about that later."*

Out loud, she said, "You said you've tried to distance yourself from your brother, from your family. Why exactly is that, Quentin?"

He took a deep breath and let go of my hand. "If you've got a supernatural expert with you"—his eyes flicked over to me briefly—"then you already know about my family."

"Why don't you just go ahead and tell me?" She gave him a brittle smile.

He sighed. His tongue flicked over his lower lip, and he glanced over at me. "The Narcisses are witches, of course. Always have been, for as far back as anyone can remember—back before the Civil War, even. The story is that we came from Haiti—Saint-Domingue—and it was there that our family . . . one of my ancestors, he supposedly made a pact with the devil, if you can believe that." He shrugged.

"You don't believe in the devil?" I blurted out.

He smiled at me. "I don't think we—any of us, really—can know what happens after death, so we make up stories so we can sleep at night, so that we can accept the deaths of loved ones." He shrugged again. "But deals with the devil? Trading your soul for power?" He laughed. "All I know for sure is that the people in my family . . . we have weird powers, powers that other people don't have." He rubbed his head. "I don't want any part of that, never did, not even when I was a kid. My *grandmere* always said I didn't have a choice, that we'd been marked centuries ago, and turning our backs on our"—he swallowed—"powers was like turning our backs on God, which was of course a sin. I don't know, it all sounded like justification to me, you know? I don't see these powers as a gift, you know? I've seen members of my family who embraced their power consumed by it. Power corrupts. I've seen it." He shook his head. "I choose to embrace God and his light, not the darkness. We all have a choice—my choice was to not use the power. Once I was old enough, I broke away from the family." He gave us both a brittle smile. "I went to college. I have a job. And I have no powers. I renounced them."

"I saw you come out of Sebastian's house a little while ago," I said.

He shrugged. "For some perverse reason, he left me his house. I'm rebuilding it so I can sell it. I want no part of that house."

"Because of the murder?" Rachel leaned forward.

Quentin's face flushed. "Of course you know about that." He sighed. "That poor kid, his poor parents—he was their only child, you know."

It took me a second to realize he was talking about *me.*

"I can't imagine what kind of pain that must be," he went on. "But that was Sebastian all over. He never gave a shit about anyone else. He probably thought it was funny to leave me that damned house." He scratched his head. "I guess I'll never know why he did it. I mean, I'd like to think he did it to, you know, try to reach out to me—make amends of a kind, I guess."

"He's lying," Rachel whispered in my head. *"He knows more than he's saying."*

"How can you be so sure if you can't read his thoughts?"

She gave me a look. "So, you don't know what your brother was up to before he died?"

He looked away. "It sounds crazy when you say it out loud."

"See? He didn't cut his family off completely." "Trust me, Mr. Narcisse," Rachel said, "there's nothing you can say that will shock or surprise us." She gave him a very thin smile. "You wouldn't believe the things we've seen."

Quentin got up and walked over to the French doors. He stood there for a moment, framed in the light from the street, before he turned back around and gave us both a terribly sad smile. "I never believed in any of the family stories, you know." He folded his arms and shuddered. "The notion that we were destined to rule over all the witches . . .

no, I couldn't believe that." He shook his head. "If the Narcisse family truly had such a destiny, then why had we spent so many generations living on boats in the swamp?" He laughed bitterly. "Delusions of grandeur—stories spun at night after dinner to make sense of a poverty so intense... What good had witchcraft done my family? So much death and destruction, none of it made any sense to me, but Sebastian?" He walked back and sat again on the edge of the bed, leaning forward. "He believed it. He believed every bit of it. He thought our family was stupid to sit around and wait for it to happen. He thought we—*he*—could make it happen...." His voice trailed off for a moment. "I don't know what he did to get his money, how he came to own that house. But he left the swamp when I went to college. I came here to go to school—and he came too. We shared an apartment at first, up near the campus on the lakeshore. I had hoped coming to New Orleans would change his mind, once he saw there was a life, that there were possibilities outside the swamp." He shook his head and gave us both a little smile. "We used to dance, you know—at the Brass Rail. It was what we did for money. For me, it paid my way through college. Sebastian? He moved into his own place—said he needed to have his privacy."

"Why?" I asked, although I thought I knew.

"You want to fuck him, don't you? Should I leave you to it, then?"

"Get out of my head, you bitch!"

"I don't know," he replied with a shrug of his muscular shoulders. "I figured he was branching out into escorting." His face flushed. "We both got offers at the Brass Rail when we danced there, but he stopped dancing once he got his own place." Quentin laughed harshly. "He told me once it was his powers that provided for him when I warned him about it, you know—that he needed to be using condoms and taking care of himself." He absently scratched his stomach. "But even after I got out of school and got a job— I work at the Whitney Bank as a loan officer—Sebastian . . . I don't know. Does this all sound as crazy to you as it does to me?"

"What about your parents?" Rachel asked, giving me a warning glance.

"We never knew our parents. They died when we were young. We were raised by our grandmother Narcisse, on a houseboat in the swamp." He made a face. "We were the last of the Narcisse. Our father was the only son of an only son. And she supported us by telling fortunes, lifting curses, performing exorcisms on ignorant swamp people. Our powers." He laughed. "The demented ravings of a sad old woman living on the edge of a swamp and Sebastian trying to tell me he was using his powers here in New Orleans. The last time I saw him was a week or so before he died. He was all excited—he'd figured out a way to become even more powerful and wanted me to join him in his plan. Because we were identical twins, together we could obtain even more power. He was insane, of course. And he killed that college boy." His voice was bitter. "And you wonder why I wanted no part of him or his life?"

I closed my eyes and remembered lying on the bed in the back room of the house on Orleans Street, my ankles and wrists tethered to the bedposts, the candles burning while Sebastian chanted his spell, fearing that he was going to kill me—as he slit my wrist and drank my blood to add the power of a vampire to that of a witch.

"Well, thank you for your time, Mr. Narcisse," Rachel said with a smile, standing and offering him her hand.

I reluctantly stood up and shook his hand. Again, I felt the same electric shock I had the first time our hands came into contact with each other.

But this time, from the look on his face, I could tell that he'd felt it this time too.

CHAPTER 7

I couldn't get Quentin out of my mind as we went down the stairs in his building. I wondered what his skin would feel like. I could remember how silky Sebastian's had felt before things had turned so ugly, before I found out that he wasn't interested in *me* but wanted to drain all of my blood and drink it.

"Can you go more than five minutes without thinking about sex?" Rachel said snidely from behind me. "Not that I mind, usually—gay sex is so much hotter than hetero, or even lesbian sex, for the most part—but you're wearing me out already."

I opened the door at the foot of the stairs and stepped out into the damp night air. It had gotten cooler while we were inside, and the air felt wet. I looked up, and while the clouds still had that pinkish tint to them, they were definitely darker and moving faster than they had been. It meant rain was coming. "So, are you a lesbian?"

"I'm a vampire," she replied as we started up Orleans. "When I was a human, I considered myself a lesbian. Since I turned"—she shrugged—"sometimes, when I'm in the mood, I have sex with a man." She smiled at me. "I think a lot of it had to do with fear, but since I'm a vampire now, I don't fear any man. Any man who tries to overpower me or force me into anything"—she made a snapping sound with her tongue—"crack goes his neck."

"Charming." We crossed at Bourbon.

She gave me a sour look. "We're vampires, Cord. Get used to it. We're predators. We survive on the blood of humans, and we can kill them."

"So it's okay for us to be sociopaths?" I climbed the steps to my front door and unlocked it. "Killing humans every chance we get?"

"I didn't say that. Are you always so literal?" She slammed the door shut behind her and plopped down onto the couch. "Our job is to protect humans, you know. Vampires who go around killing, well, that's what part of our job as Nightwatchers entails."

I turned the dead bolt just as the entire house lit up with a flash of lightning. "What exactly does that entail?"

Rachel said in a rather snotty voice, "Your primary concern should be Jared, you know—not what the Nightwatchers do or whether you'll get to fuck Quentin Narcisse this evening."

Stung, I started to answer her when I realized something didn't feel right about the house. I closed my mouth and walked over to the pocket doors, sliding one back, just as thunder roared so loudly the entire house shook. Rain started pounding against the window on the far side of the room as I walked over to the bed and looked down at him.

Jared was still lying there on his back, his eyes closed, his bare chest moving up and down as he breathed shallowly. I sat on the bed and leaned over him, staring intently at his face. *It's not him,* I thought, looking around the room and seeing everything exactly the way I'd left it. *What's different? What's wrong with the house?* I closed my eyes and tried to sense it, put my finger on whatever it was that I was feeling.

"What is it?" Rachel stood in the doorway, her arms

folded over her breasts. "What are you feeling?" She smirked. "This doesn't feel like another one of your pornographic daydreams." She walked over to the bed and gently brushed Jared's bangs off his forehead. She lifted first his right eyelid, then his left. "He's okay, and from the looks of it, his conversion is going well—his body is adapting to the second infusion of blood from Nigel." She looked over at me and said gently, "I know you worry about him. He's going to be okay."

I turned around and glared at her. "No, he isn't going to be okay. He's never going to be okay again—"

"Stop." She reached over and grabbed my wrist. "Listen to me, okay? What's done is done. Are you going to feel guilty about this for the rest of eternity?" She shook her head. "I may have been a vampire for only twenty years, but I know that we can't hold on to things the way we could when we were human. Trust me, I've seen what happens to vampires who obsess. . . ." She dropped my wrist and shuddered. "You don't want to end up like that. Just trust me on that one." She looked at me, and her eyebrows knit together over her nose. "What are you feeling? I can sense something—"

"I don't know." I got off the bed. "Something's wrong. I just can't figure out what it is." I shivered and closed my eyes as there was another roar of thunder.

"Just focus," she replied, also standing up. On the bed, Jared rolled over onto his stomach and mumbled something. She leaned down and pulled the blanket up to cover his bare butt. "Pretend like the feeling is a string and grab on to it with both your hands—in your mind, I mean."

"Everything seems okay to you?" I tried doing what she suggested, but it didn't work. Whatever it was, was just outside my mind's eye. I pushed past her and walked down the hallway, opening every door and checking every room.

They were all empty, exactly as they were the last time I'd looked at them. But as I searched that side of the house, the feeling that something was wrong kept growing stronger. I walked back into the living room, and into the kitchen and down the other side of the house. I opened the door to the back gallery and walked out. A cat glared at me from the top of the wire table and proceeded to clean himself.

The rain was pouring off the roof into the courtyard like a waterfall. The pavement was under a couple of inches of water already. Lightning flashed again, close enough so that angry red spots filled my vision and the hair on my head stood up. I started to say something, but the clap of thunder was so loud Rachel couldn't hear me. She looked at me quizzically.

"I can't figure it out," I said, sitting in one of the chairs.

"I know it's frustrating," she said, sitting across from me at the wire table. "I mean, I can sense what you're feeling—"

Get out of my head!

"—but I don't feel it other than that." She made a face. "Which doesn't make any sense. *You* can't be more sensitive than I am. If you were, you'd be able to . . ." She ran her hands through her hair. "Maybe . . ."

"Maybe what?" The cat glared at us both and jumped down from the table. He walked over to the edge of the gallery and looked up at the steady stream of water coming down from the roof. He looked back at me, leaped onto the fence, and down into the yard next door.

"Nigel didn't want me to say anything—he didn't see any point in worrying you unnecessarily—but there's always issues when witches are involved." She frowned. "It's possible that Sebastian changed you somehow. Did you notice anything odd before you came back here?"

I shook my head. "Other than being a vampire?" I asked sarcastically. "Having to sink my teeth into humans and drink their blood in order to survive? Gee, what could possibly seem odd to me? Let me think for a minute."

To my surprise, she threw her head back and laughed, long and hard. When she was able to finally speak again, she grabbed my hands with hers and pressed them to her lips. "Oh, Cord, Cord! I'm beginning to understand what Jean-Paul saw in you. You remind me—" Her voice broke off. She looked stricken and turned away. "You remind me of my friend Philip." Her voice shook as she said the words.

"Philip?"

"It's a long story. Maybe someday I'll tell you about him." She looked away from me, watching the streams of water coming from the roof. "After we solve this problem and everything's okay around here, yeah." She turned back to me. "We might even end up as friends, you know." One corner of her mouth went up, and she raised an eyebrow. "Most people find me charming."

I found that unlikely but didn't say it out loud. Maybe she didn't mean it that way, but it was annoying to be referred to as "a problem."

But while she'd distracted me from thinking about it, whatever I was sensing in the house had faded away into nothingness, as if it had never been there. I took a deep breath and walked back into the house, leaving her sitting there on the gallery. I shut the door behind me and closed my eyes. I focused, like she told me to do earlier. I could feel it, and reached out for it in my mind, grabbing it with a mental hand.

And there it was—a faint greenish glow, a kind of essence of something that was slowly fading away, even as my mind was finally able to see it.

It was gone in another instant.

"Okay, what the hell was that?" I whispered as I walked

through the kitchen. I could see that the rain was lessening—the storm was moving on.

Rachel's words came back to me.

If there *was* something wrong with me—if Sebastian had done something to me, altered me in some way—why hadn't Jean-Paul or any of the others ever noticed? Why hadn't Nigel—and Rachel, for that matter—noticed? Especially Nigel. If he'd been around since the beginning of human history, surely he could sense if I wasn't a normal vampire.

As if there was such a thing as a normal vampire.

The whole thing was making my head hurt.

I walked into the bedroom and watched Jared. He had rolled back over onto his back. His chest still rose shallowly as he breathed. He'd shrugged off the comforter again, and he was aroused.

It was a really remarkable cock.

I sat down on the bed and stared at him, willing myself to not become aroused. It was wrong. He was gestating, converting from human to vampire, and taking advantage of him while he was in that state was no better than raping a girl passed out from drink, the way some of the brothers back at Ole Miss used to do.

But it was tempting—oh so tempting.

"Are you constantly horny? You're worse than a thirteen-year-old."

"Stay out of my head, Rachel." I closed my eyes and imagined a wall going up around my mind, keeping her out.

"Nicely done," she said, her voice fading.

I touched his forehead. His skin was cool, and I could feel his breath on my arm.

I remembered meeting his parents, how kind they'd been to me, and once again felt sorrow and guilt at what I'd done to him rising within me.

What story would be concocted to explain to them what happened to their son? Undoubtedly they were worried—he hadn't come home that night; he'd simply vanished. Had they already contacted the police? Was there an alert out for him? I closed my eyes.

I'd never really known how Jean-Paul had fixed things with the fire so my parents had believed me to be dead. All I knew for sure was there were two bodies in that house when it burned—Sebastian and another who had been identified as me. I'd been an only child. My birth had been difficult, and after a long, horrible labor that had almost killed her, my mother had been left unable to have another child. She liked to remind me of how difficult my birth had been when I disagreed with her or disobeyed. By the time I was a teenager, I could say the words along with her. But because she couldn't have another child, she had clung to me—they both had. I sometimes wondered why they never considered adopting—it certainly would have made sense with their deep religious faith—but as far as I knew, it was never even considered an option. As much as I'd hated them for trying to control every aspect of my life, planning my future and forcing their hateful religion down my throat, I had loved them, which was what had made trying to break free from them so difficult. My high school friends had envied me my parents, who'd never missed a game or a play or anything I did. There was never a question I'd go to college, and they'd bought me a secondhand car when I got my driver's license. So many of the kids I went to school with had parents who could barely afford to clothe them, let alone send them to college or get them a car or give them an allowance.

But it was all a trap too. How could I tell them that their much-loved only son was gay, was an abomination in the eyes of the religion that was so much a part of their lives? Could they turn their backs on the Church of Christ and realize I was actually born this way, gay by the grace of God and not by choice?

I feared they'd cut me out of their lives. My uncle had done so to his oldest son when he'd left his wife for another woman. "The church forbids divorce," he'd said in a tone that left no doubt that he no longer considered his oldest son his child.

It was either tell them or live a lie for the rest of my life, and I didn't think I had the courage to tell them. But I'd been so desperate to escape that decision that I'd been easy prey for Jean-Paul. It had been easy for him to convince me that being a vampire was the best possible escape for me. They'd think I was dead and I would be free to live my own life for all eternity.

But sitting on the edge of the bed, staring at Jared and what I'd done to him, I began to wonder if I had made the right choice.

The bitter memories were pushed aside and I began to remember the good things about my parents. There had been laughter, love, and above all else, joy. Birthday parties and high school football games when I could pick out the sound of my father's voice shouting from the bleachers over all the other noise, and coming home after the game, staying up for hours discussing and dissecting the game with him at the kitchen table. Both of my parents had wonderful senses of humor and loved nothing more than to laugh. I remembered the summer vacations on the sugary white sand beaches of the Florida panhandle, where my skin turned brown from the sun. There had been trips to Six Flags in Atlanta, and my father had ridden everything with me, enjoying the thrilling rides as much as I had.

A lump rose in my throat as I remembered again how much pain my "death" in the fire must have caused them, was probably still causing them.

Rachel's hand touched my shoulder, caressing it gently. "There's no use in thinking this way, Cord. The pain will not help. It will only make you bitter if you dwell on it." She sat down next to me on the bed. "What's done is done. There's no point in regret—regret is the path to madness for a vampire. You have to put all of that behind you now. It may not seem this way to you because you're so young, but humans live and die in no more than a blink of our eyes."

Eternity stretched out before me, and I caught my breath at the vast emptiness I saw.

"I cannot imagine what it must be like to be Nigel's age," she went on, putting her arm around my shoulders. "The things he has seen—he is my creator, and I am so incredibly young next to him. I've been a vampire for only twenty years, and I have seen some of the people I cared about grow older, some of them sicken and die. I try not to think about it too much—you have to learn to deal with it, to separate your feelings from your reality or else you'll go mad." She took a deep breath. "And you—you're just a baby. I could strangle Jean-Paul for his irresponsibility! You shouldn't be on your own—not for at least another century. Nigel wouldn't even consider letting me on my own until I have passed my first century—and possibly not even then. What Jean-Paul has done is no different than putting a newborn out in the forest to fend for itself."

"Tell me about your old life, your human life," I said, struggling to keep my voice from shaking. I wanted to hear her story, to forget my own, to push the melancholy and sadness from my consciousness.

"I was a singer." She stroked the top of my head gently.

"I came to New Orleans to be a musician. I worked in a coffee shop during the day and sang with a band at night. I was quite good too."

Jared muttered something and shifted again in his sleep. She had pulled the comforter back up over him, so his erection was hidden.

"I know, I enjoyed listening to you play," I replied, smiling at her. "You really have a remarkable voice. You could have been a star."

"You think?" She took me by the hand. "Come back out into the living room and I'll play something for you."

She pulled me along and pushed me down into a wing-back chair while she sat down at the baby grand. "I've always loved music," she said as she began running her fingers along the keys. "Even now, whenever things become too much for me to bear, I can simply sit down and play and forget everything."

She began to play a song I didn't recognize, but it was melodic and beautiful. I closed my eyes and allowed my head to rest against the back of the chair. The music washed over me and carried me away from everything.

"Why are you so difficult?" Jean-Paul shouted at me, his eyes blazing angrily. "Why can't you simply enjoy yourself? Why must you turn everything into some stupid soap opera?"

"Because I love you," I retorted, pulling my knees up to my chest and wrapping my arms around them. "Why is that so hard for you to understand? Do you even know what love is?"

He stood there, fists clenched, his enormous swollen cock slapping against his lower abdomen as he literally shook with anger. "Sex isn't love," he replied, walking back over to the bed and grabbing a fistful of my hair in one hand, pulling my head back and exposing my neck. He leaned down and ran his tongue along my Adam's apple down to the base of my throat. "You don't know the

difference between the two—and you don't care, really, do you?
You're just a little pig who wants to get fucked and be fucked and
fuck and be with as many men as you can."

His angry, insulting words washed over me, but I didn't care. I
didn't care as long as he was touching me. I didn't care as long as
he was feeling something for me, even if it was anger.

Anything was better than nothing.

I moaned as the ecstasy pushed the anger from my mind, my cock
swelling in response as the pressure on my hair increased as he
pulled harder. "You want it rough, don't you?" he whispered as he
pushed me down against the mattress, slamming a leg roughly in
between mine and pushing my legs apart.

"Fuck you," I spat as his weight pressed down on me. He held
both of my wrists with one hand over my head, and I was helpless,
even as I writhed and tried to buck him off me.

"No, I'm going to fuck you, you nasty little bitch boy," he whis-
pered into my ear, biting down on my earlobe. "I am going to fuck
you long and rough and hard, just the way you like it, the way you
want it."

I gasped as his mouth worked its way down to my nipples, and he
began licking and sucking on them, moving rapidly back and forth
from one to the other until my entire body was shaking and trem-
bling with need and desire, my cock straining against his body as
one of his hands started rubbing over the head, and as much as I
was hating him in that moment, I didn't want him to stop. He was
right—I liked it like this. I liked him forcing me. I liked him hold-
ing me down and calling me names. It made my cock ache and my
balls clench, and I wanted him inside me, pounding away at me,
driving his hardness into me, slamming me with such force that my
head hit the wall. He released my hands and sat up, releasing me.
I gulped in breaths of air as he toyed with my nipples, flicking them
with his fingers.

"Look at you. You're just a little bitch in heat who wants my
cock so bad he'll beg for it," he taunted me.

"Go to hell, asshole!" I shouted the words at him, my face twisted in a sneer. I shoved his fingers away from my nipples and tried to sit up, but he grabbed hold of my legs and pulled them up in the air and forced them down again.

He placed his mouth right next to my ear as he pressed his weight down on top of me. "You're just a little bitch, aren't you?" he whispered into my ear as he kept rubbing the head of my cock. "You want to be forced, don't you? You like it rough, don't you, bitch?"

"Fuck you." I managed to breathe the words out again somehow, even as my eyes were rolling back in my head from the waves of pleasure emanating from the head of my cock as his fingertips continued to tease it, playing with the slit as my precum began to slowly ooze from it.

"I'll fuck you, all right," he said, and slapped me across the face. My eyes welled with bloody tears as I started fighting against him, trying to push him off me. But he was too strong, and he somehow managed to get both of my wrists in his free hand and push them over my head, holding them there. He stopped the pressure on the head of my cock, and I gasped for air as my body's trembling stopped, blinking back the tears as he tied my wrists to the headboard, the way Sebastian had.

"Oh yeah, the witch knew what he was doing with you, didn't he?" His voice was contemptuous. "He knew what you like, didn't he? He tied you up and you loved it, didn't you? You teased him with your tight little ass just like a bitch in heat until he couldn't take it anymore."

"Fuck you! Fuck you!"

He straddled me, sitting on my stomach and smiling down at me, his blue eyes glinting in the candlelight. "What are you going to do now, bitch?" His voice mocked me, and he leaned forward, rubbing his cock on my lips. I could taste the salty sweat, smell its masculine mustiness. His heavy balls rested on my chin, and I wanted him, God help me, I wanted him.

"You want to suck my cock, don't you? You want to lube it up with your saliva before I shove it up your ass, don't you, boy?"

"Fuck you," I whimpered as he slid down my body, grasping my cock and his with the same hand, rubbing them together as his hips began moving back and forth, grinding into me, and I started gasping again because it felt good, it felt amazing, and I wanted him inside me, because even though I hated him, I loved him and I wanted him inside, I wanted to feel him thrusting angrily into me, and then his mouth was on my right armpit, licking and kissing and nibbling, and involuntarily I cried out, almost sobbing from the intensity of how good it felt, how absolutely amazing he was making me feel. No one else on earth could make me feel the way Jean-Paul could, no one, and then his mouth was on my other armpit, but there was another mouth on the other.

I opened my eyes and there was Clint, his bald head gleaming in the candlelight, and Armand was also there, his eyes glinting as he stroked himself. Norman was at the foot of the bed, and he leaned forward. His tongue began darting between my butt cheeks, and I stifled a scream as Jean-Paul maneuvered off me, and I pulled against the restraints. There was nothing I could do, other than writhe and scream and moan, but at the same time it felt extraordinary, and someone was tying a handkerchief over my eyes and I couldn't see, everything was dark, but I could feel their mouths, their tongues darting over my body, and someone took my cock into their mouth.

Another mouth was nibbling the tender skin of my left armpit while fingers pulled and pinched and tweaked at my nipples, while another mouth was on my asshole, the tongue and lips teasing the skin around it, and every so often the tongue would penetrate, making my entire body stiffen, but there was nothing to do but moan, nothing to do but surrender to the pleasure.

"You want to act like a little bitch, then you're going to be treated like one," Jean-Paul breathed into my ear.

And a cock entered me, rough and hard, shoving inside and

tearing me apart. I opened my mouth to scream but another mouth came down over it, a tongue shoving into my mouth, lips closing over my tongue and sucking on it, and my whole body began to shiver and tremble as the cock stopped pushing; it was completely inside of me, and I relaxed, welcoming whoever it was inside of me, and the animalistic side of my brain pushed everything aside.

"Yes, fuck me. Make me your little bitch," I demanded when my mouth was released again. "Come on, fuck me! Do it! Give it to me! I doubt all of you combined can satisfy me!"

I strained against the ropes, trying to push myself down farther on the cock, to get it all inside of me, and it began to withdraw and I was gasping from the feeling as everything closed up behind its retreat, and I growled, "Fuck me fuck me make me your bitch I want you inside of me," and then it was forcing its way back in as I screamed, but the pain crossed the line into pleasure and it was intense. It was like I was a virgin and this was the first time I'd ever taken a cock inside of me, and I wanted them all inside of me. All I wanted was cock in my mouth, in my ass; there wasn't enough cock to satisfy me, and he kept fucking me, and I got my wish as a thick one was shoved into my mouth, and I lapped at it, closing my mouth around it and toying with his head with my tongue, sucking and bucking my hips upward as the other cock plunged deeper and deeper inside of me, and I gripped with my ass, and I felt that one tremble and cry out as he came inside, and the other began pumping his cum into my mouth, pulling it out, raining the cum down on my face as I lapped for it with my tongue. I wanted to taste it all; I wanted more. And then a different cock was forcing its way into my ass, and I laughed, because I wanted more. I wanted to just be used and debased and humiliated over and over and over again. . . .

The music stopped and I opened my eyes. I took a deep breath as the memory faded away.

I looked over at Rachel, who was watching me carefully, her eyes narrowed to slits. "Did they often treat you like that?" she asked, her voice quiet and still and sympathetic. "You know that was gang rape, don't you?"

"Please." I stood up, my erection straining against my jeans. "Please stay out of my head, Rachel." My legs were wobbly.

She nodded and turned away from me. She began playing the piano again, this time a classical piece. I think it was Rachmaninoff, but I wasn't sure, and I knew I had to get away from her pity, away from her loathing.

Embarrassed, I headed for the front door. "I'm going for a walk. I think I need to get some air."

She merely nodded again without looking up.

CHAPTER 8

It was all too much for me.

The night sky was clear of clouds, a beautiful deep midnight blue with a gorgeous half-moon casting light down on the city. The sidewalk was slick and wet, and the gutters were filled with clear water. I stood at the top of the steps, breathing in the clear air. The French Quarter only smells clean after a heavy rain. It always took an hour or so for the stink to take over again.

I looked over at Sebastian's—no, *Quentin's*—house. That was really where it all started, wasn't it? The debasement, the dark shameful desires that drove me to illicit encounters with men who had no names, whose faces I couldn't remember, who were nothing more to me than a body with an erection and an ass to plug?

Since I had fled Palm Springs and come to New Orleans, every night had been filled with strangers. I fed from all of them, sinking my teeth into that spot on the neck where the juicy jugular vein was most prominent, feeling their bodies shudder with pleasure as my lips closed around the gushing holes and lapped their blood. Sometimes there were as many as four a night, fucking and sucking and licking and kissing until my cock was nearly rubbed raw.

But the beauty of being a vampire was those raw friction sores always healed quickly, sometimes before the trick of the moment had finished putting his clothes back on and disappeared into the night. There was the back room at Rawhide where conversation wasn't even required, where I could just go stand in a corner and wait for someone's hand to brush against my crotch, and my ability to see clearly in the dark gave me an advantage over my human counterparts. I would take off my shirt and toss it aside, open my pants and expose my cock and balls for anyone with a hungry mouth and a need to worship another man to pleasure me. There was the upstairs room at the Phoenix over on Elysian Fields, where I could find a moist hole to pound as they pressed a bottle of poppers to my nostrils as my cock took them to heights of pleasure they never imagined existed.

I'd been lost in a nonstop orgy for over two weeks.

And that was really why, a few days ago, I'd decided to test myself by seeing how long I could go without feeding. A stupid, self-destructive decision made because my heart was aching, because there was an emptiness inside of me because Jean-Paul hadn't loved me, had never loved me. I'd tried to fill that empty space with strangers.

I might as well have set myself on fire and been done with it.

Jared was paying the price for my self-destruction.

I wasn't human anymore.

And that, too, had been a thoughtless decision, one that should have received more consideration, more thought put into it. But I had so desperately wanted to be myself, to be able to enjoy the love of another man that I traded my humanity for it.

Was it worth it?

I wasn't sure any longer.

I wandered down Orleans Street, not really paying attention to what I was doing or where I was going. I just needed to get away from that house, from her, from what I had done to Jared. The guilt—how did vampires live with such guilt? Was it something that came with time, the longer you lived the less you cared about your victims?

I wasn't sure I wanted to be that person. I wasn't sure I could ever stop caring, stop feeling guilt. If anything, being a vampire had made me care more.

I walked past the cathedral and Jackson Square. I didn't look down Chartres Street, where this whole mess had begun—was it just a day or two ago? I wasn't even sure anymore. Leaving Palm Springs and Jean-Paul had clearly been a mistake. I had been immature, stupid. So Jean-Paul wasn't in love with me? So I was nothing more than another beautiful young man who excited his desire and lusts? There were worse things. And I did miss the others, especially Clint. He had always been almost a surrogate father for me, much more so than selfish, self-absorbed Jean-Paul. He was handsome, with his gleaming bald head and gentle blue eyes, the strong, thick muscles. He was the one who always took care of me, made sure I'd fed and was okay—not Jean-Paul.

I missed him.

Maybe once this entire mess was cleared up, I could go back to Palm Springs and find Clint. The two of us could leave Jean-Paul and the others and make our way through the world. Surely he was tired of the parties and the drugs, the crowds of sweating musclemen flying high on one drug or another, the thumping dance music, the anonymity of it all.

I crossed Decatur Street, smelling the coffee and beignets frying in oil at Café du Monde as I went up the ramp. I crossed the streetcar tracks and climbed up the last steps to the very top of the levee. I turned back and looked at the beautifully lit cathedral. Jackson Square was locked for the night, quiet and lovely in the night lamps. I smiled and turned back to watch the river. It was peaceful up here on the levee, with the river making its endless journey to the Gulf of Mexico. A huge barge was going past on the river, and I sat down on a bench, resisting the urge to bury my face in my hands. I watched the currents swirling and wondered what would happen if I simply jumped into the cold, muddy water. Could a vampire drown? Would I simply be swept out to the Gulf by the treacherous and tricky currents?

I don't know anything, I reminded myself. *Jean-Paul taught me nothing, nothing at all, about being what I am now, what he created of me. Why was he so careless?*

I vaguely became aware of someone walking up behind me, but I didn't turn and look. Whoever it was came around the bench and sat down next to me. "Are you okay?" a male voice said softly. A warm hand came down on my bare shoulder.

The contact sent an electric shock through me.

I turned my head and was more than a little startled to see Quentin sitting there. He had put on a pair of khaki shorts and a blue tank top, and he was slouching down, his legs spread out widely in front of him. A gold cross on a gold chain hung around his neck. "What are you doing here?" I asked, not quite sure I was completely comfortable to be alone with him—even in public. He seemed to ooze sensuality, and I could make out his nipples through the cotton of his tank top. They were hard.

"I saw you walking," he explained, slouching down a few more inches on the bench. "I like sitting out on my balcony, and I saw you. You seemed upset about something, so I came down. I saw you walking across the square, and I followed you here." His knee brushed lightly against mine, and I again felt that strange electrical current pass from his skin to mine.

"Why would you care?" I asked, shifting slightly away from him on the bench. The last thing I needed right then was to be hit on by the twin of the witch who'd almost killed me two years earlier.

Even if he was incredibly sexy . . . even though I wanted him to hit on me, I knew this was a mistake. I knew I should probably just get up and walk back to the house, sit inside dutifully and listen to Rachel play the piano while we both waited for Nigel to come back.

He shrugged slightly. "I don't know. I probably shouldn't, but for some reason I do. I can't explain it. If you want me to go away and leave you alone, I will."

"No," I said automatically, without pausing to think. "I'm glad you're here."

"I find watching the river to be incredibly calming," he replied. "I like to come down here whenever I need to think, sort things out, you know? I think maybe it's because no matter what happens to me, this river is going to keep flowing by here, just like it always has. The river is eternal." He smiled at me shyly. "If you need someone to listen—"

"Thanks." It was difficult not to laugh. Oh, sure, it's one thing to talk about witches and so forth; it's entirely another to say, *Oh, yeah, by the way, I'm actually a vampire, and the real reason we came to talk to you was we're trying to figure out whether or not your dead brother—you know the one, the one you think embraced darkness—might have put some kind of curse on me before he died. And oh yes, I'm the reason your brother died. I'm the other one everyone thinks died in that fire, along with your brother. And no, I don't know how Jean-Paul worked that. I just know that somehow he did.*

"So, you're some kind of expert on the supernatural?" Quentin asked, his knee brushing against my leg again, making me shiver slightly. "It's so nice to be able to talk to someone about all that shit, you know, someone who isn't going to think I've completely lost my mind or am stupid or superstitious or something." He laughed. "Everyone up in Bayou Shadows believes my grandmother's a witch, you know. They really believed my brother and I were too. It made life kind of hellish for me growing up."

"Bayou Shadows?"

"It's this little Podunk town on the edge of the swamp where I'm from." He rolled his eyes. "They believe in all that kind of stuff up there. There's supposed to be a family that has the rougarou curse up there too."

"Rougarou?" I started to ask what that was but stopped myself. I was supposed to be an expert on the supernatural— and one had to assume an expert would know what that was. "Really?"

He rolled his eyes. "I told you, crazy shit. It's a town full of superstitious people, believe you me." He shook his head. "You don't know how glad I am I got out of there."

"Actually, I bet I do know," I replied, relaxing a little bit and slouching down on the bench a little more. "I'm from a little rural town too. I grew up in the hills in northwest Alabama. You want to talk about backwards places? The whole time I was a kid, all I did was pray I'd get older so I could get the hell out of there. Although we didn't have superstitious people who believed in witches and stuff. What we had was way worse."

"What could be worse?" He looked at me.

"Fundamentalist Christians." I winked at him. "I'd much rather grow up around people who think witches and rougarous are real than the self-righteous." I shook my head. "You know the type, I'm sure—the ones who are convinced they are the only ones who know what God really wants, and if you don't do exactly as they say, you're going straight to hell." I shivered as a cool breeze came off the river. "You can imagine what that was like for a gay kid."

"We had some of that in Bayou Shadows too," Quentin commiserated. "There was a horrible little church there called the Church of Repentance. Talk about a bunch of whacked-out nutjobs. You know, they actually used to talk about burning my grandmother at the stake, and they were serious." He rubbed his forehead. "One of the preacher's kids tried to beat me up one day when we were in grammar school. I kicked his stupid little bitch ass." He laughed. "No one ever tried that again, let me tell you. I imagine Stevie Hebert is running that stupid church now. He used to make me wish that I actually was a witch, you know?"

"Yeah." I laughed along with him. The truth was, just being around him made me feel better. There was something about him that was calming, that seemed to put me at ease. "Thanks, Quentin." I allowed my knee to brush against his again and wondered if he, too, felt the electricity when our bare skin touched. "You've made me feel better, and I appreciate it, man."

"No problem, bro. Why don't you come back over to my place?" He peered into my eyes. "We can open a bottle of wine and talk some more." His tongue darted out and licked his upper lip.

I nodded, and when we stood up, our arms brushed against each other. Our eyes met, and there was no mistaking the desire in his. I smiled back at him and reached out, taking his strong hand in mine again. We walked back to his apartment, hand in hand. Every so often, as we walked, we lightly brushed against each other. I followed him up the stairs inside his building, watching the way his round, beautiful ass moved, my cock beginning to stir to life inside my jeans. He unlocked his apartment door, and I sat down in the chair I'd taken earlier. He opened the wine and poured us each a glass, handing me mine. I took a sip. It was good.

He pulled his shirt up over his head and tossed it into a laundry basket before sitting down on his bed. He smiled at me. "Your partner was a little on the intense side—she really made me nervous." He made a face. "Sebastian's been dead now for over two years, and I still haven't been able to shake him, you know? It's so weird. My grand-mother..." He paused.

"What about your grandmother?" I leaned forward. I stared at the deep valley in the center of his chest, the trail of wiry copper hair trailing from his navel to his shorts, the bulge in the front.

He sighed. "She thinks he hasn't moved on, if you can believe that. She thinks he's still tethered to this world somehow and can't move on." He rubbed his eyes. "She thinks I can help him move on and wants me to come back up there so she can do a ritual. I don't know. I mean, I don't really believe in that shit, but at the same time it kind of scares me."

"Why don't you?" I asked. "What can it hurt? If you don't believe in any of this, and if it makes your grandmother feel better..." I let my voice trail off. "I mean, where's the harm? Sometimes we should just do things, you know, for the people we love. Isn't that what it's all about?"

"I never really thought of it that way," Quentin said slowly. He got up and refilled his wineglass and walked over to the window. "I've spent most of my life running away from all this stupidity, you know."

He stood there, his back to me, facing the cathedral. The huge shadow of the statue of Jesus cast by the spotlight on the back of the building seemed to be almost beckoning me to get up from my chair and join Quentin. I couldn't help staring at his broad back. It was beautifully sculpted underneath his tawny gold skin. His shoulders were thick and capped with perfectly shaped muscles, and his back tapered down to a narrow waist. There were two dimples in his lower back just above where the curve of his perfectly shaped ass began. His khaki shorts were loose, and as before, I could read UNICO on the waistband of his underwear. There was a small patch of dark gold curly hairs in the center of his back just above the shorts. The shorts hung down to his knees, over defined, thick calves.

I got up and walked up behind him. I leaned against the frame opposite him, but we were still very close. I could smell him—a mixture of cologne and sweat that seemed deeply masculine and remarkably sensual and arousing.

He was more muscular than Sebastian had been, and Sebastian hadn't exactly been a ninety-eight-pound weakling.

I wanted to kiss his thick, sensual lips, put my hand on his muscular chest.

But I wasn't completely sure if my attentions would be welcomed, if he could feel the electrical current flowing between us. I swallowed nervously.

He looked at me and smiled. "Would you be interested in coming up to Bayou Shadows with me?" he asked. "Watching the ritual might be interesting for you—in your work, I mean."

My work? I gawked at him for a moment before remembering Rachel had introduced me as an expert in the supernatural. "Would you like me to?" I asked quietly.

"I think I'd like that very much, Cord." He reached over with his free hand and traced his index finger along the side of my face. "You're a very beautiful man." He took another step toward me until we were so close we were almost touching.

I licked my lower lip and placed my left hand directly

onto his chest. His skin was silky and incredibly warm, almost feverish, to the touch. I could feel his heart pounding beneath, and I was glad I'd fed so deeply from the stripper the night before. The hunger wasn't there, and there was no worry I might lose control with him and sink my teeth into his neck.

But I couldn't help but wonder how his blood would taste.

He leaned closer, and his chest pressed against mine. He placed his lips against mine. He tasted of wine, and I opened my mouth and allowed his tongue to slip inside. I closed my mouth around his and sucked on his tongue as he pressed his hips against me, and I could feel the enormity of his erection through our clothes, its need and urgency.

I put my left hand on his ass. It was hard and solid, and I let my other hand drift down, our mouths still pressed together, and grabbed hold of his erect penis. He clenched his ass and pushed against me, and I raised my left leg and wrapped it around his, pulling him deeper and closer into me. His hands cupped my ass and lifted me almost effortlessly until I was up on my toes. He was so strong, and desire raced through me, desire and the need to be naked with this remarkably beautiful man.

He pulled his head back and smiled, his eyes half closed. "I wanted you from the moment you walked in here this afternoon," he confessed in a low voice. "All I could think of when I saw you was how badly I wanted to fuck your pretty little ass." He squeezed my ass again, and I bit my lower lip, my eyes closing. "I knew it was hard as a rock, just like the rest of you. You are so beautiful . . ." His voice trailed off as he stepped back from me. He walked back into the apartment, undoing his shorts and stepping out of them as he headed for his bed. His red underwear had ridden up slightly into the crack of his big muscular ass, exposing hard smooth cheeks that only heightened my desire.

He turned as he sat down on the edge of the bed, and I could see the head of his enormous cock sticking out through the waistband of his underwear. He smiled at me and lay back, beckoning me forward. I pulled my shirt over my head, dropping it on the floor as I walked toward the bed. A cool breeze came through the open doors and kissed my skin. I shivered slightly as I undid my shorts and slid them down until I stood naked before him. I stepped out of them and put both of my hands on my hips. My cock strained up against my stomach.

He smiled at me. "You're even more beautiful out of your clothes than you were in them," he whispered, licking his lips.

I knelt between his legs and grabbed his cock with my hands. I leaned down and flicked the head with my tongue. His body trembled.

"That's nice," he breathed. "Oh, yeah, baby, that's good." His voice deepened. "You want to suck that big dick, boy?"

I looked up at his smiling face and replied, "Oh, yeah."

I slid his underwear down and off his feet, tossing them over my shoulder. I ran my tongue from the head all the way down the underside of his cock until I reached his thick balls. I took one of them into my mouth gently, sucking on it before gently letting it slip between my lips and taking the other one inside as well. I spit on my left index finger and traced it down from his balls to the entrance between his muscular ass cheeks. I tapped his hole with my fingertip, smiling as his entire body began to slightly tremble with anticipation. I let the other ball slide out and ran my tongue up the underside of his mighty cock again. A drop of precum oozed out of the slit, and I smeared it with my right index finger as I slowly began working the left finger inside of him. I looked up at his face, above the rippling abdominal muscles and the thick slabs of his chest. He had a nipple in each of his hands, twisting and pinching them. His eyes were closed, and he pursed those beautiful red lips.

I took his cock into my mouth, tightening my lips around it as my tongue continued to lick and toy with the head. I slid my mouth slowly down the big shaft, stopping about halfway down as my gag reflex involuntarily reacted. He was so big I wasn't sure I could take all of him inside of my mouth, let alone into my ass. I'd never seen a cock this large outside of Internet porn. Jean-Paul, Clint, and the others were all nicely endowed, but nothing on this scale.

Even Sebastian, whose cock had been thick and long, paled in comparison to his twin.

I closed my right hand around the base of the massive thing and continued working the top with my mouth as I started stroking him with my hand.

"Oooh, baby, that feels so good," he whispered, and I felt his hand on the top on my head. "I want you to fuck me, but I don't want you to stop that."

I let his dick pop out of my mouth, and I gave him a lusty grin, relieved that I wouldn't have to take that monster inside of me. "Baby, I'll fuck that hot ass of yours into next week." I winked. "And I bet it's hot and tight, isn't it?"

I pushed his legs farther apart and stuck my tongue into his musky hole, tasting him and working the rim with my lips as I moved my tongue in a circle inside of him.

He was gasping for air, his hand still on the top of my head as I continued working him. His ass tasted strangely sweet to me, almost as though it were some strange kind of nectar my body needed, craved, and desired.

I took my mouth off him and slid up his body until we were face-to-face, cock-to-cock. I ground my cock into his as I forced my tongue into his mouth, hoping he could taste himself in my mouth.

He brought his legs up, pressing his ass against my hard-on. He reached over to the nightstand and pulled out a bottle of lube, squeezing some into his palm. He massaged some into his hole and then slicked up my cock before pointing its head directly into him.

"Ride me," he demanded, his voice urgent. "Fuck me, make me your bitch."

I grinned down at him and shoved myself as deep inside of him as I could go. I got a few inches inside before meeting resistance, and rather than forcing my way in, I stopped, allowing the head to rest against the obstruction.

His breath was coming in tiny little gasps as I stayed there, half inside, not making a move to go any farther, just teasing him.

I put my mouth next to his ear. "You want that cock, don't you, bitch?" I nibbled on his earlobe.

His back arched upward. "Yes, please, oh God, yes, please I want you . . ."

With a nasty smirk, I started sliding back out of him.

"No, don't, please—"

"I want you to beg," I replied, not sure where this side of me had come from. But it was what I wanted, what I needed to hear. I wanted him to beg me to fuck him, beg me to ride that beautiful, muscled ass, to just fuck him and fuck him until he was blowing out a huge load all over himself while I blew one inside of him. I just wanted to fuck him and fuck him and fuck him, but first I wanted this big, beautiful muscleman to beg me to do it. I wanted him to be mine, to own him completely, to dominate him and ride him, to fuck him like no one had ever fucked him before so he would remember how I felt deep inside him, so he'd never forget, so that he would remember when he was alone and tugging on himself, his eyes closed, remembering how my cock felt, how much of a load I shot into him, and make him my willing sex slave, who'd want me to tie him up, spread-eagled so he was defenseless while I worked and teased and toyed with his ass, that big round hard beautiful muscled ass.

And I finally understood how erotic it was to be dominant, to use your cock solely for the pleasure of another man, to drive him insane with desire and pleasure and lust while you pumped him and filled him completely, and I understood finally why Jean-Paul had done some of the things he had done to me.

I understood how erotic and arousing it was to have your man tied to the bedposts, unable to move, unable to resist you, unable to do anything other than whimper and moan and beg and plead.

And I slammed deep into him, and the resistance I'd encountered finally gave, relaxing and surrendering to me almost the very instant my cock's head reached it.

Quentin relaxed and took me, accepting me as his lord and master, his dominant top, and I knew he was mine when the deep guttural moan of pleasure came through his amazing lips, as his eyes half closed and all I could see were the whites because the pleasure was making them roll back up.

I plunged all the way inside of him, my balls slamming against his muscular cheeks, grinding my hips from side to side as I tried to get my entire body inside of him.

His eyes bulged open and he let out a long, drawn-out moan of pleasure.

And I started riding him, pounding away at him, in and out, harder and faster, listening to him and taking joy in the sound of him unable to catch a breath, gasping from the intensity of the pleasure my cock was giving his beautiful ass, looking down at his magnificent body as sweat began dripping down my face, drops falling from my chin and my nose onto that beautiful smooth velvety skin, his skin becoming moist from his own rising sweat, the hair in his pits becoming wet as rivulets of water ran down the sides of his face, and I kept pounding at him as he gasped and groaned and moaned from the intensity of it all.

And his mouth opened and a guttural cry roared out of him as thick, stringy ropes of milky white cum began shooting out of him, each shot accompanied by a scream and an incredible twitch.

And I slid out of his trembling, shaking body, shooting my own onto his torso, mingling mine with his.

And then I reached out and put my mouth on his, laying my torso against his, the sticky mixture of our juices smearing onto both of us as we kissed, our hearts pounding together.

I rolled off to the side and stared up at the ceiling fan, which was slowly turning over us, cooling our slick, hot skin.

He got up, his legs slightly trembling, and tossed me a towel to wipe myself down with as he took another towel and did the same.

He smiled at me. "Wow." He was breathing hard, and a trickle of sweat ran down his chest.

I smiled back at him. "Yeah."

He crawled back into the bed with me, putting his arms around me and pulling me close. I kissed his cheek and lay there for a while.

But finally, I knew I had to go, so I got out of the bed and slowly began to dress.

He watched me, his eyes still half closed. "You can't stay?" he asked.

I shook my head.

"But you will go to Bayou Shadows with me?"

I nodded. I wrote my phone number down and placed it on the nightstand.

"I'll call you when I've made the arrangements with my grandmother." He followed me to the door and kissed me again.

I placed my finger on his lips. "I look forward to seeing you again, Quentin."

And I walked down the stairs and out the front door.

CHAPTER 9

"Well, it's not a bad idea," Rachel said carefully, tilting her head to one side and scratching her chin. "And it does go along with what you found out, Nigel." She gave me a snide smile. "But it wasn't absolutely necessary for you to fuck him, was it?"

"I don't know why it's such an issue for you." I stuck my tongue out at her. "I don't know why you hate sex so much. Maybe if you tried it sometime, you wouldn't be so jealous and nasty when someone else does."

They'd been waiting for me when I got back to the house. As soon as I walked in the front door and saw them sitting there, I could tell by the bitchy look on Rachel's face that she'd known exactly where I'd been and what I'd been doing. Nigel, on the other hand, I couldn't read his face. He was like the sphinx. He hadn't spoken since I'd walked in, instead merely sitting there watching and listening to our back-and-forth bickering without even changing his expression.

Rachel simply gave Nigel an exasperated look and a slight shrug, like she was saying, *See? I told you so.* She turned back to me and sneered, "Aren't you even curious as to what Nigel found out, baby? I thought you were so very concerned about your *friend*." Her voice went into an even nastier tone. "Or has your dick taken control of your brain again?"

She was worse than Jean-Paul. But her bitchy attitude didn't make what she said any less true. I squirmed a little in my chair. I glanced over at Nigel, whose face was still impassive.

"Don't bicker, children," he finally said, sounding more tired than anything else. "Although I have to agree with her, Cord—it wasn't the smartest thing to sleep with Sebastian's twin brother. We don't know anything about him other than what he has told the two of you. He could be no better than his brother was—could be worse, in fact, and may have reasons of his own that aren't in your best interests, so getting involved with him in any way could be dangerous." He tried to lessen the sting of his words by giving me a tired smile.

I stopped myself from responding angrily, instead doing what my parents always told me to do when in danger of losing my temper—I counted to ten while taking deep breaths. When I reached ten, I felt calmer, and exhaled. I took another breath and was able to smile and nod at him. "You're right, of course, Nigel. I wasn't thinking. But I don't think he's a danger. I didn't sense any from him."

"Did you sense danger from Sebastian?" Rachel asked sweetly.

"I wasn't completely a vampire when I was with him, I was transitioning," I replied in the same tone. "It may have been a mistake, yes. But it's done, and I can't change that now." Rachel's eyes narrowed; I sensed she wasn't happy I hadn't reacted the way she'd expected, which was more than fine with me.

For all I knew, she was inside my head anyway.

"No, she isn't." Nigel waved his hand tiredly. "I don't allow that in my presence—and she knows I disapprove." Her lips narrowed at this rebuke, but she simply bowed her head. He shook his head.

I opened my mouth but didn't say anything out loud. *"But it's okay for* you *to be reading my thoughts?"*

"I don't need to read your thoughts—they're written all over your face." Nigel reached into his satchel and removed a file folder. "I did my research, and what Quentin told you wasn't untrue—although whether he was telling the truth about everything remains to be seen." He shrugged. "I cannot say; he has the witch bloodline—that much I do know is true." He sighed.

"I couldn't read his thoughts," Rachel said, her voice meek.

I shot a startled glance at her. This was a side of her I hadn't seen before and I wasn't sure what it was about. Was she always this deferential in Nigel's presence?

There was still so much I didn't understand.

"I cannot sense him," Nigel went on, "no matter how much I concentrate. So these Narcisses are a very powerful bloodline." He shook his head, his longish white hair bouncing. "But there is very little about them in the Night-watcher records and histories, which makes no sense to me." He rubbed his chin thoughtfully. "It's hard to believe any family of witches could have escaped our notice, especially one so powerful."

I sighed. I knew Nigel was a Nightwatcher, but I was also really sick and tired of both of them acting like I knew what exactly that meant. "Nobody's perfect," I replied, "and certainly not even the great Nightwatchers, whatever the hell that means. Can you two tell me exactly what Nightwatchers are? I'd greatly appreciate it." I crossed my legs. "Some kind of supernatural police force? Is that what you both are?" I waved a hand. "Come on, would it kill you to be up front with me about this stuff? The Councils and everything?"

Rachel inhaled sharply, but Nigel just smiled at me. She started to say something, but he grabbed her wrist, and she closed her mouth, bowing her head. "Now, Rachel, you've complained endlessly about how poorly Jean-Paul educated young Cord, and this is simply another example of just how uneducated Cord is about his new world—since Jean-Paul didn't teach him, we shall have to." He clicked his tongue while he shook his head.

"Yes, Nigel," she said meekly.

"Were you a good student, young Cord, when you were in school?"

I really didn't like being called *young* Cord any more than I liked Rachel calling me a baby, but then if he was indeed thousands of years old like Rachel had said, *young* probably wasn't a strong enough description of how I seemed to him. Besides, if it meant the old man was finally going to tell me what the hell was going on, I'd gladly let him call me anything he wished. I raised my chin proudly. "I had a three-point-nine GPA at Ole Miss," I replied, giving Rachel a snide look, "and I was valedictorian at my high school. So, yes, I was a good student. I learn quickly and I retain what I learn."

"Right," Rachel whispered, her voice barely audible.

"The Nightwatchers—how best to describe what we do?" Nigel mused. "In a way that you will understand?"

"You're right, Cord. We're like a police force." Rachel broke in, returning my snide look. "Only we deal with supernatural beings, rather than the mundane human crimes regular police have to handle. Humans don't know we exist—

which is safer for us—so we are charged with making sure they don't learn of our existence. It's our job to make sure no supernatural creature exposes us all to danger. It took centuries to convince humans that we are mythical—centuries of hard work." She shook her head. "So, sometimes when one of us, for example, is too obvious or isn't careful enough or goes mad, we have to step in and clean up the mess." She leaned back in her chair and stared at me coldly. "Which is why we are here now." She gestured to the bedroom door. "Cleaning up the mess you created."

"So, where were you when Sebastian was trying to turn himself into a witch-vampire hybrid?" I matched her stare. "Seems to me that was a job for you Nightwatchers."

"There was no need for us to become involved," Nigel replied before Rachel could say anything. His smile didn't falter. "We were aware that Jean-Paul and his fraternity were on the case, as it were, and Jean-Paul is not a fool, no matter what you might think and despite how ignorant he kept you. He knew the danger if Sebastian was allowed to complete his conversion. I was monitoring the situation, and had Jean-Paul not done his duty, we would have intervened. Our intervention wasn't necessary, as it turned out." He shrugged. "But then again, we are perhaps being too hard on Jean-Paul. I am sure he thought he had a lot more time to educate young Cord—and it's only been two or three years since his conversion."

"And two years is nothing compared to eternity, of course." Rachel sighed. "Although letting this one out on his own so young, so unaware of the dangers—"

"ENOUGH!" I shouted, making them both jump. I got up and paced over to the double doors, sliding them open. Jared still lay there, exactly as he had the last time I'd seen him, on his back with his mouth open. His bare chest rose and fell slightly as he inhaled and exhaled. I sat down on the bed and stared at my former best friend. I reached over and brushed an errant lock of hair from his forehead. I was sick to death of them and their constant talking in riddles, their treating me like a stupid child. It galled me to no end that I couldn't order them out of the house the way I wanted to, because I needed their help with Jared.

And ultimately, I would swallow my pride and my dignity. I would take Rachel's insults and condescension—because Jared needed them.

"Please accept my apology," Nigel said from the doorway behind me. I turned my head in time to see the front door shutting behind Rachel. He walked over to the wingback chair in the corner and very carefully sat down, crossing his left leg over the right. "I asked her to leave us alone so I could speak frankly with you."

"I try not to let her bother me," I replied. "I know she's not really mad at me, is she? It's Jean-Paul she's really angry with."

"There is bad blood between the two of them, yes." He nodded. "She had a friend . . ." His voice trailed off, and he shook his head.

"Philip?"

"Ah, she told you, then." Nigel sighed, and for a moment I could see how old he truly was. "A terrible tragedy. We have yet to find him, you know, and we've been looking for him for twenty years."

"She didn't tell me the whole story—just that I reminded her of him. What happened?"

He stared at me for a few moments, and just when the silence started to get uncomfortable, he said, "He was converted by a rogue vampire, one who had gone mad. Gunther's story is actually rather sad. Several centuries ago, he fell in love with a beautiful young German peasant, and they were lovers. Gunther had hoped to convert the young peasant to be his companion, but when he found out what Gunther was, he ran from him and fell to his death. It drove Gunther mad. He spent all of his time trying to find his lost love. For centuries he searched for him. And then, twenty years ago here in New Orleans, he found Philip and was convinced Philip was the reincarnation of his love."

"How . . . sad." I shook my head. "Poor Gunther."

Nigel wiped at his forehead. "I'd been hunting Gunther for quite some time—he was quite powerful—but as his madness grew, he was exposing himself and his true nature to more and more humans. I followed him here and sensed his discovery of Philip. But he was able to hide himself from me. I came so close so many times only to have him slip through my fingers, and so I found Rachel to help me find them. He had already taken Philip, had started converting him. We were able to rescue Philip, but Gunther escaped. And I converted Rachel—recruited her to become a Nightwatcher. Her potential, you see, was so strong. It had been centuries since I'd come across one such as her, and she has been an invaluable associate." He sighed again. "But the tie between Philip and Gunther was too strong— Philip ran away from us and joined Gunther. We've looked for them everywhere since then, with no luck."

"So that's why she's such a bitch," I said without thinking. "Was she in love with Philip?"

"No, Philip was gay. He was like family to her—they were very close." He looked at me and smiled. "And yes, I can see why you remind her of him. There's something about the shape of your face, and the eyes, and your build is very similar." He reached over and took my hand. "So, try to understand Rachel, and be kind to her. I know she's been rude to you, and abrupt, but seeing you is very hard for her. You remind her of what she's lost, and she still feels that pain very deeply." He rubbed his eyes. "When you're as old as I, sometimes it is very easy to forget what it's like to be young, how difficult it is to let go of someone."

"How old are you?" I asked, wondering if he would actually tell me.

"Your mind cannot comprehend how old I am, Cord. I am older than the pyramids." Nigel looked off into the distance, his voice growing softer. "I was old when the pyramids were built. I've seen thousands of years, millions be born and die. I saw the rise and fall of Rome. I stood on the walls of Troy and watched the Greek fleet land. I witnessed the great Flood from the Old Testament. I remember what is called in your religion the Garden."

My jaw dropped. I could think of nothing to say to him in response. Thousands of years old? "The Garden of *Eden?*" I swallowed. I was twenty-three. That was like the blink of an eye to him. He was right; his age wasn't something I could wrap my mind around. "So, you knew Adam and Eve? How is that even possible? Are you saying that there were vampires before there were humans? I . . . I don't understand how that could be." He didn't answer me; he just met my eyes, and his were so incredibly sad I had to look away from him. It was like looking into them was a window through the centuries, and my mind couldn't handle it.

"Jean-Paul should never have let you go off on your own, Cord. Never. It was criminally negligent, and when we are finished here, I shall have to talk to him." He held up a hand. "Oh, yes, I am sure you were quite exasperating to him. I am sure you pushed his patience to its limit; I can see that within you. But that is still no excuse. What he did was tantamount to a death sentence for you—and one thing we have always stood for, from the beginning, was the protection of our vampire children." He swallowed, closing his eyes and taking several deep breaths.

"I'm not completely helpless," I protested. "I mean, I may not be able to do the mind-reading thing or—"

"Of course you aren't. I didn't mean to imply that you were." The old man flashed a warm smile at me. "You're much less helpless than you would have been had you remained merely human, after all. You're stronger, you can see in the dark, you don't need as much sleep"—he shrugged—"and the more time passes, the more blood you ingest, the stronger you will become, the stronger your heart will become. Humans truly aren't a threat to you—but humans aren't the only creatures out there." He closed his eyes. "Witches, werewolves, fairies, shifters, and pixies—all of those things are real, not simply creatures from horror novels or bogeymen to frighten small children into behaving. And some of them are dangerous to vampires. You've already encountered a witch with delusions of grandeur." He shook his head again. "And don't think for a moment that there aren't others out there like Sebastian Narcisse. For centuries, we have all peacefully coexisted and abided by the rules set by the Council. But things are changing for some reason, Cord, and I don't understand why that is. Sebastian isn't the only witch with the desire to become a god—and a vampire as young as you, with a heart as weak as yours currently is, you're easy prey for a powerful witch. That's why Rachel and I are so concerned about this...*relationship* you've begun with his twin. His twin, Cord." He ran a hand through his mane of white hair. "*Identical* twin. Identical twins are identical in every way—so why would Sebastian be gifted with great power while his twin was not?"

"Quentin said he wanted nothing to do with the family powers," I replied slowly, beginning to see his point and beginning to feel more than a little afraid. "That he didn't believe in them and turned his back on them, on his family. I believe him, Nigel. He meant what he said."

"I don't doubt his sincerity, Cord. But not believing in his powers doesn't mean he doesn't have them, you know. Perhaps now he doesn't want them, but if he ever experiences that power...power corrupts." He smiled at me sadly. "Even your power as a vampire can corrupt your soul. I've seen it happen to vampires, ones who thought we should take over the world and enslave humans, reduce them to nothing more than milk cows to feed our need for their blood. There was a war..." His voice trailed off for a moment, and he shook his head. "Anyway, that means Quentin can still be dangerous to you. You didn't feed from him, did you? He doesn't know what you are?"

"No." Everything he said made terrible sense, one that made me afraid. They were right—I needed to stay away from Quentin.

The thought made my heart hurt.

Jared muttered something and shifted on the bed.

"What did he say?" Nigel moved so quickly I didn't even see it—one moment he was sitting in the chair, the next he was leaning over Jared on the other side of the bed.

"I didn't hear him," I replied.

Jared shifted again. He started moving back and forth, writhing like he was having a terrible nightmare, and his lips moved in a slight groan that shaped itself into words. I still couldn't make out what he was saying.

"You could if you focused," Nigel's voice echoed inside my head. *"I understand what he is saying. Focus, young Cord, and you will too."*

"Don't do that," I replied as Jared rolled over onto his stomach. His legs flailed a bit and the covers slid down his back, exposing the beginning of the curve of his ass. I pulled the blanket back up.

Nigel straightened up, and narrowed his eyes. He relaxed a bit, but he said imperiously, "You can guard your mind from us, you know. You simply have to learn how."

"Great, something else I need to learn," I replied sarcastically. I gestured at Jared's sleeping form. "So, what exactly did he say?"

Nigel walked over to the door and gestured for me to follow him into the living room. I slid the pocket doors closed behind us and leaned back up against them, folding my arms while I waited for him to answer me.

"He said *Sebastian still lives.*" Nigel slid down onto the sofa and closed his eyes. "I don't know how that could be possible, though. Sebastian is dead. I saw it happen—"

"You were there?" I gaped at him.

He didn't look at me or answer my question. "And his body was destroyed in the fire. They found two bodies— and one was definitely Sebastian's." He glanced over at me. "When one is going through the conversion process, like young Jared is, their powers are being turned on like a series of switches." He nodded. "Yes, that's the best way to describe it. As the human mind, through the vampiric blood, becomes more powerful, awakens to its full and true potential, it begins accessing the power that will eventually become second nature to use." He tapped the right side of his skull with his left index finger. "But when he returns to consciousness, his human brain will again limit his abilities—until he is trained in how to use them."

"Rachel said that it comes with time, and age," I replied.

"So, you're saying that I can do everything you and she can—I just don't know how?" I liked the sound of it.

"Your mind, yes." He was nodding. "Your body—to achieve the ability to fly, to move in the blink of an eye, to become invisible to humans—that will take years to achieve, and right now your heart, your blood, isn't powerful enough. But it will come in time, and your mind already has the ability to speak telepathically, to communicate with the dead, for example, or see things. Humans could do it, if they knew how. Humans don't use even ten percent of the power of their minds." He gestured at Jared. "He said *Sebastian still lives*, which is very peculiar. His mind cannot tell lies—his mind right now is operating much like a supercomputer, processing everything at rapid speeds. So, he must somehow be sensing something that I cannot." He sighed. "You're absolutely certain that this Quentin is not actually Sebastian?"

I started to deny it, but stopped myself.

I didn't *know*.

There were differences, but—

Sebastian was a witch, and a powerful one.

"Witches can't cheat death, can they?" I asked slowly. "They are mortal, aren't they?"

"They are more than human, yes, but they are still bound by the same physical law of mortality as humans," Nigel replied. "Only vampires have life eternal. Witches and werewolves, other nonhumans, they might have slightly longer life spans, but not so much as to make humans notice."

"Wouldn't I have—"

"Noticed?" A slight smile played across his lips. "It's not like the two experiences were similar, were they? I believe your experience with this Quentin was what would be considered more *normal*, while the experience with Sebastian was perhaps a little more perverse, in the way humans understand and perceive sexuality?"

I remembered the powerful urges I'd felt, the desire to hurt and dominate him in ways I'd never felt or wanted to before. I swallowed. "It was more traditional, I suppose, but . . ." I didn't know if I could tell him.

Of course, I didn't have to say anything. He could see into my head whenever he wanted. His eyes narrowed. "Actually, what you were experiencing, what you wanted to do to him was similar to what Sebastian had done to you before Jean-Paul and the others rescued you?"

"Yeah. It was strange."

"Twins." He stroked his chin. "Yin and yang. Witch twins are often two different halves of the whole. Opposites. What Sebastian did to you would of course be what Quentin would want done to him."

"You're saying it was really *Quentin* who made me want to do those things?"

"It's very possible—which would, of course, mean that Quentin isn't Sebastian." He shook his head, the long white locks bouncing. "Unless somehow their two souls joined when Sebastian's body died . . ."

"Well, he said his grandmother claimed Sebastian is still tied to this world." I nodded again. "Maybe going up to Bayou Shadows to see his grandmother, and talk to her, would be helpful—she might be able to release Sebastian and put an end to all of this." *No matter what Rachel thinks.*

A cramp seized my stomach.

"And you said he cursed me," I went on, ignoring the cramp, hoping it would go away. I knew what it meant—the desire for blood was coming on. "Wouldn't releasing his soul break the curse?" I closed my eyes and willed the cramp to go away.

But I could feel the dryness coming on in my mouth, the slight ache in my right temple. My eyes began to burn a little bit. The cramp faded, but I felt hollow and empty inside.

It's a truly horrible feeling.

"Yes, it would release you and break the curse, whatever it is." He got up and walked over to the bookcase. He ran his fingers along the spines of the books, and some dust flew up. "Sebastian Narcisse was a terrible person, consumed by his lust for power." He turned back to me. "The Council of Witches had already warned the Nightwatchers about him—but I still don't understand why there is so little information about the bloodline in our records. As powerful as he was—"

"Why don't you come to Bayou Shadows with us?" I replied. "You can ask his grandmother for yourself. Maybe she knows. Maybe they've just managed to fly under the radar for a long time. Isn't that possible?"

"Anything's possible." He sounded tired again. "But witches cannot be trusted," he mused. "It's entirely possible . . ." His eyes widened. "No, it can't be."

"What?"

"The curse. Of course." He threw open the pocket doors and sped into the room, sitting on the bed beside Jared. Jared's restlessness had passed, and he lay still. Were it not for the slight rise and fall of his chest, I'd think he was dead. Nigel stared at me. "He cursed you in the most horrible of ways." He shook his head. "What a bastard! We do need to free his soul so it can burn." His voice was venomous.

"What do you mean?" I could feel fear rising inside of me. I didn't like the way this was going.

"*Gunther.*" He stood up and started pacing. "I wonder if he was cursed as well? It never occurred to me...How could I have been so blind? So stupid? And there was a witch family in that village. I'll have to check the records."

"What are you talking about?"

He turned back to me. "The curse that Sebastian put on you? If you ever feed from someone you care about, someone you truly love, the wounds won't heal. They will die—unless you turn them."

"But..." A chill went through me, followed by yet another cramp, this one so powerful I gasped out loud.

"Vampires have been cursed before by witches, and usually the curse dies with the witch, but your curse survived Sebastian's death—in fact, he somehow managed to cast the curse as he died, and it still hangs over you." He leaned forward. "Now tell me again. Are you *certain* Quentin is not Sebastian?"

"I can't be certain of anything." I stood up and stretched. Another cramp shot through my system, and this time it was so strong I doubled over. I gasped as yet another one ripped through my stomach.

It had never been this strong before. Even when I'd so foolishly tried to see how long I could go without feeding, the cramps had not been so strong. I'd simply felt hunger and need, felt hollow and empty inside, nothing as strong as this.

"You need to feed." Nigel was at my side in a moment, his hand under my chin and forcing my head up. He stared into my eyes. "Your body—it metabolized the stripper's blood too quickly. You need to go feed."

"I—"

"Feed before it's too late. Go!" He waved his hand in dismissal.

I walked out the front door, closing it behind me as yet another cramp ripped through me. I gasped and had to put my hands against the door to keep from falling down. I staggered down the steps and became aware of the scent of blood, the beating of a heart, very close . . . oh so close.

I staggered down the steps and somehow managed to make it to the corner before another cramp doubled me over yet again and an involuntary cry came out of my mouth. I wanted to get to a gay bar, have nothing to do with the crowds on Bourbon Street. I could smell blood in the air; someone's heart was beating stronger, and I followed it like a beacon. I turned on Dauphine. It was always a quiet street, even though the insanity of Bourbon was a mere street away. I wasn't aware of anything other than the smell of blood and the sound of that strong heartbeat, beckoning me forward. I staggered down the sidewalk, looking like yet another idiot who'd had too much to drink. I felt so hollow, so empty. *Must find the blood . . . must find that heartbeat.*

And there it was.

There was a young man leaning against a building about a half-block up Dauphine Street. He was talking on a cell phone. I could see his jugular vein pounding in his neck.

Drool filled my mouth. I was so damned hungry. . . .

"Look, buddy, you're being a real dick. Just calm the fuck down. You don't own me—we're just friends, remember? Isn't that what you said? That was *your* choice, not mine, and now you bug out and get jealous because I met someone? No, fuck *you!*"

Angrily he disconnected the call and slammed his other fist into the wall.

"Hello," I said as I neared him, barely able to keep from shoving him against the wall and sinking my teeth into his neck. I needed his blood. . . .

He just looked at me and smiled. "I've been waiting for you, Cord."

He held up the hand holding the phone.

He was wearing a ring with an enormous stone in it.

Green.

Everything went green.

Green...

CHAPTER 10

Green.

Everything was green.

It looked like someone had put a green filter over my eyes—everywhere I looked, everywhere I turned my head, there was nothing but green. Dark green, light green, every conceivable shade of green I could imagine and even some that I couldn't. It was starting to make me slightly sick. I didn't know where I was at first, but as I adjusted to the weird, disorienting green, I realized I was in my bedroom at the Orleans Street house. Bright green light was coming through the windows, feeling hot on my skin. I got out of the bed and closed the curtains, and realized I was naked. I picked up my robe from the floor and draped it around my body. I heard a noise from the front of the house and walked down the hallway. As I walked past the front bedroom, I could make out Jared's naked form lying there—also in shades of green. He had a raging hard-on, and even though his eyes were closed, he was playing with himself, absently pulling on his erection like it was an afterthought, like there was no driving need for him to be doing what he was doing.

I went around the corner and there, in the living room, sat my parents. On the couch.

And the green faded, and everything became normal again.

"Is it true?" my mother asked. Her eyes were red and tears

stained her cheeks. Her dark brown hair was now streaked with gray, and she looked like she'd aged twenty years in the two years or so since I'd seen her. "You're not only a demon but you're also a homosexual?"

"I told her there was no way a son of ours could have turned his back on God and started worshipping the devil," *my father's voice boomed out. His arm was around her shoulders, and he was giving me a reassuring look. His voice was strong, but there was a hint of uncertainty to it, almost like he was saying,* Tell me it isn't so, son, so we can be finished with this foolishness.

"It is true," *I replied.* "I'm gay, and I'm a vampire."

My mother started wailing, and my father turned away from me and started comforting her. I didn't know what to do, what to say, so I just stood there stupidly staring at them both.

"I can take care of this for you," *Jean-Paul's voice whispered in my brain.* They don't deserve to live, do they? With all that hatred in their hearts? Wouldn't it be better to release them from the horrors of this world so they can go be with the God they worship and obey so mindlessly?

"No," *I said out loud, but in the blink of an eye, they were all there—Jean-Paul and Clint and the others, holding my parents down and drinking from their veins and they were both screaming and I wanted to go to them, help them, push the others away from them, but I couldn't move. I was stuck in place, and then everything began to go green again, first around the edges of my vision and then it spread, everything going green. . . .*

And then the colors became normal again, and I was once again tied to the posts of Sebastian's bed, in his bedroom with all the candles lit, but there were two of him, one on either side of the bed, both of them naked, mirror images of each other. One had to be Quentin and the other Sebastian, but although I remembered there were subtle differences, I couldn't remember what they were, and my eyes moved back and forth between them, and then they both were standing at the foot of the bed, each holding the other's erection, stroking, and they started kissing, two identical twins kissing and I knew it was wrong, it was incredibly wrong, but then they stopped and turned their attention back to me.

"Don't you want us?" the one on the right asked. "Don't you want me to climb up on that bed and flip you over and shove my cock so far inside of you that my come will shoot out your mouth?"

"And while he is fucking you"—the other turned and bent over, pulling his muscular ass cheeks apart—"you can fuck me like you did earlier, make me your little bitch, and we'll all be satisfied. Isn't that what you want? You want me to be your bitch while he makes you his little bitch?"

And despite everything, I heard myself saying, "Yes, yes, that is what I want, please," and everything began going green again until it was all green, that strange shade of green I'd first seen on the street. . . .

I opened my eyes, and the hunger was there—a gnawing sense of agony that pushed everything else out of my head and consciousness.

What had happened? I tried to piece it all back together, but my head was aching, and there was that horrible ravenous hunger, the emptiness inside that made my eyes water and was so damned all-consuming.

I'd needed to feed, yes; I remembered that. I remembered talking to some old man with long white hair and cramping from the hunger; it was so intense I could barely stand, yes.

Another cramp tore through my body and instinctively I tried to curl up into a ball, but my arms and legs were restrained. I opened my mouth and howled from the agony. It hurt so much I could barely stand it. I was going to go mad from the hunger if I didn't feed soon.

The cramp unclenched, and I gasped in dank, musty air. My eyes were still watering, and I wasn't able to see—and I needed to be able to see.

Focus. I needed to focus. Focus and remember.

I'd walked out of the house . . . Oh, yes, I'd gone to feed after the old man (*Nigel, his name is Nigel*) told me some bizarre story I didn't quite understand, about why Rachel was such a bitch—

Someone she loved was killed, a victim of a rogue vampire, killed and then converted. He had disappeared, and they'd been looking for him for the last twenty years. He'd also told me about witches cursing vampires—I'd been cursed apparently by Sebastian, and the curse hadn't died with him, and we needed to figure out a way to break the curse and then the hunger had consumed me, which hadn't made sense because I'd just fed the night before; I should have been good for at least another day. I'd drunk deeply from the stripper, whatever his name was, the one in the underwear with the incredibly hot ass.

And I'd gone out of the house to feed; he'd told me to. I'd heard a heart beating and I'd smelled blood—someone on Dauphine Street—so I'd walked around the corner and . . .

Yes, the boy on the cell phone.

That was the last thing I remembered, walking up to him and then everything went green.

I had no idea how I'd gotten here, wherever I was, or what he had done to me.

He'd known who I was, had called me by name, said he'd been waiting for me.

Who the hell was he, and what did he want from me?

I tried remembering what he looked like, but for some reason whenever I tried to picture his face, his body, what he'd been wearing, all I could see was green haze.

I blinked rapidly a few times, and the water cleared. I needed to get an idea of where I was before the next hunger pang consumed me again.

The room was dark as pitch, but of course I could see

through the darkness. I tried again to sit up but my arms were restrained at the wrists. I tried to raise my head, but there was also some kind of restraint around my neck. I was tied down, spread-eagled, so that I could barely move.

And I was naked.

This is exactly the way I'd been restrained by Sebastian that night.

I swallowed and closed my eyes again. Surely that couldn't be a coincidence, could it? I opened my eyes and turned my head to one side. I could make out the wall—it looked like it was cinder block. There were no windows on that side, so I rolled my head the other way to stare at another wall of cinder blocks. There was a small rectangle up near the ceiling that could be a window, but it was completely blacked out. I sighed and looked up at the ceiling, moving my eyes as much as I could—but there was nothing I could detect that would be helpful up there, either.

I strained to listen, to see if I could hear anything beyond the walls; there was nothing but silence.

Of all times for that stupid bitch to not be listening to my thoughts, I thought angrily. *How was I taken without them knowing anyway?*

I opened my eyes and looked around the room again, as much as I could without being able to lift my head. I felt the cramp coming and started breathing more rapidly in an attempt to lessen its exquisite agony. When the pang came, it was even more blindingly intense than the last one. With no other choice, I opened my mouth and screamed as loudly as I could. It seemed to go on forever; it felt like my body was on fire and being ripped in half.

Death would have been preferable.

It faded away, leaving me gasping for air, tears streaming out of my eyes.

If I didn't feed soon—

I heard a door swing open, and the room filled with a dazzling light from above as a switch was flipped. I couldn't see who it was but could sense him—for it was definitely a male. Men and women smell profoundly different.

And more important, I could smell his blood, hear his heartbeat. It took all of my strength not to growl in anticipation.

"You're hungry, aren't you?" the man said in a soft, low voice. I heard him shuffle across the room until he was at my side, and I rolled my head to the left so I could look at him.

He was dressed in a black silk shirt that was open to just below his rib cage, revealing smooth skin and a deep valley between his pectoral muscles. His pants appeared to be made from clinging black velvet that outlined the strong muscles of his legs. There was a prominent bulge in the crotch area. He had long, curly blond hair that fell gently to his shoulders and deep green eyes that almost glowed in the darkness on either side of a strong, sculpted nose. There were dimples in his pale cheeks as he looked at me, and his lips were thick and sensual.

Around his neck was a gold chain, from which hung a green stone.

The green stone—it was like the one in the boy's ring.

As I stared at it, it started glowing.

He stretched a white wrist to my mouth, and with his other hand stroked my forehead. "Go ahead, bite my wrist, drink from me," he instructed in a soft, gentle voice. He smiled. "You are so beautiful, so much more beautiful than I thought you would be, than I could have possibly hoped for. Go ahead, don't be afraid—I'm not going to hurt you." He leaned down and whispered in my ear, "Can't you hear my heart beating? Can't you smell my warm blood?"

But it wasn't just his blood I could smell. Oh, the metallic coppery smell of his blood was definitely there, and there was an underlying sweetness that was unusual—and I could feel my cock beginning to harden from its scent—but I could smell his essence above that.

It wasn't quite human.

Don't drink from him—it's a big mistake.

The hunger tore through me again, and I sank my teeth into his wrist, even if I knew somehow I shouldn't. I had to stop the agony, make it go away, do whatever it took to never feel that way again. My canines sliced through his skin and the blood . . . I could taste it at last and nothing else mattered.

His eyes closed and he moaned as I tore into his skin, ripped it apart in my need. I closed my mouth around the jagged holes, and his warm blood flooded my mouth. I gulped hungrily, greedily, yet even as I lost myself in the unspeakable pleasure of replenishing myself, I knew there was too much blood. No one I'd ever drank from before had filled my mouth so quickly.

Something was definitely wrong here.

The blood tasted sweet, as though it were mixed with raw honey, and it was also more viscous than most. I gulped it down and felt intoxicated from its power and taste. I could feel my muscles growing stronger with every swallow, my veins almost on fire as this blood absorbed into my system and ran through me. My eyes began moving rapidly from side to side, and my cock got harder, my balls were aching and demanding some form of release, and I could feel it; an orgasm was beginning. I was going to come, but I didn't care, not as long as I could drink from him. Who was he? What was he? I didn't care . . .

"That's enough," he whispered in my ear. "Let go of me."

It was a command, and even though the bloodlust was

still driving me, I withdrew my fangs from his arm and opened my mouth.

He held the wrist above my mouth and allowed more blood to drip into my mouth. "You know what to do," he whispered, and my tongue darted out, licking the tears and getting the last drops, until the wounds closed.

He smiled and waved his arm. The blinding overhead light went out, and candles mounted in sconces on the walls burst into flame, casting flickering light and shadows through the room.

"I find candlelight to be more pleasant than electric light, don't you?" he asked in a slightly bemused tone.

I used my tongue to get every last drop of blood on my lips and dribbling down my chin.

"For such advanced creatures, vampires are truly little more than animals," he said. His voice was full of both wonder and amusement.

"Why have you taken me?" I asked. "Let me go." I pulled against the wrist restraints.

"That isn't possible," he replied. He held up the green stone, which sparkled and flashed in the candlelight. "It wasn't my idea to take you in the first place. I think this is a terrible mistake—"

"We all know what you think, Nico," a similar yet deeper voice said from the doorway.

I strained to see him, but the bond around my neck wouldn't allow me to raise my head enough to see this newcomer.

"He was responsible for Sebastian's death," the voice continued.

I could hear his footsteps as he walked into the room. He, too, I could smell—his essence was very similar to the one he called Nico. He moved to my side, directly opposite

Nico, and I turned my eyes that way so I could get a good look at him.

He was very similar to Nico; they were identical in every respect, only where Nico was fair, this stranger was dark. Thick, dark curls cascaded to his shoulders. His eyes were almost black under broad dark eyebrows. His skin was swarthy rather than pale, like Nico, and he wore a white silk shirt, open so I could see the almost identical chest development. But where Nico was smooth, thick curly black hair covered the skin of his chest, and the bulge in the front of his white velvet trousers was bigger than of the man on my other side. It was almost like one was the negative image of the other, identical but somehow reversed.

Two halves of a whole.

Sebastian and Quentin.

Twins—yin and yang—the most powerful witches came in pairs. Twins.

"Sebastian was a fool who played with fire and asked for death, if not from this one than from another, more powerful one," Nico replied with a toss of his head that made his curls bounce defiantly. "Why avenge the death of a fool?"

"Fool or not, he was our master, and his spirit will not rest until we avenge him," the dark one replied. "You know that as well as I." He looked down at me and stroked my cheek with his hand. "He is beautiful, though. Such a waste of masculine beauty. Perhaps..." He smiled. "We don't have to kill him right away, you know. We can have fun with him first." He leaned down so his eyes were gazing into mine, and I could smell his breath. "Would you like to have some fun with us, honored guest?"

"I'm sorry, Cord." Nico sniffed disdainfully. "My brother, as you can see, while extremely brave, is also exceptionally stupid." He crossed his arms, and I could see the veins in his forearms. "Sebastian was as big a fool as you, my brother. He tried to do something forbidden without the help of his twin. We can work together." He smiled. "And be much stronger than Sebastian ever could have hoped to be."

Quentin. Sebastian had wanted my vampire-tainted blood so that he could be a god—could he have succeeded had he been working with Quentin?

What were these two going to do to me?

I could feel strength, power, coursing through my veins. My muscles felt stronger, the fibers thickening as though my skin couldn't contain them as they grew, and my eyes, my vision, I could see even better than I could before.

What had his blood done to me?

Witch blood—was I becoming an abomination? A hybrid of vampire and witch?

"Why am I here?" I asked again. "What are you going to do to me?"

The dark one smiled at me and reached down to run his fingers along the side of my face again and then down my neck. I thrilled to his touch; his fingertips felt like they were sending currents of electricity into my body, and involuntarily my head turned to him, like a flower turning to the sun. "You see, Nico?" he said mockingly. "He turns to me rather than you, as they all do eventually."

"And they always leave you in the end, too, don't they, Lorenzo?" Nico said in an equally mocking tone. "One after the other, they run as quickly as they can, to get as far from you as possible."

"Just my touch makes his cock hard," Lorenzo continued in his taunting tone, as though Nico hadn't spoken a word. He moved his fingers down my throat and down the center of my chest, toying with my nipple. I closed my eyes and bit my lower lip.

He was making me incredibly horny, damn him to hell.

"His cock was already hard, you fool." Venom dripped from every word. I sensed something violent radiating off Nico.

"Why am I here?" I asked yet again, not expecting an answer. "Just let me go."

"Our master demands you be sacrificed in order that he might find his eternal rest," Lorenzo said dreamily as his fingertips continued to brush against my skin, moving from my clavicle down my stomach. His index finger slid into my navel, and he scratched the inside of it softly, gently. Desire shot through me, and I wanted him in that moment. No, I wanted both of them—

The green stone hanging around Lorenzo's neck began to glow brighter, and out of the corner of my eye, I could see that Nico's stone was glowing also.

"He cursed you," Lorenzo went on as his fingertips grazed the skin just above my pubic hair, "and his mark is on you. You keep him tethered to this world, this dimension, and he longs for peace."

"Then maybe he shouldn't have cursed me." My voice sounded weak, wavery, and breathless to my ears, and my breath was coming in quick little gasps as his fingers continued to stroke the skin between my navel and my cock, the tips barely brushing against the skin—enough contact to make me tremble and ache with need and desire, but just barely, and all I could think was how I wished I was free of my bonds so that I could hold both of them against me, kiss them both even if they were brothers.

"It isn't the curse that keeps him here," Nico interrupted my reverie, and I wished he would touch me in the way Lorenzo was, "and you know that, Lorenzo. You simply want revenge because Sebastian was with him and you're jealous. Sebastian wanted his blood, yes, but Sebastian also desired him, could have loved him in time, and you—"

"Silence!" Lorenzo roared so loudly my ears rang, and even worse, his fingers were no longer in contact with my skin. I could feel anger coming from him now—the violence was still radiating from Nico, and the two energies met just above my stomach, and I could almost see it.

Their stones were glowing so brightly the room seemed to be alive with green fire.

"Perhaps we should leave him, my brother," Nico said smoothly, but his breath was shallow, almost panting, "and continue this discussion in private?"

"Don't leave me here alone, please," I pleaded as their eyes locked over my prone body. The green stones began to dim as their faces relaxed and they smiled at each other. They both leaned over and kissed me on opposite cheeks, and they joined hands over me and walked out of the room.

The door shut behind them.

I let my head fall back and closed my eyes.

I was a prisoner, and this all had something to do with Sebastian.

Sebastian had been their master, and they wanted me for something. Maybe they wanted the same thing Sebastian had wanted, to drink my blood and become gods. They loved each other, but at the same time they were competitive, almost to the point of hatred and violence.

And what were the green stones?

But, I reasoned, at least this proves that Miss Know-It-All Rachel was wrong about Quentin. He doesn't have anything to do with this.

Small comfort. I was still the prisoner of this strange pair of twins.

Sebastian's soul was still tethered to the earth, and I gathered from what Nico said that he was something more to Lorenzo.

Yet neither of them was the boy from Dauphine Street

who had mesmerized me with his own green stone. Who had that been?

How many of them were there?

Rachel and Nigel couldn't possibly have any idea where I was. They hadn't even known I was being taken, so I couldn't hold out any hope they would come to my rescue. Besides, if these two were witches—and what else could they be?—Nigel and Rachel wouldn't be able to read their thoughts or find them. I didn't know how long I'd been gone, yet surely they knew I was missing by now.

But maybe, just maybe, they could find me.

I cursed Jean-Paul for not teaching me the vampire telepathy trick.

I might as well give it a try.

I closed my eyes and concentrated, pictured the two of them sitting around in the living room of my house. I focused on both of them and thought with as much concentration and energy as I could muster.

"Rachel! Nigel! I've been taken prisoner! Please come find me!"

As I repeated the thought over and over, I felt power surging through my body—power I'd never felt before. The candles flickered as I kept focusing, and I closed my eyes to shut out other distractions. My body was tingling, every hair on it standing on end.

There was no answer.

I don't know how long I tried, but when I finally opened my eyes again, exhausted and frustrated, the candles had burned about halfway down.

Angrily I yanked my head to one side—and to my surprise, the metal cuff holding my neck down snapped free of its hasp. Stunned, I sat there for just a moment, not sure what had just happened.

The surge of power I'd felt . . . Had drinking Nico's witch blood somehow made me stronger, more powerful?

I closed my eyes and tried to raise my arms, focusing on the muscles in my upper arms and shoulders. They strained, but I felt the surging power and strength, and those cuffs, too, snapped as if they were made of paper.

I sat up and rubbed my wrists, which felt stiff and a little sore from being so rigidly restrained.

I looked around the room, but I didn't see my clothes anywhere. I slid down the stone slab, and in a matter of moments snapped my ankles free. I hopped down from the stone slab and stretched. The only window was far over my head, the one I'd noticed before that had been blacked out, and I couldn't reach it. I pressed my hands against each wall in turn. They were stone, and cold, and there was a cold breeze blowing from a vent above my head. I looked up at it, but the ceiling was easily fifteen feet above the floor; besides, even if I could somehow reach it, it was far too narrow for my body to fit through. I went to the door and turned the knob. I almost laughed out loud as it turned in my hand and opened.

No need to lock the door when you have me tied up, right, guys?

I hesitated before walking out, though. Surely Nico had known what his blood would do to me? And the door being left unlocked—maybe it was a trick, a trap of some sort.

I peered out the doorway into a long hallway with other, similar doors in even intervals its entire length. Candles burned in sconces mounted on the walls. There was no one around, so I slipped out into the hallway. I checked in every cell, but each was empty. I was apparently the only prisoner in this building. I hurried down the hall, keeping an eye out for anything I could use to cover myself with. I had to find clothes of some sort—there was no way I could walk around outside stark naked once I managed to escape this building—with no luck. Finally, I reached the end of the hall. I opened the door and found myself staring across a long lawn of perfectly manicured grass to where a huge mansion stood, surrounded by massive live oaks, beards of Spanish moss hanging from their heavy branches. The mansion was ablaze with light. There was a long driveway on the other side, lined with huge oak trees. There were an awful lot of cars parked along the driveway, which made me curious.

Something was going on at the house.

With no clothes, I certainly couldn't make a break for the road the driveway surely ended in. The last thing I wanted was to draw more attention to myself. With no other choice, I started making my way across the lawn to the wide veranda, glancing back and forth to make sure there was no one else around. I passed an empty gazebo, and as I drew nearer to the veranda, I could see there was a lazy river just beyond, with a dock jutting out into the black water.

I paused for a moment. That couldn't be the Mississippi River. It wasn't muddy nor wide enough, nor was the current as fast and strong. Where the hell was I?

I crept up the steps to the veranda and could hear music from inside—a piano playing some classical piece I'd heard before but didn't recognize—and then the song ended. There was a lot of applause, and unable to curb my curiosity, I crept over to the nearest window and peered inside.

There was a crowd of people inside, and I immediately spotted the twins sitting in the very first row, applauding as a young woman in a period costume from French colonial times, with coffee-colored skin, curtsied in front of the company.

It was so completely surreal I didn't know what to think, but I shook my head. I could worry about all of this later, once I was dressed and on my way back to the house on Orleans Street. I darted down the veranda to a door, which was unlocked. I slipped inside the house. There was an open door to my right leading into the room where the music audience was and another one to my left. But just beyond the door to the music room was a carpeted hanging staircase. I took a deep breath and ran toward it, hoping no one happened to glance out into the hallway as my naked form dashed past.

I went up the stairs as quickly as I could and found myself in another hallway. I went into the first door I saw and found a furnished bedroom. I smiled as I found an armoire full of clothes. The shirt barely buttoned over my chest, and the pants were a little too long, so I had to roll them up, but the shoes fit perfectly.

I looked at myself in the mirror and smiled.

"Leaving us already?" Nico said from the doorway. "But the fun's about to start."

CHAPTER 11

Nico smiled, leaning against the door frame. He brushed a lock of curly blond hair off his forehead. "You look good in my clothes," he said, looking me up and down. His smile turned lascivious. "Although I suspect you'd look better in my bed."

I took a deep breath. I could hear the pianist beginning to play yet another selection downstairs. "Just let me go," I replied, feeling a surge in my strength again as the green stone hanging on his chest began to glow softly, tinting the smooth skin around an eerie pale green. "I don't know—or care—why you and your brother brought me here, or what you're up to. I don't care about Sebastian. None of that was my fault. He came after me, and he would have killed me if Jean-Paul and the others hadn't come for me. Please, just let me go so no one else gets hurt."

He laughed, a sweet, musical sound, and stepped into the room. He softly closed the door behind him and leaned back against it. His black silk shirt fell open all the way to the waist. His skin was completely smooth—there wasn't even a happy trail from his navel down to the crotch. "Silly Cord," he said, his tone teasing, a big smile on his face. "Why would we let you go when we've gone to such great trouble to bring you here?" He looked me up and down. "And before I've had the chance to sample your wares? It's only fair, you know. I gave you my blood, didn't I? What else do I have to do to convince you I don't want to hurt you?"

"You and your brother kidnapped me off the street. You could at least do me the courtesy of explaining to me what I'm doing here," I said, involuntarily taking a step backward as he drew closer to me. *You're a vampire. What are you afraid of? Overpower him and make your escape!*

But somehow I couldn't do it. There was something about him that was frightening to me. He was slighter of build and shorter than I, and of course he was human (*are you sure?*), yet I couldn't bring myself to raise my hand against him. And his green eyes—they were so beautiful and his skin so soft and silky.

One of his slender hands reached up and slid inside the silk shirt I couldn't close. The other lightly grasped my right bicep. His smile got even bigger, his strong, even white teeth glinting, his green eyes twinkling. "You're so muscular," he breathed, stepping even closer to me as he pushed my shirt open and moved his hand to the center of my chest. The palm of his hand sent that same strange current through me, a wave of almost overpowering desire that went straight to my cock. "You cannot resist me," he whispered, leaning into me and brushing his soft lips against the base of my throat, "nor can you ever leave me."

The feel of his lips brought up goose bumps all over my body, and I felt my heart begin to race.

"What have you done to me? You and your blood?" I somehow managed to whisper. I wanted to run out of the room, down the stairs, and out the front door of this strange house, and not stop until I reached the road at the end of the driveway. But as much as I wanted to escape the danger

I sensed in this place, somehow I couldn't move. I was completely under his spell. "You're a witch, aren't you?"

His hand was undoing the clasp of my slacks, and the other was caressing my ass, his index finger stroking the bottom where my hole was, and I didn't want him to stop teasing me. "Witch?" he laughed as my pants fell to the floor in a heap at my feet. "I suppose you could say that, but it's such a vast oversimplification—it really is an unworthy description of what we all are." He winked up at me as his tongue darted out and made a slithery circle at the base of my neck, producing a moan from me. "But I suppose *witch* will do, in a pinch."

He leisurely knelt in front of me and tilted his head back so I could see his delighted smile before his tongue darted out and licked the head of my cock. I moaned again, cursing my traitorous body for responding to him, for not obeying me and getting me the hell out of there.

I wanted him now. I wanted release. He had teased me into a state of arousal that demanded satisfaction.

He smiled up at me. "Are all vampires as beautiful as you, Cord?" He breathed out, blowing on the wet head of my cock.

I closed my eyes again. "Are all witches as beautiful as you?"

He answered by taking me into his mouth, his tongue working the vein on the underside. His mouth was warm and he suckled on my cock, and there was no resistance possible against the pleasure coursing through my body as his mouth moved back and forth over my aching erection. I'd never felt anything like it before—no one had ever sucked me this way. His mouth felt like warm, moist, crushed velvet as it worshipped me, and it was like the greatest drug ever conceived by man was exploding through my veins. Every nerve ending in my body was alive, alert, firing pleasure synapses to my brain. My skin felt incredibly sensitive—the cool air being pushed down from the rotating blades of the ceiling fan felt like thousands of fingers stroking my skin. It was like I'd taken several hits of Ecstasy, but even better. I could feel every strand of hair on my body, goose bumps popping up everywhere, and my nipples were so hard they felt like they could cut through glass, like a diamond. I brought up both of my hands and pinched each nipple, my body trembling in response as heat radiated out from the flash-point center of my nipples. I could hear myself moaning, and he kept working on my cock with that amazing mouth, up and down while his tongue slithered along the dark vein on the underside, and my balls contracted and ached for release. One of his fingers slid inside the crevice between my buttocks, at the very top, and I shivered as the finger gently pushed its way down until it found an opening and started tapping slowly and gently. My legs began to shake.

And I could hear Rachel's voice saying in a disgusted tone, *Must you fuck everyone you come into contact with?*

I didn't know if she actually was there reading my thoughts or if it was just my imagination, but if she was there, I knew I needed to focus and somehow lead her and Nigel to me, but the pleasure was so incredibly intense I couldn't form the words. I couldn't think about anything except the animalistic pleasure I was feeling, and all I wanted to do was go with it, keep feeling it. The tip of his finger slid inside of me, and an involuntary cry burst out of my throat, and the only thing I could think was, *Maybe if you got laid once in a while, you wouldn't be such an uptight bitch when other people are getting some,* and his finger was going deeper inside, wiggling and moving, tapping and turning and rotating as it sought the magic place, and then he found it and started rubbing and tapping it and my eyes rolled back in my head as pleasure like I'd never experienced, never thought humanly possible, washed over me like waves crashing onto a beach, and I couldn't think; I couldn't even form words in my head. Not even Jean-Paul at his most sensual had ever made me feel like this, not even Clint or when all of our little fraternity had been naked and having an orgy, nothing had been this intense. How was this even possible? No one should be able to make anyone else feel like this. . . . This was more intense than any drug, any alcohol. . . . I wanted him to *fuck* me. I wanted his cock inside of me, but still his finger worked on me as his mouth and tongue continued working my cock, and I could hardly stand it and then I felt my cum rising. I was going to come—

And his finger stopped.

His other hand clamped around the base of my cock as I shuddered and tried to shoot my load, but it was trapped inside of me by his hand. I could feel it trying to get past, my body lurching with each spurt being trapped inside of me, and it felt like I was going to explode.

He smiled at me as I shuddered and tried with all of my willpower not to let out a scream.

"No sound, my beautiful Cord," he whispered, licking his lips as I shuddered. His green eyes flashed at me until the spasms passed. "We don't want anyone downstairs to hear us, do we?" His eyes narrowed. "Especially not Lorenzo—we don't want Lorenzo to know what's going on up here, do we?"

I couldn't speak, so I just nodded as I gulped breath. The orgasm was over, and he smiled as he let go of my cock, and I shuddered as a few drops of cum slid up my channel and out the slit. His tongue shot out and licked them up, and the touch of his tongue on my cock's head sent another sliver of agonizing pleasure through my entire body.

"Your head is really sensitive right now," he said with a low laugh. He licked his thumb and began sliding it back and forth over it.

My knees buckled and I almost collapsed, it was such an incredibly intense feeling, and then I felt his finger slide out of me. He stood and pressed his lips against mine. I could taste my own cock in his mouth, and as his tongue pushed inside my mouth, I couldn't help but suck on it and my arms went around him as he unbuttoned his silk shirt and shrugged it off his shoulders. I ground my bare cock against the crotch of his velvet trousers, my balls feeling heavy and sore and aching but needing to be worked. My cock wanted to be inside of him, but I also wanted him inside of me. I imagined his beautiful body on top of me, between my legs, his hips thrusting his cock deeper inside of me as I locked my legs around him, pressing him, and I felt his trousers loosen and drop to the floor.

I became aware through the pleasure that my feet were no longer on the floor and the trousers bunched around my feet had fallen away. I opened my eyes and saw that his eyes were closed—

And realized we were rising in the air! We were about five feet above the floor.

How is this possible? I wondered as he pressured me into turning, and we rotated in the air, and he was then forcing me backward, and I felt myself falling back through the air, and then I was lying on the bed and he was on top of me, his crotch grinding against mine, and I wanted to suck him, taste him, get his cock inside my mouth and worship him the way he'd worshipped me, and so I moved my head back, rolling him over onto his back.

He moaned as my mouth slid from his lips to his throat, and I could feel his moan vibrating through the skin of his throat, and I knew he was feeling pleasure just as intensely as I was, but I wanted him to feel even more. I wanted to drive him insane with pleasure. I wanted it to push every other thought out of his head until all he could feel, the only thing he could think about, was spattering his load all over himself. I wanted to see his cock squirting cum all over his beautiful torso, and I would lick him clean, tasting both his incredible skin and his delicious seed at the same time. I wanted to run my tongue all over his entire body. I wanted my tongue to seek and explore every crack and crevice of his body, to tug on his nipples with my teeth, to drink his sweat and join our bodies together until we were one flesh, one skin, one person.

I found the deep pit at the base of his throat and licked it, kissed it, and nipped at the skin with my teeth, not hard enough to draw blood but to tease and torment, and his back arched, his cock rubbing against my stomach, and I moved my stomach from within so that his cock had its hardness to serve as friction and I felt a sticky wetness as some of his precum oozed out against my skin and I smiled to myself. I hazarded a look up at him and his eyes were closed, his head tilted back, and I moved my mouth down, my tongue darting in and out as it traced a path down the center of his chest, leaving a wet trail behind, and his skin tasted both salty from his rising sweat yet sweet as honey at the same time, and I could hear his heart pounding through the bones of his rib cage. His heart was leaping about with each beat, yet rather than a bloodlust it only served to push me further. My desire for blood had already been sated with his sweet blood earlier, and I brought up both of my hands and pinched his nipples, tugging on them, and they were as hard as his firm chest, and he gasped again, and I could feel his moan of pleasure echoing and reverberating inside his diaphragm as he pushed his hips against me again, and I felt his hardness against my stomach, his balls growing heavier and more demanding with each movement, and I knew he was getting close—

And so was I.

I let go of his nipples and pushed myself up into a sitting position. His legs were around my waist and I looked down at the silky white down of his pubic hair, his long pink cock, the heavy pink balls hanging below them, the blue veins in his throat, the swollen hard nipples glistening in the light from my spit, the clear drop oozing and glistening from the slit in the round pink head of his cock.

He was beautiful, simply beautiful.

He opened his eyes. "Don't tease me," he breathed out through his thick lips, his voice thick with desire, need, the heat radiating from his skin in waves.

"I can't decide," I replied in a seductive whisper, "if I want to fuck your pretty ass or take that beautiful cock inside of me." I reached over and smeared the glistening drop over the head.

His eyes closed and he groaned again. "I want you to fuck me . . . oh God, please, please fuck me with that big beautiful cock."

I grabbed his ankles and shoved them forward until his beautiful hard white ass was in front of me, and I buried my face between his buttocks. My tongue ran around the rim of his asshole, and I felt his entire body trembling as I teased his hole with my tongue, and in that moment I knew I was going to fuck him. I wanted to fuck him more than I'd ever wanted to fuck anyone in my life, and I knew fucking him would be better than anyone I'd ever fucked, better than anyone I'd ever fuck in the future. There was only Nico for me now; anyone else would be a vast disappointment. I could search until the end of time for another lover, but I would never find another to be his equal. Maybe this was what they meant by soul mates and love. And my tongue went inside of him and I could feel his legs shaking and I knew he was feeling it, too, and I licked and lapped at him, looking for the spot that would send him to the moon and yet bring him back at the same time.

You really are a disgusting pig.

Fuck you, Rachel.

I pulled my head back and wiped my mouth with my arm. His eyes were half closed as he looked up at me, the green stone twinkling in the light from the chandeliers. I got to my feet and pointed the head of my cock into him.

He resisted at first, but gravity was pulling me irresistibly down into him.

He shoved his arm into his open mouth to muffle the scream as I plunged deep into him.

I fought gravity myself. I wanted him to slowly open to me as I entered him bit by bit, making him want me even more the slower I went, and his eyes opened, and when he moved his arm, I could see his teeth marks on his forearm where he'd bit down to muffle the scream. They were deep but hadn't drawn blood, which was a good thing, as I knew damned well there was no way I could have stopped myself from drinking him dry once the scent of his blood was in the air. I would have drained him until there was nothing left but a hollow husk of what had once been a beautiful man, an oh-so-beautiful man, and I realized he was pushing himself up against me, trying to get me deeper inside of him, and his green eyes were wild with passion, desire, almost inhuman in their need for me to plunge into him, and I could see into his mind . . .

Oh God oh God yes Cord fuck me I need you to fuck me tear me in half my God your cock is so amazing so perfect it feels like nothing I've ever had inside me before you're so amazing you're so beautiful come on bitch fuck me make me your whore make me your pig I want you come on give it to me come on pound me pound my

*ass put my head through the fucking headboard you know you can
do it stud I want to be your whore your bitch come on fuck me fuck
me I want you deeper in me I want you all the way inside come on
fucker fuck me come on come on stop teasing me oh my God oh my
God that feels so incredible oh dear fucking God please don't stop
please don't please please please . . .*

And I smiled down at him as my own need to be inside of
him took over and nothing else mattered, nothing else in
the world existed other than the two of us and my cock inside his ass and I stopped resisting and let gravity work, and
I plunged all the way down inside of him, stopping only
when my balls struck skin and his eyes opened so wide I
thought they might pop out of his head, and they began to
glow, just as the stone around his neck did, and I remembered that was the last thing I'd seen on Dauphine Street.
Something was telling me I needed to stop, but there was
no way I was going to stop, not until I'd shot my load deep
inside of him, until he was coated and dripping with his
own and I grabbed him by the wrists and lifted him, slamming him back down on the bed, only now with his back
resting on the bed and I slammed into him again and his
eyes were glowing and I felt myself being sucked into
them, and everything was green. Everything around me,
everything inside and outside my head was going green,
and I started moving my hips back and forth, fucking him
mindlessly and I could hear him grunting and groaning,
groaning as I plunged into him, grunting as I slid almost all
the way out before burying myself back inside of him.

We existed outside of time, outside of everything.

All there was, all that mattered, was the two of us.

And I was aware we were floating again, up into the air
above the bed, but I didn't care, didn't question it. All that
mattered was the intensity of my fucking him, and I wanted
to go on fucking him forever. I never wanted to take my

cock out of him. I never wanted this incredible feeling to end. I just wanted to fuck and fuck and fuck, never leave this room, never leave his side. His ass felt like velvet and silk and satin as I slid in and out of it faster and deeper and faster, and he was tensing and trembling. He couldn't stop and that increased the friction on my cock and I could feel it was going to be soon as my balls tightened and ached and that rumbling feeling began to gather inside of me and I saw his shooting out of him, raining down on his chest and stomach, some shots going over his head, others landing on his face and his hair, and it was so beautiful, so intense and erotic that I felt his entire body relax as I let out a cry and my entire body went stiff as my cock released inside of him.

And we fell back out of the air, landing on the bed, gasping and shaking and trembling.

I leaned down and pressed my lips to his.

Chapter 12

"You're hungry, aren't you?" Nico asked.

I didn't know how long we'd lain there together, sated. The sounds of the piano still floated up from downstairs, and I'd been more than content to continue lying there, my right arm around him while his head rested on my chest.

The moment the words left his mouth, the all-too-familiar pang shot agony through me. How had he known before I did?

What exactly was he? He said he was more than a witch, and while I didn't know exactly what all a witch could do, I was more than willing to believe his claim.

"Lorenzo and I have some sport planned for later this evening, you know," he whispered, "and you'll be able to drink your fill then. But if you need something to get you by until then"—he pressed his wrist to my mouth—"by all means have some of my blood." He smiled at me. "They never tell you how arousing it is when a vampire feeds from you. It was almost better than sex." His hair fell forward into his face, and he brushed it back again. "But sex with you was better than any I'd ever had before. I don't want you to ever leave here."

I could see the blue veins in his forearms, pulsing with each heartbeat. I could smell his sweet blood through his skin. I stopped myself just when I was about to sink my teeth through his skin.

"What are you?" I asked him as I stroked his golden curls. "You're more than human; that's for sure. The only other witch I've known was Sebastian, and he didn't..." I hesitated for a moment. "He wasn't like you, Nico. You're different somehow."

"Does it really matter?" he asked, pulling his wrist away from my mouth and letting it gently graze my cock, which rested, spent and exhausted, over my balls. "But you're wrong—we *are* witches." He kissed my chest again. "The witch blood has run powerfully in my family for hundreds of years." He waved his hand around the room. "All of this—this house, this property, all of our wealth—is a result of our witch blood."

"Okay," I replied. "I believe you." I nuzzled my lips against his warm neck and smelled the sweet blood coursing through his jugular vein.

"The most powerful witches come in pairs—as Sebastian well knew, even if his brother rejected his heritage," he murmured.

I could feel the vibration of his voice through the skin of his neck.

"Yet, Lorenzo said that Sebastian had been your master," I said, ignoring the next pang of hunger inside of me. The blood scent was rising from him, sweet and pungent. But I also remembered the feeling of power his blood had given me—how it had made me strong enough to break the bonds that had held me in my prison in the outbuilding. "If you and Lorenzo are so powerful, how was it that Sebastian was your master?"

"Sebastian was a natural leader," Nico replied, starting to

tease the head of my cock with his thumb and forefinger again. "Neither Lorenzo nor I felt any need to be the witchmaster. And it's often better if the witchmaster isn't the most powerful—power corrupts, you know, and the last thing anyone needs is the most powerful to be also the most corrupt."

"Did you not know what his plan was?" I asked, closing my eyes and feeling my cock beginning to grow again. "You know what he wanted me for?"

"Look at this," he said, glancing down at my cock. He looked back into my eyes. "Sebastian wanted your vampire blood. He thought with his power and your blood he could become a god." He rolled his big green eyes. "Sebastian could be really stupid at times. Like that would ever be allowed. He'd have been destroyed in either case."

"But your brother said that I needed to be sacrificed to free Sebastian and allow him to rest in peace. Does that mean you and your twin plan to kill me?"

"My brother has always been a fool." Nico turned, placing both hands on my chest and resting his chin on his hands so that he could look me in the eye. "Almost as big a fool as Sebastian. They were lovers, you know—Lorenzo and Sebastian. Often my brother and I share our lovers, but we didn't share Sebastian." He sat up. "And now he claims Sebastian's soul can't move on until you die."

"And you don't believe that?"

"Even when we were children, he was a fool. He's stronger than I—the dark is always stronger than the light—but the light is always smarter than the dark. That is why the light always wins in the end." His eyes flashed at me. "I am a witch—just as Sebastian was, and as his foolish brother is, no matter how much he tries to deny who he is, his heritage. But witches come in all different shapes and sizes and styles. We all have our own powers. Some of us can command the winds and raise storms. Others can cast spells or command animals and insects. Some, like Sebastian, are incredibly strong while others are remarkably weak. If the bloodline is weakened by intermarriage with nonwitches"—he shrugged and brushed a lock of curly hair from his face—"then the power is weakened. It used to be forbidden for witches to marry nonwitches just for that very reason." He laughed. "But the heart wants what the heart wants. Don't you find that to be so?" A dark look crossed his face. "So, at the time of the great scattering, the rules were relaxed and in many cases the bloodlines were diluted. But not in our family. Never in our family. In our family, witch married witch."

"The great scattering?" I stared at him. "What do you mean by that?"

"It happened so long ago, no one is sure if it really happened or if it was just a legend, but there have been many other, smaller scatterings." He dismissed my question with a flick of his wrist. "But in our family, the bloodline has never been diluted. The Narcisse? It has been diluted—Sebastian and his brother are the most powerful Narcisse to come along in many a generation."

"But you said that he wasn't as powerful—"

"If his brother hadn't been a fool, the Narcisse would be the most powerful twin witches in centuries—but the brother was a fool." He smiled at me, his eyes twinkling. "Do you understand now?"

I didn't, and said so. "I don't understand what you want with me, though. If you don't want to kill me—"

"I don't want to kill you—Lorenzo does." His eyes widened. "It would be such a waste of a beautiful vampire." He lowered his head and kissed my chest again. "So, yes, you are our prisoner. I wish it weren't so, but maybe once Lorenzo realizes how foolish he's being about this whole Sebastian thing... It's more about revenge, I think, than anything else. I hope you'll want to stay here with me."

"So, I'm nothing but a prisoner?" I touched his lips with the fingers of my left hand. "After what we just did, you can say that to me?"

I didn't trust him in the least, and I certainly didn't trust his brother. But if I was going to be their prisoner, I'd rather be in the mansion than in that dreadful building I'd been in before escaping. I hated playing a game with him, but I wanted to live. I didn't want to die here in this place. So, I was going to do whatever I had to do in order to survive until I could escape. If it meant earning his trust, then I would do whatever was necessary to do so.

His blood, though, had made me stronger and I didn't understand how or why that was possible. It didn't make any sense. But then, there was so much I didn't know. Maybe vampires were forbidden from drinking the blood of witches, but for some reason Nico hadn't had a problem with giving me his blood. He'd offered me more—and I was hungry. That didn't make sense either.

Why was the hunger not being sated the way it usually was? I'd drunk from the stripper and yet had been hungry again the next day. I didn't know how long I'd been unconscious and bound to that slab, but Nico had fed me more than enough blood to last me for at least a day or two—yet I was hungry again. I wasn't certain if I should drink more of Nico's blood until I knew for certain what effect it was having on me.

Sebastian had wanted my vampire-infected blood to increase his own power—perhaps it worked in reverse as well? If a vampire drank the blood of a witch... It was so infuriating being so ignorant of everything! I muffled a cry as the hunger twisted my bowels into another brutal cramp.

He pressed his wrist against my lips immediately. "Drink from me, my love."

I sank my teeth into his wrist again, and this time he cried out. The cry soon turned into a moan as his blood washed into my mouth and I drank, closing my lips around the torn flesh and sucking, drawing blood from him faster than his heart could pump it.

It crossed my mind that I could completely drain him before he realized what was happening, and then I could escape.

As I drank, he continued to moan, and he moved his body on top of mine, rubbing his hardening cock against mine as I kept lapping up his sweet-tasting blood. He was so besotted with the pleasure of my feeding he wouldn't realize I was taking too much until it was far too late to do anything about it, but how much blood did he have? As I drank, my mouth continued to fill almost as fast as I could gulp the sweet, sticky elixir down.

And sure enough, my veins began to flame again with strength and power as every nerve in my body sprang to alertness and sensitivity. I felt alive, strong, and powerful, like I could fly, like I could tear this house down brick by brick with my bare hands, tear Nico and Lorenzo both limb from limb without the slightest bit of effort.

I felt like a god, as though the world were mine for the taking, and the power was so intoxicating. I was getting drunk on his blood, drunk on the power it was giving me. My muscles longed to be flexed, put to use, and tested. It felt like my muscles were growing, getting bigger. I made a fist with my left hand and saw the veins bulging in my forearm and over the biceps. The muscles did look larger than they had been, my chest felt like the muscles had expanded some, and even my cock was bigger than it had been. I felt invincible.

He gently pushed my head away, and my tongue darted out, licking up the last of his blood before the wounds closed and healed. "You feel the power of my blood, don't you?" His eyes glittered, and the stone around his neck began to glow brighter again.

"What is it doing to me, Nico?" I whispered, grabbing him by both wrists and flipping him onto his back. I straddled him, pinning him down on the satin sheets, and leaned down so that my face was close to his. "What is your blood turning me into? Will a vampire who drinks the blood of a witch become a god as well?"

His pupils were expanding. "Why would I create a god if I couldn't control him?" he whispered, his right arm slipping out of my grasp. He held up the green stone, which was glowing. "Imagine . . ."

"What is this jewel?" I asked, reaching for the pendant. He pushed my hand away. "Don't touch it!"

"This is how I was taken prisoner, kidnapped off the street," I replied, still staring at it. "The boy on Dauphine Street—that wasn't you or Lorenzo. Who was the boy? How did he do it?"

"He's a novitiate in our coven, one of us," Nico replied, a smug look on his face. "You saw how many of us there are— the entire coven gathered here tonight for a celebration."

"To celebrate my death and Sebastian's release?" I replied, angry.

His face darkened. "Please stop. Let me go, please."

"It isn't just your death we intend to celebrate," a voice said from the doorway behind us.

I turned my head and watched Lorenzo strut into the room. He walked with the swagger of a supremely confident man who was getting exactly what he wanted. It made me want to kill him, frankly.

He shut the door behind him and removed his shirt as he

approached the bed. "Did you honestly think you could escape from your shackles and I wouldn't know about it immediately? Do you think I am that stupid, foolish?" he asked as he stood next to the bed.

"Sebastian was overconfident," I replied, rolling off Nico onto my back and watching Lorenzo as he dropped the white silk shirt to the floor.

He reached down and pinched my left nipple. "Or that you could rut with my brother and I wouldn't be aware of it?" He laughed, a low chuckle that was more of a growl than anything else. He undid the clasp of his white velvet pants, and they slid down his muscled thighs. His cock wasn't quite as long as his brother's, and it was darker, almost purplish, and much thicker. His legs weren't smooth like his brother's, but like his chest, they were dusted with curly, wiry black hairs. His muscles were also thicker, and he grasped his cock with his right hand. A little drop oozed out from the slit.

In spite of myself, I felt a strong attraction to him, and my cock was thickening again. I almost could hear Rachel's voice again, mocking me and calling me a whore. I pushed her out of my mind and met his eyes.

"Don't you want to touch it?" he whispered, leaning against the side of the bed so it was closer to me, within my reach. "Don't you want to know if I can take you to the same heights of pleasure that my beautiful blond brother did? Or higher?" His tongue darted over his thick lips. "Because, as in all things, I am superior to my brother as a lover."

I could not take my eyes away from his and was aware that the green stone around his neck was also glowing. I sensed rather than saw Nico climbing out of the bed on the other side. I could hear his footsteps as he walked over to the French doors, and the click as he pushed them open.

"You were so beautiful when you were bound that I wanted to fuck you right then and there. Oh, yes," he said when I flinched, "didn't he explain to you that we are the two halves of the whole? I am the dark; he is the light. I am the top; he is the bottom." He reached down and took his cock into his hands. "You want me inside of you, just as you wanted to be inside of him, don't you?"

And God help me, I did. I wanted him on top of me, his cock inside of me.

My asshole twitched with desire.

"You are such a whore," Rachel's voice echoed inside my head, exasperated.

I dismissed her. *"If all you're going to do is bitch at me and not rescue me, then go to hell and shut the fuck up."*

"You need rescuing from a good fuck, Cord?" Her voice mocked me. *"Since when? I can read your thoughts, remember? You want him inside of you, don't you, you disgusting pig."*

"Rescue me or shut the fuck up."

He climbed onto the bed and stood over me on all fours—his knees inside of my legs, his hands on either side of my head. His long, luxuriant dark hair glinted chestnut in the chandelier's light and hung on either side of his head down toward me. He leaned down and pressed his lips against mine.

He tasted succulent and rich, sweet yet an entirely different kind of sweet from his brother. His lips worked against mine as he lowered his pelvis down on top of me, and I felt his thickness pressing against my now-hard cock. Nico had been warm, but Lorenzo radiated heat like a fire, and his skin burned against mine as he took my tongue inside his mouth.

His kisses are the opposite of Nico's, I thought crazily. *They truly are yin and yang.*

"That's right, two halves of a whole, bound together," he

breathed against my ear, "and as you fucked him so hard, I will fuck you even harder." His teeth closed on my earlobe, pulling on it slightly. It felt incredible, and I wanted him to bite me harder.

What is happening to me? I thought crazily as his teeth kept chewing lightly on my ear, as I arched my back and pressed my crotch up against his, my legs coming up and closing around his waist, locking tightly and pulling him down harder against me.

It's not like I'd ever objected to sex, but when had I turned into such a pig?

Rachel was right. But then desire pushed everything else out of my mind, and I wanted more.

His tongue ran from my ear along my jawline, and I shuddered, barely able to stand how good it felt. The pleasure was so intense it almost hurt; it was almost more than I could stand. I wanted him to stop, but I also didn't want him to stop. Ever. I wanted him to mount me, make me his little bitch, his little whore. I wanted him to shove that thick monster inside of me, to rip me in half, to make me scream and beg and whine and grunt like a pig. I wanted him on top of me. I wanted him to take me from behind and slap me, pull my hair, claw me until my vampire blood was spilling. I wanted his teeth to tear at my ear, gnaw on my lips, bite my nipples until they ached, and then I wanted him to put all of his fingers inside of me.

His tongue lapped at my throat as he started flicking my nipples with both hands. My entire body started trembling. I had no idea where Nico was, if he was even still in the room with us or if he'd fled. I didn't care—in fact, the thought of him watching his brother, his dark identical twin, driving me insane with pleasure was somewhat thrilling to me, arousing me even more than I already had been, which I didn't think possible. These two clearly were witches,

witches who could give and take pleasure, take me to heights of pleasure and depths of depravity I'd never dreamed of before.

Then his teeth closed around my right nipple and I felt myself rising from the bed. I opened my eyes and could see the top of his head, my legs locked around his waist, and we were indeed rising from the bed. I looked through the open French doors out onto the broad veranda, and I saw Nico's naked form at the wrought-iron railing, leaning over it, his perfectly formed, beautiful white ass almost beckoning for me to come up from behind and take him yet again. I opened my mouth to call out to him, to ask him to come back inside, but all that came out of my throat was a guttural gasping for air as Lorenzo nibbled on my nipple.

My head fell back and before my eyes stopped focusing and closed, I could see the bed several feet below us.

I heard Lorenzo laugh and say in a low voice, "Yes, you like that, don't you, bitch? You want to be my little whore, don't you?"

"Yes," I breathed out, "make me your bitch. I'll do anything you want. Just don't stop, please, don't stop..."

My voice trailed off into a scream as his teeth closed on my other nipple, hard enough that it felt like he was trying to bite it off. For a brief moment, pain drove everything else out of my mind, but the pain transformed almost instantly into pleasure, crossing the thin line that separated the two, and I wondered how that was even possible, but then the thought was driven right out of my head again as I felt one of his fingers probing between my ass, looking for a way in, and I braced myself for the invasion I knew was to come.

There was no playing around, as Jean-Paul and so many others liked to do. Once his finger found what it was looking for, there was no hesitation, no pause.

Instead he shoved it inside.

My entire body stiffened as everything inside and out-side contracted, fighting to keep the invading digit out of me, resisting it, not wanting to surrender and give in to it, and my breathing was fast, so fast that I couldn't get enough oxygen into my brain, and I knew I was about to hyperven-tilate. I was going to pass out from the pleasure, but was that even possible for a vampire? And then with a loud gasp and a cry, my entire body relaxed and his finger went all the way and began moving around inside of me, making an enormous circle.

"Oh, yes, boy, you like that, don't you? Think you can handle another finger?" he whispered.

Before I could answer, another finger slid into me.

He spread them apart and wiggled them.

I couldn't think.

I could barely breathe.

My entire body felt like it had been doused in gasoline and set on fire.

Another finger slid into me.

How was that even possible?

"Because you're a whore, Cord, just a big hole waiting to get plugged by whatever creature comes along big enough to satisfy you."

"Fuck you, Rachel! Get out of my head!"

It was almost like her taunting voice inspired me to greater depths.

I pushed him until he was on his back, and I was strad-dling him. I pulled his fingers out of my ass and grabbed his cock.

"You want to fuck me, big man?" I hissed through clenched teeth. "You think that cock can satisfy me?"

I shoved the head into my ass and a half scream erupted

from my lips. I'd had big men before, but it was like his was growing inside of me, getting thicker somehow now that it was on the inside.

As I slid down the shaft, it seemed like that, too, was somehow getting longer, thicker.

How was that possible?

Witchcraft.

And he was filling me up.

He was huge, so fucking big—

My eyes stopped focusing.

Everything was turning green.

And finally it was all inside of me, every last inch of it, every piece of it, and I sensed he was smiling, enjoying the feel of my ass against his thick balls, and I just sat there, not moving, just resting with his enormous cock throbbing inside of me, and he tried to move his hips, tried to move it a little bit out of me, but I would have none of it.

"You'll pull out when I let you," I snarled, my voice almost animalistic as I gripped it with every muscle I could.

He slapped me, my head spinning off to the left with the force of the blow, my eyes filling with liquid and my ears ringing.

He shoved me off and down through the air, until I hit the bed with such force I heard the frame crack. He landed on top of me and slapped me again.

"You don't make the rules, whore. If I want to fuck you, I will fuck you. Do you understand me, you little bitch?" he snarled, grabbing my ankles and holding them up as he slammed his cock inside of me so hard that my head hit the wall. He slammed a fist into my stomach, knocking all the air out of me as he pulled his cock back out and slammed it back inside of me.

I tasted blood in my mouth and the taste of it, my own blood, only raised my passion and desire to a higher level, and he slammed his cock into me again, my head hitting the wall again with enough force to crack the plaster.

"I knew you liked it rough," he snarled, slapping my face again with the other hand.

"You think you're man enough to make me come?" I snarled. "I don't think you are, little man. You think you can satisfy me? You're not man enough, do you understand? Better men than you have tried and failed, so come on, man, come on, give it to me!" I'd never been so wild, so determined, so out of control.

He slapped me again, his face contorted with anger, almost purple with his rage as he grabbed my hair and yanked.

The pain was exquisite, and I gasped, almost blowing my load as he pulled my head back even harder.

I slapped his face.

His eyes got wide with anger, and he slammed deep into me until I gasped. He pounded his big thick dick into me a few more times, and then he pulled almost completely out, just watching me with a sly look on his face.

"What are you doing?" I gasped out.

"Beg me."

"You fucking bastard," I snarled.

He flipped me over onto my stomach and pulled me up to my knees and slammed into me again.

He started fucking me harder, deeper, building up a rhythm and the pleasure was so intense I couldn't think of anything except that cock, his mighty cock, deep in me. I wanted it so far inside me that when he came, it would shoot out my mouth. I wanted to be bruised and battered and slammed and treated like the nasty whore I was. Yes, I was just a pig with no pride or shame; I wanted to be fucked and raped and spanked, smacked around like the bitch I was. No wonder I'd left Jean-Paul; neither he nor any of the others were man enough to give me the kind of fucking I wanted, the kind of fucking I deserved, the kind of fucking I had to have. No, they weren't men. I'd needed a real man, with a cock the size of a baseball bat that could slam into me over and over again, make me beg, make me debase myself. I could feel drool spilling out of my mouth, but I didn't care. I didn't ever want him to stop. I wanted him to pound me until the end of time. Nothing mattered except that huge dick inside me, and maybe if I got lucky he'd bathe me in his cum. I wanted to be covered in his cum and his sweat and his man juice. I wanted him to treat me like the whore I was—

And I felt it, I was going to come and there was nothing I could do. There was no way I could stop it, and it exploded out of me.

And I felt him blowing his own all over my ass, my back, my hair, my head until I was drenched, the droplets running down my sides.

And spent, I collapsed onto the mattress.

And he leaned forward and whispered in my ear, "Who's your master, whore?"

"My God," I breathed. "My God, my God, my God."

"Yeah, you liked that, didn't you?" he whispered, slapping my ass with his right hand. "Rest up, bitch, and I'll give you some more."

I closed my eyes and tried to catch my breath.

I opened them again when I felt a towel wiping Lorenzo's cum off me. I looked up and saw Nico. He gave me a sad little smile and walked away.

I rolled over onto my back and felt sore everywhere. Lorenzo's eyes were closed, and he was sleeping. His hair was slick with sweat, and drops of sweat glistened in his body hair. I sat up, wincing a bit.

Nico walked out of the bathroom and sat down, naked, in a wingback chair next to the hall door.

I got out of the bed and walked on shaky legs over to him. "Nico—"

His eyes glistened with tears. "It's okay, Cord. I'm used to it," he said quietly. He wrapped his arms around himself, the picture of misery. "It's been my whole life, you know." He gave me a weak, sad smile. "That's why I was glad I got to you first. If I hadn't, you never would have given me a second glance."

I knelt in front of him, my legs protesting as I did. "Nico, just because"—I bit my lip—"what just happened did, that doesn't mean I don't want you anymore."

He looked at me, his wet green eyes alive with hope. "Do you really mean that? Will you stay here with us?"

"Of course I will." I stood up and reached my hand out for him. "Come lie down with us."

I turned my back so he couldn't see my smirk.

CHAPTER 13

Nico slipped into the bed behind me, placing his arm over me. I pressed his hand to my lips, and I felt him sigh. His touch sent an electric current through my body, and again, I felt like I was on a drug of some kind, but it was a better drug than anything Jean-Paul had given me.

I closed my eyes and tried to keep my breathing even, focusing on each breath going in and holding it for a second before releasing it completely, blowing out until my lungs were empty. I could hear my heart racing, pounding in my ears, so powerful I could see it pulsing in my eyelids. My mind was alive with consciousness—I was aware of a multitude of different voices besides my own inside my head. I tried to push all the noise aside and wondered again what was happening to me. I could hear birds rustling in trees outside the house, the whisper of the grass moving in the wind, the gentle lapping of the river against the shore, the slight noise the current made as it moved out in the center, the intense playing of hands on the piano downstairs.

My skin was so hot it was like being on fire, and heat was radiating out of my veins. And my heart kept pounding, so loud I wondered that neither Lorenzo nor Nico could hear it. I focused on my breath, not wanting to start panting, not wanting to let either one of them know anything was different with me. I didn't know why I didn't want them to know, but somehow I knew it was important.

Something was happening to me—and not just to my physical self, but to my mind.

I was changing, and in the deep recesses of memory, I knew that my conversion from human to vampire had been something similar to this, several days of this burning fever, of doors inside of my mind opening.

What had these twin witches done to me? I wondered as I opened my eyes and realized I could see every individual strand of hair on Lorenzo's head, that I could feel every soft, downy, almost invisible hair on Nico's arm brushing against my skin, and it took all of my willpower and self-control not to tremble.

Whatever was happening to me wasn't over, and I didn't know how long this was going to last, but there wasn't any point to panicking, so I allowed myself to relax a bit. The first time I had done Ecstasy had been something similar to this—the feeling had been so overwhelming I'd tried to resist it, which had only made it worse. Jean-Paul and Clint had talked me through that brief scary moment, convinced me to let go and ride the waves. And even though this was so much more intense, resisting it wasn't going to make it stop.

So I let myself go, gave myself to the fire burning in my veins, and when the sensations and noises and voices crowded back into my mind, I didn't try to fight them.

And as I'd figured, eventually they faded until my own consciousness, my own self, was the most clear and more powerful.

I nestled up closer against Lorenzo, just to see if my body felt hot to the touch. He didn't move, didn't adjust at all, didn't even shift or try to move away from me. He simply relaxed his muscles more so that some of his weight was now pressed against my chest. Clearly, this burning feeling was for me alone. I wasn't radiating heat to either of the twin witches. Although I still felt as if I were burning alive, their skin remained pressed to mine on both sides of me. Their skin felt deliciously cool, and I could feel Nico's even breathing behind me, and as soon as I thought about his breath on my skin, my skin began to tingle and I allowed my entire body to go into an involuntary shudder of pleasure. Their breathing was even and gentle, not labored, so they were both slumbering—and I could sense their minds at peace, not dreaming, just images dancing through their brains without any coherence. I didn't know how it was possible, but whatever was happening to me and my body and my mind, the vampiric powers that Rachel had told me I would gradually develop over time were now developing and very quickly, at that.

I listened again, and heard the sound of the wind moving the grass on the lawn, then limbs and leaves in the trees on the far side of the lawn being kissed by the same wind.

And as they were both deep in slumber, I wondered if I could ease myself out from between them and escape.

But whenever I shifted, even the slightest bit, I sensed their consciousness swimming up from the darkness of sleep and knew they'd be awake in a moment if I tried to get out of the bed.

But as my veins continued to burn inside of my skin, I felt my muscles getting stronger—the feeling I remembered from when I used to go to the gym and work out, that tiredness and soreness of muscle tissue being torn down and rebuilt. I opened my eyes and looked at my shoulder, and as I looked at it, it seemed like I was able to see through the skin down to the muscle fibers themselves, and they were growing, getting stronger, bigger, storing power.

When this was over, whatever it was, I suspected neither Nico nor Lorenzo would be able to stop me from leaving, even with their magic.

And I no sooner thought that than a voice whispered inside my head, *"Why do you want to get away? You have two gorgeous studs right here, ready to service you whenever you need it. And they're witches—powerful creatures who can work magic. What do you have to go back to? What have the vampires ever done for you? Jean-Paul didn't love you, remember? He loved you being young, not you. You could have been anyone. So what's out there for you, Cord? All there is for you is that lonely, musty old house on Orleans Street! And do you really think the old man and the bitch give two shits about you? It's not like they've come looking for you or anything. That should tell you all you need to know about them...."*

Jared. There's Jared.

Could I really just leave him there with those two?

Didn't I owe him something?

I closed my eyes and concentrated on him, wondering if he was all right.

And a window in my mind opened, and I could see him just as clearly as if I were standing in the front bedroom of the old house, next to the bed he was stretched out on. Once again he had shrugged the covers aside, pushing them down to the foot of the bed. His eyes were still closed but were moving beneath the lids, his mouth slightly open, a spot of drool in the right corner. His chest was moving up and down with each breath he drew in and blew out. His beautiful chest, flat stomach, and of course, the enormous erection just above the heavy balls, straining and aching for release . . . it was like being there. I could smell the mustiness of the house, the dust, and the strong man scent coming from him, the mustiness from his damp armpits. Drops of water nestled in his underarm hair and dotted his hair along the hairline. As I looked down at his beautiful body, I wanted him, wanted to straddle his massive cock and ride it, let him fill me up and—

And I closed the window in my mind firmly, and I was no longer in the room with him but back in this bedroom in this weird mansion of the twin witches.

I wouldn't allow myself to think about Jared that way. I only could hope he didn't remember what had already happened, and I felt guilt bubbling up inside of me. *Had I taken advantage of him when he was clearly not in his right mind? What was it my women's studies professor had said—oh, yes, if someone can't think clearly enough to give informed consent, it is rape.*

I'd raped him.

I pushed that thought out of my mind. I'd deal with that some other time.

I wondered if I should try to communicate with Nigel or Rachel, but another voice whispered, *You don't know if any of this is true, or if they've given you some kind of drug that's making you imagine all of these things. Can you trust what you're feeling? Jean-Paul used to give you drugs that made you imagine all kinds of things, didn't he? And you loved them . . . you loved them so much you would have taken them all the time if he would have let you. It's no wonder you don't know anything about being a vampire, about what's happening to you now. All you wanted to do was take drugs, drink some blood, and fuck. Shame on you!*

That voice in my head sounded like my father's.

I pushed that voice aside, realizing my cock was hardening again as it pressed against Lorenzo's hard, hairy ass. He shifted in his sleep slightly and pulled my arm tighter across his chest. Again, a tingle went through my body, and I felt the heat coming back, even hotter and more intense than before, and I wondered if I could slip inside of him, ride him, make him my little bitch the way he'd branded me as his earlier.

What is wrong with me? What have they done to me, these brother witches?

A memory of him riding me as we floated up in the air, him driving deep inside of me and me begging—no, *demanding*—that he keep pounding away made me blush a bit, but my asshole also twitched, and I realized that not only was my hard-on pressing tight against the crack of Lorenzo's ass but also I could feel my ass pressing against Nico's crotch behind me.

Rachel's voice echoed in my head: *"You're really just a disgusting whore, aren't you?"*

"Go to hell," I responded. *"There's nothing wrong with sex, you prude."*

That was the Church of Christ way. Sex was dirty, wrong, something you had to keep secret and never talk about, even though obviously members of the church did have sex—some of them had as many as eight children. Our high school had plenty of teen mothers, and the county was full of married couples whose oldest child was born less than nine months after the wedding. Everyone pretended those babies had been premature, but if that were true, someone from the CDC or EPA would surely have done a study on Fayette County to find out why there was such a high rate of premature births there.

Every last one of them was a fucking hypocrite. But the indoctrination of "sex is sin" was so strong and powerful, I still couldn't completely break free of it, and I wasn't even a human anymore.

And since escaping from my prison and coming into this big house, I'd been sexually obsessed—almost perpetually horny. I slid my hand down to my aching erection. I had already come several times within the past hour, yet somehow my cock wanted more, and I felt the heat burning inside of me. *Fuck him, you know he wants it,* my cock seemed to be urging me on. *If not Lorenzo, you know Nico does—he's a nasty little pig who can't get enough of your cock. They both want you. That's why they brought you here, really, to be their sex slave. They'd wear a human out too soon, so they needed a vampire, someone superhuman, who can get hard again and again and get off again and never be completely satisfied and what's wrong with that? There's nothing wrong with it, Church of Christ boy, and isn't having all this gay sex the ultimate fuck you to the church and your parents and the way you were raised? So do it, just go ahead and do it, you know . . .*

I shook my head to clear it.

Something was happening to me, all right.

Sure, back when I'd only been human, I'd been horny a lot. At the time, I thought there was something wrong with me—surely no one else was so driven to jack off as much as I was? The fear of sin I'd been raised with, the belief that sex was sin, made me feel dirty, perverted, and disgusting, but no matter how much I prayed, I'd had to jack off several times a day—which wasn't easy in the fraternity house, since I was always afraid Jared might come back to the room unexpectedly. It had been much easier in my parents' house, when I could lock my bedroom door or go into the bathroom and lock the door behind me and know I was safe and secure from being walked in on. But the fraternity was a nightmare of almost-discovery. There were always guys around, I shared my room with Jared, and you never knew when some wasted brother would confuse your room with his and use his student ID to pop the door open when his key failed to work and his mind was too addled with drink or drugs or both to realize it wasn't working because it was the wrong door.

And there had been times I'd woken up in the middle of the night with a hard-on so intense I had to do something about it, so I'd slipped down to the communal bathroom and gone into a stall, hoping none of the other brothers would wake up and need to relieve themselves.

I was always scared about something at Beta Kappa—scared someone would catch me beating off, scared someone would catch me watching them in the showers, scared someone would figure out that I was gay.

But as a vampire, the need for sex wasn't quite as strong. Not that I didn't enjoy the hell out of it—nothing could really compare to the feeling of shooting your load—but it wasn't the same. While I slept or rested, I never woke up with the aching need to be inside someone or have someone inside of me. I would feel desire when I saw a man to whom I was attracted, and of course I responded to touch, and the feedings . . .

And it hit me at that moment.

I'd fed from Nico.

He had cut his wrist and held it to my mouth, and I drank his sweet witch blood.

Before I drank his blood, I couldn't break free from the restraints.

After I drank his blood, they snapped like twigs when I tried to free myself.

Sebastian had wanted my blood to convert himself into a witch-vampire hybrid, to become a god.

So what happened to a vampire who drank witch blood?

The fire in my veins—was it actually a new power I was feeling, a strange hybrid mixture of vampire and witch? Maybe it wasn't my vampire powers developing faster than they were supposed to—maybe it was witch power. Or the witch blood was working as an accelerant. My muscles definitely felt stronger, more powerful, and were getting stronger with each passing second. I could sense their strength increasing; every muscle in my body felt like it was coiled, waiting to unleash itself.

Surely Nico knew the effect his blood would have on me?

He had to. Sebastian had been their master; they had been his seconds in command. They'd known what he was trying to do.

Nico had given me his blood deliberately so this would happen.

"*Of course I did,*" Nico's voice cooed inside my head. "*I told you—Sebastian was a fool. He never really understood. . . . Shhh, Lorenzo is waking. He doesn't know, and I don't want him to know anything just yet.*"

Lorenzo moved under my arm, shifting again. He pushed my arm away as he sat up. I opened my eyes, focusing on him. His broad shoulders tapering down to his narrow waist, the hard fullness of his muscular ass—

I wanted to grab him, force him down on the bed and shove myself into him, pound his ass until tears came out of his eyes, use him as contemptuously and as thoroughly as he had used me, teach him that no witch can be the master of a vampire—

"*Control yourself. There will be time enough for Lorenzo's humiliation later. And believe me, I've been waiting for that for many years. So be patient. We can both wait a little while longer. Our vengeance on him will be that much sweeter for the waiting. Trust me, my darling vampire, on this.*"

Lorenzo stood up, stretching to his full height with his arms going above his head as he went up on his toes. I wondered how delicious his blood would taste in my mouth. My cock ached even more as I imagined his blood gushing into my mouth, his muscles going slack in my arms as he became submissive to my needs and my desires—

"*Ease up, Cord! Patience!*"

I shook my head, trying to calm myself as Lorenzo dressed, and I felt Nico's arm tighten somewhat around me. His hand slid down to my cock and wrapped around it. I closed my eyes.

"Once he's gone I will relieve you, okay? But stop thinking about him, stop thinking about the power—I don't know how much he can sense from you. He may not be able to sense anything, but I don't want to take the risk. I'm not as strong as he is, but together he will be easy prey for us."

Lorenzo pulled his shirt on and turned back to the bed, fastening the buttons over his broad hairy chest. He smiled, but it wasn't a pleasant smile. "I will go down and see to our guests," he said, his voice sneering, and I knew then he was cruel; he enjoyed dominance because he was arrogant and superior and liked to inflict pain.

And I could see a man tied by the wrists to two posts, his arms stretched out and his shoulders aching from the strain. His back was to me, and his skin glistened with sweat and oil in the light from two burning torches. He was wearing a leather thong that dropped between the two marble globes of his ass, and he was pleading, almost whimpering, for mercy.

Lorenzo's face was a cruel mask as he snapped the whip, and its tip licked at the skin of the man's lower back, an angry welt forming where it had touched him. The man's entire body tensed and trembled with the pain from the lash, and Lorenzo coiled the whip in his hand again, and I turned my head to watch him.

Lorenzo was wearing only tight calfskin pants, and the bulge in his crotch gave away how much he was enjoying whipping the man—

"And remember, dear Cord, we have some entertainment for you—and our guests—in just a little while." Lorenzo walked back over to the bed and put his fingers beneath my chin, and despite myself I trembled with desire at his electrifying touch, the tips of his fingers burning the flesh beneath my chin. "And don't think you can escape, my pretty young vampire. I have bound you to this room." He snapped his fingers in my face. "And only I can release you from it. Vampires are strong, but no vampire is strong enough to defeat magic."

He lightly slapped my face, nothing more than a tap, yet blinding pain seared through me. My eyes filled with tears that I blinked away, and I felt a rage building inside me. I saw myself twisting his neck until it snapped, and the sound gave me pleasure.

What the hell was wrong with me?

I could hear the music still coming from downstairs. It seemed crazy that all that had happened in this room could have, yet all the while the musicale continued below our feet. While their guests remained in the music room, perched on their chairs and sipping wine from crystal, giving their full attention to the young woman at the piano, just above their heads the twins had gratified their lusts and desires with me.

I found that thought to be completely and utterly gratifying.

Lorenzo smirked down at me. "You belong to us now, vampire, but don't worry your pretty little head about it. You will enjoy your stay with us. I'll make sure of that." He stepped back from the bed and finished buttoning the silk shirt.

I felt Nico shift behind me and sit up. "You'll get everything ready?" he asked.

Lorenzo walked over to the door and looked back at the bed. "Yes, brother, I'll take care of everything—like always." His tone was mocking, and it filled me with rage. Again, I envisioned myself crossing the room in a second, slamming him against the wall, lashing at his face until it dripped with blood and gore, sinking my teeth into his neck and draining him until he was nothing more than an empty husk to be tossed into the trash.

Nico's hand touched my shoulder—again, I felt as though

electricity coursed through my body at the touch—but he squeezed softly, and the strange rage left me.

The door shut behind Lorenzo, and I heard his mocking laughter as he walked away.

"What have you done to me?" I whispered, turning so that I could see Nico.

He turned his back to me and walked over to the French doors. He wrapped his arms around himself as he stood on the threshold leading out to the veranda, his round butt and milky skin almost aglow in the moonlight. "Sebastian wanted to drink your blood, and he thought it would make him a god," Nico said softly. "It has been forbidden from earliest times for a witch to become a vampire, or for a vampire to feed from a witch."

Great, I thought, *yet another rule I didn't know about and have broken.*

"The legends always said that it wasn't possible," he went on. "That such a creature would be an abomination and would go mad and destroy itself." He turned back to me with a sweet smile on his face. "Yet Sebastian didn't die from drinking your blood, did he?"

"My blood wasn't fully vampiric," I replied, rising from the bed and walking across the room. I felt like I could fly, like for some reason the law of gravity no longer applied to my body. I grabbed at the carpet with my toes, scrunching them up, grabbing carpet with them. I was trying to tether myself to the floor because I felt like I was going to float off if I didn't. "I was still partly human, was only transitioning."

"Of course. He hoped that the blood would continue to transition inside him—it had never been tried before. That's why he had to have you." Nico didn't turn even as I came up beside him. "What were the odds he'd ever have access to a transitioning vampire again?" He laughed bitterly. "It was much safer—and easier—you see. Vampires are too strong for us. Our magic and spells can hold them for a little while, but not for long."

"Lorenzo said I couldn't defy his magic," I said.

He laughed. "He wants you to think that. If you believe it, you won't try to escape." He sighed. "No, we can hold a vampire for only a short time. And imagine the anger of a vampire, to come out of a spell and discover a witch had drank from him! No, it had to be you." He tilted his head to one side. "Besides, the stories always said that a witch would go mad and would be consumed if he drank the blood of a fully developed vampire. Sebastian was very brave, but very foolish." His voice sounded sad.

"I thought it was Lorenzo who loved him," I said, putting my hand on his bare shoulder.

The instant our skin came into contact, there was a flash of something, but I could see that Nico felt nothing; only I had felt the rush of power from him.

And I felt even stronger now.

Nico smiled at me, and I felt a rush of love for him, the emotion just as powerful as the rage that had coursed through me earlier. "I have made you a god." He reached out a hand, and his fingertips ran down the center of my chest, making my entire body tingle and tremble. "I gave you my blood to drink, and it has changed you—is changing you. Can you feel the power within you now?"

"Yes." I lay back down on the bed, resting my back against some lace-edged pillows that cushioned my weight. "You said you've made me a god. Why would you do something like that?" I asked, raising my eyebrows. "Isn't it forbidden?"

"Rules." He waved his hand contemptuously. "What use have we for rules? Rules that were made only to keep us from achieving our true potential? Rules that keep us hidden, cowering in the shadows, while humans destroy themselves, refusing to learn, making the same mistakes over and over again?" His white body gleamed in the moonlight. "Councils of witches, councils of vampires and other creatures, all with their stupid petty rules and petty politics, all threatening us with destruction if we don't conform and go along with their idiocies." He turned back around, his arms folded across his chest. "Sebastian was a genius, you know. He saw how stupid it all was, how for millennia we have all denied our true natures rather than developed our abilities and our potential, all because of some stupid rules made when humans still hadn't figured out how to wipe their asses." His lip curled in scorn. "Sebastian's mistake was that he thought *he* was the one who would be able to combine the powers of a vampire with a witch." He shook his head. "He was a genius in many ways, but his own ambitions blinded him."

"The key was to give a vampire witch blood to drink," I said slowly.

He nodded. "Vampires are practically immortal; witches are not. You feel the power, don't you?" Nico stepped back over to me. "Your body is already changing." He reached out and grasped my right bicep muscle. Again, it felt like a current flowed through his hand through my skin and into my arm. "Your muscles feel harder, bigger." He smiled. "Together we can rule the world."

I pulled my arm away from him. "The Nightwatchers will never sit still for this."

He laughed, and it sounded harsh to my ears. "The Nightwatchers are fools whose time is past. It is time they were overthrown and destroyed." His lips grazed my cheek in a kiss. "I will teach you how to be a witch, and you are already immortal. Together we can destroy anyone or anything that stands in our way." He put his mouth to my ear. "And admit it—you want to destroy Lorenzo, don't you?"

"Yes," I replied, feeling the urge growing within me. "I want to punish him. I want to fuck him and humiliate him before I kill him."

His eyelids came down about halfway. "I've had a life-time of humiliations at his hands," he smiled nastily. "I will help you."

He put his arms around me and dropped to his knees in front of me, taking my cock into his mouth.

As he began to worship me, it was as though his mind opened to me, and images began rushing through my head.

I saw myself walking down Bourbon Street, eyes wide open as I walked around people. Beads were flying down into the crowds gathered beneath balconies, and I could hear the sound of a march-ing band and crowds yelling behind me, back at Canal Street.

It was the night I met Jean-Paul.

And I saw myself bumping into the vampire I would later know as Clint, shirtless in the intersection at Bourbon and St. Ann, dance music competing from the bars on opposite sides of the street, and as Clint looked me over, with what I thought then was attrac-tion to my body but I know now was simply the lust for my blood as well as for my body, and he led me inside to where the rest of the coven was dancing in the midst of the crowded dance floor, and I knew later that evening Jean-Paul was going to feed from me and give me some of his own blood to drink, starting the process that turned me into what I am now.

And then I was back, lashed to the bed in Sebastian's house as he lit candles and chanted an incantation, preparing me for some rit-ual going back to ancient times, a ritual he'd discovered, some spell he could cast to protect himself from dying from ingesting vampire blood and then the others were bursting into the house to protect me, to rescue me, and destroy Sebastian for his great sin.

Only this time, I watched as Sebastian was tortured by my vam-pire brothers. I saw Jean-Paul carry my limp and naked form, wrapped in a blanket, out of the house and across the street, where he gave me more of his blood to revive me and finish the transformation.

And I watched as my brothers gagged Sebastian so he couldn't speak, couldn't work his magic, and somehow I knew that witches had to be able to speak the words out loud, else their magic had no power.

They tied him spread-eagled to the bed in the same fashion as I had been, only they tied him facedown so that his big muscular ass was turned up to the air, and I saw Clint step out of his pants and mount him and start fucking him.

And I watched as they all took their turn mounting him, humiliating him as they raped him, as he screamed through the gag in his mouth, and tears of humiliation and anger and rage streamed from his eyes, and despite what he had wanted to do to me, what he had planned to do to me, I could not help but feel pity for him, for I would not wish such a fate on any other person.

And when they had satisfied their lusts, their desire to exhibit their vampiric power over the witch who'd dared to capture a baby vampire to drink from and kill, they slit his throat, and blood gushed everywhere, and I saw their eyes glitter with hunger for it.

And then Jean-Paul returned, carrying a boy in his arms, a beautiful young boy whose body was similar to mine, whose coloring and bone structure of his face could pass as mine from a distance, and I knew the boy was dead, his neck broken because there was no way anyone's head could lie at that angle and still be alive, and I knew then what I'd always known but refused to acknowledge—that they'd murdered some boy to take my place.

And Jean-Paul and my brothers took the candles and started fires, setting the house aflame as they worked their way back to the front door, and by the time they closed the door behind them, the back of the house was a roaring inferno, and the roof caught fire, and there was the scream of fire sirens through the misty night as they locked the door of our house behind them.

And I saw myself standing in front of St. Louis Cathedral in the twilight, watching a young man walk across the square while talking on his cell phone, and I saw myself start to follow him, and then—

I came, my entire body jerking, and I was out of the vision and back into the bedroom of the big mansion, and I was looking down in horror at Nico as he drank my ejaculate.

"It was you," I whispered, and I knew it was true. "You set everything in motion so I would wind up here."

He stood, wiping his mouth. "And be with me always. Together, my darling Cord, we are going to rule the world."

CHAPTER 14

He stepped closer to me and slipped his arms around me, his smile so warm and inviting it was hard to conceive that one so angelic-looking could conceive of something so evil as what he had set in motion.

And as our bare chests came together again, once again I felt another surge of power. I felt like a battery being recharged, power rushing through my veins and into my muscles. I wasn't on fire anymore—this was more like when I accidentally touched the electric fence that kept the cows in back on my grandfather's farm, yet somehow not as unpleasant.

This felt good.

I felt like I was about to levitate, and once again tried to grasp the carpet with my toes. I focused on my breathing until the power surge passed. I didn't want him to know—somehow I knew that he shouldn't know, because I felt like I was draining away his power and if that was true, he would surely kill me to get the power back. My mind was racing, and I knew that I had to get away. No matter how tempting it might seem to stay here in this big mansion, being serviced and servicing the twins every night—every night being an endless erotic dream of sensual pleasure—I couldn't stay here. Of course the twins wanted my stay here to be pleasurable. They didn't want me to ever leave; they wanted me to stay here forever and be their slave, use my power somehow to do their bidding.

Lorenzo didn't know his brother's plan was even more evil than he could possibly imagine, that his brother was planning on using me to kill him.

Killing Lorenzo ... the very thought made my blood rise, made my dick get even harder than it already was. As much pleasure as he'd given me, as much as I wanted him to give me more, I also knew that I hated him, that he was cruel and evil, and that wasn't my father or the Church of Christ condemning sexuality. Lorenzo enjoyed hurting people, was what my psychology teacher back at Ole Miss would have called a *sociopath*.

Lorenzo had to die, and I might have to play along with Nico to make sure that happened.

And then I would worry about getting away from Nico.

My head was spinning, and my feelings were all jumbled up inside me. Sure I was a vampire, but the Christianity was still deeply ingrained in my psyche—*thou shalt not kill*.

But those rules only applied to humans, and I was no longer human. Hell, I was no longer just a vampire. I was something more.

"Just be patient." Nico pressed up against me again. My cock was still hard and sensitive as it pressed against his smooth stomach. He was smiling up at me, and I could see the love in his eyes. I had feelings for him, but they certainly weren't feelings of *love*.

Loving him wasn't possible. I was grateful to him—without him I'd still be restrained in that other building, just something to be used and abused by Lorenzo. He had given me his blood, given me more power than I'd ever dreamed was possible.

But he was the one who had set everything up. He was the reason I was a vampire. If not for him, I would have graduated from Ole Miss, would have come out to my parents—all the things that once seemed so horrible and unbearable and impossible to me when I was still human.

And while it was possible becoming a vampire had indeed been the best possible thing for me, I couldn't forgive him for what happened to Jared.

If I had not become a vampire, Jared would still have his own life—and he would not be in that house on Orleans Street, transitioning into a creature he'd never even dreamed existed outside of books and movies.

And as I looked deep into Nico's beautiful green eyes, I could see it all happening. His eyes were like windows into his memory, and I wanted to see it, experience it like I'd been there that night.

Nico had been there, all right.

Jared was getting out of his car. He had parked on Esplanade Avenue, between Royal and Chartres. He was happy, in a good mood. He'd just left his office in the Central Business District and had had a great day at work. He loved his job, and everything was going great. He was living in the carriage house behind his parents' big home in Uptown to save money—he wanted to buy a house sooner rather than later. The only shadow in his life was the fact that he still missed Cord, even felt some guilt about his death. Maybe he shouldn't have let him go off by himself, but they had both been young and didn't think anything bad could ever happen to them. But he'd already discussed it with Tori. They were going to name their first son Cord Logan Holcomb. He marveled again that he was so lucky. He'd met Tori Crawford the very night Cord died, on the parade route at St. Charles. She was beautiful, slender with blond hair and perfect, flawless skin. She was a student at Tulane, originally from up north. She was a couple of years older—she'd graduated from the University of Wisconsin and was working on her master's in public health at Tulane while she worked for a local AIDS nonprofit. She was smart and she was driven and she called him on his shit. After a few hours in her company, he was crazy about her, and when the news about Cord had broken, she'd been great. He didn't think he could have made it through that time without her. He started coming home to New Orleans every weekend, and finally when he graduated and got a job, he asked her to marry him.

He was whistling as he unplugged his iPhone from the car charger and slipped it into his pocket. As soon as he did, it vibrated. He locked the car with a click of the fob attached to his key ring, and clipped his keys to a belt loop. He pulled the phone back out and grinned as he read the text message. He leaned against his car—a gray Lexus SUV—and using his thumbs typed out a response.

"Just parked. Be there in a few. Love you."

He slipped the phone back into his pocket and walked up to the corner at Chartres Street. There was a spring in his step, and he really felt like he could just burst into song at any moment. He was the luckiest son of a bitch who ever lived. He was meeting Tori and his parents at Café Amelie on Royal Street—it was Tori's favorite restaurant in the Quarter—and they were not only having dinner there but also making wedding plans. Tori wanted to get married in the beautiful garden at Café Amelie, and he couldn't blame her. It was beautiful out there, and why not get married in the heart of the French Quarter? His mom had wanted them to use the backyard of the house in Uptown, but Tori's heart was set on getting married in the Quarter—and she didn't want to get married in one of the hotels.

He turned right when he reached the corner and started walking toward Jackson Square. The sun was setting and a cool breeze was blowing off the river. He probably could have gotten a parking place closer—or paid to park in a lot, for that matter—but it was a beautiful night and he didn't mind the walk. He kept whistling as he walked, his walk still jaunty. He'd changed out of his suit into a pullover cardigan and a pair of jeans before he left the office. He looked up at the sky. The clouds looked like pink cotton candy.

When he reached the corner at Ursulines, he paused for a moment, looking up the street, as though trying to decide whether it was better to change direction or keep going. With a shrug, he turned the corner and headed toward Royal Street. Café Amelie was on Royal Street, after all, and he might as well head up now.

He'd taken only two steps when a black cat howled behind him.

He stopped walking and looked back. The cat meowed again, and lay down on the sidewalk. He smiled and walked back. The cat was purring.

"Aren't you a pretty kitty?" he said, kneeling down and scratching the cat's ears. The cat kept purring and rolled over onto his back. His phone vibrated again in his pocket, and he stood again so he could retrieve it. He looked at the message on his screen—Plz hurry starving!—and smiled down at it. The cat was now winding his way in and around his legs, still purring. But before he could kneel down again, the cat darted across Ursulines Street. "Hey!" he called after it, and crossed the street. The cat kept going up Chartres and Jared followed, forgetting about walking over to Royal Street completely.

About halfway down the block, the cat sat and started licking his paws. When Jared approached, the cat darted through a gate into a long hallway leading to a courtyard. Jared looked through the black wrought iron for a moment before shrugging and continuing on his way. As soon as he was out of sight, the cat began to morph into Nico, who smiled. He materialized outside of the gate and followed Jared as he walked up Chartres.

A few more blocks and a young man in a black T-shirt reading "Who Dat Say Dey Gonna Beat Dem Saints" came into view, strolling along as he talked animatedly on his cell phone. I could see myself, walking right behind him, getting closer and starting to reach out with my hands—

"Cord?" Jared said, stunned, clearly not believing what he was seeing. It couldn't be. Cord was dead; he'd died in a fire. There'd been a service, and he had to be imagining this. It couldn't be happening; people didn't come back from the dead.

And I watched as I grabbed him, pulled him into a doorway, and sank my teeth into his neck.

Had I looked up, I would have seen Nico smiling at me from across the street.

And before he disappeared, he cast a spell.

It had been Nico. It had always been Nico.

He was why I was a vampire, and for whatever reason, he'd wanted me to drink from Jared, placed a spell on him. Nigel had been right; there'd been a witch involved, but it wasn't Sebastian or his spirit.

It was this blond, angelic-looking witch who'd done it all. I didn't know how he made all this possible, only that it had been necessary for me to end up here so I could drink his blood and transform yet again.

I wanted to kill him.

"Sebastian didn't put a curse on me," I said, my voice barely audible. I was repulsed, horrified, by what I'd seen. He was the one who'd thrown Jared into my path. I focused on my breathing as the rage built inside of me, struggled to hold the power in check. "Why? Why did you do all of this? Why Jared? Why did it have to be Jared?" In my mind I could feel my hands around Nico's neck, and I could hear the oh-so-satisfying crack his neck would make as it broke in my hands.

He stepped back away from me, still smiling, but with the beginning of a little fear showing in his eyes. He looked like every depiction of an angel I'd ever seen in art—the long white-blond hair, the beautiful smile, and the perfectly shaped body. It was amazing. I'd always thought angels were beautiful—terrifying but beautiful. I wondered if it had been witches who'd inspired the mythology of angels, beautiful creatures with terrifying powers.

"Why not Jared?" He kept smiling. He shook his head, the beautiful hair moving gently. "There's so much you don't know, can't even begin to comprehend now. Of course it had to be Jared, Cord. Would you have cared about someone else? If you'd fed from the boy in the Saints T-shirt and his wounds hadn't healed, would you have cared? No, my dear, you would have just killed him and gotten rid of the body. But you would never harm Jared."

"But why did he have to be involved in the first place? That's what I don't understand."

"A vampire victim whose wounds won't heal? A baby vampire committing the incredibly grave sin of giving his blood to a human, when his heart isn't strong enough to truly convert him to a vampire?" He laughed. "That was surely going to bring the Nightwatchers on the run, wasn't it?"

"So, this was all about Nigel and Rachel?" I stared at him, not understanding.

"You don't need to understand, my dear." He walked over to an armoire and opened the doors. He pulled out a pair of black pants and a red satin shirt and draped them over a wingback chair. "All of this is for you," he said, pulling on his black velvet pants, his delectable ass disappearing into them. He looked back over his shoulder. "I've been preparing this room for you ever since that first night, the night of the Endymion parade." He slid his arms into his black silk shirt, slowly buttoning the mother-of-pearl buttons. He sat down on the edge of the bed, delicately crossing one leg over the other. "I've been in love with you since you were a teenager, you know."

"How is that even possible? You didn't know me then."

"Look into my eyes," he replied, beckoning me to come closer to him.

I didn't want to. All I could think was how badly I wanted to get as far away from him and his crazy twin as I possibly could—but I had to know.

I crossed the room, still feeling like if I didn't focus I would float untethered up into the air. I knelt in front of him and looked into his eyes.

And I was in a forest of pines, and I knew immediately where I was—Church Camp, in the woods of northeastern Mississippi, a three-hour drive or so from Fayette County. Every summer, Churches of Christ from all over Alabama, Mississippi, and Tennessee—even some from as far away as Georgia and Florida— rented out a campground and for two weeks, sent their teenagers there for Bible study and to wonder at the magnificent world God had created for us. Oh, it wasn't all just Bible study. We learned crafts and played sports and did all kinds of wonderful outdoorsy things, but of course there was no swimming. Mixed swimming was one step away from fornication in the eyes of the church. The girls never even got to wear shorts, no matter how hot and humid it got in the woods; they always had to wear jeans. I wasn't sure if the counselors were just blind or if they turned a blind eye to boys and girls sneaking off into the pitch-black woods after lights-out.

I always wondered how many babies were conceived at Church Camp.

As I saw myself, I knew immediately what was going on and re-membered exactly when it was.

I looked so young it almost broke my heart. I'd thought I was so mature and practically an adult at that age. Now I knew I was little more than a child. I hadn't even gotten hair all over my legs yet—just from the knees down, and there were just a few sprouting under my arms and on my chest.

My dick, though, was nestled in a thick bush that had started growing when I was twelve.

I was walking alone through the woods. There was a wood-working class going on for the boys while the girls were learning how to bake cakes from scratch, but I had no interest in working wood; electric saws terrified me ever since I was a child and saw my great-uncle Abe slice off his thumb with a table saw. Even the sound of them running made me sick to my stomach, so instead of making a picture frame or some other stupid thing, I'd decided to go for a walk in the woods, alone.

I was fourteen, and back home in Fayette County I had a huge crush on a junior named Keith Kennedy. I fantasized about Keith all the time—he had big, strong, powerful legs and the most amazing ass, thick sensual lips, curly reddish brown hair, big green eyes, broad shoulders—and I stole glances at him whenever I could after football practice in the locker room. He wasn't at church camp. He was a Southern Baptist, which meant he was also going straight to hell when he died, which bothered me more than a little, but he was also dating my cousin Vonda. Vonda, of course, was trying to get him to start going to church with us all at White's Chapel, but so far she hadn't had any luck. Keith's sister Sheila was my age, and she had a crush on me. We were sort of going steady, but I was only doing that to get closer to Keith. I responded to Sheila's body whenever she pressed up against me and kissed me. My best friend D.J., who lived in a trailer and didn't go to church at all, kept pressing me to have sex with Sheila. D.J. claimed to have lost his virginity when we were in junior high school to an older girl from Carbon Hill. I didn't know her, but I knew her family was trash. Fucking girls was all D.J. could think about, would talk about. It was annoying, but I put up with it because D.J.'s constant horniness meant he was always needing to beat off. And while we wouldn't touch each other, seeing him pulling on his dick and seeing him naked and seeing him come was the closest I could get to actually being with another boy at that time, and it was better than nothing. I wasn't all that attracted to D.J.—I only had eyes for Keith—but D.J.'s laptop didn't have parental controls on it. When I stayed overnight at D.J.'s house, I could wait till he was sound asleep and then go online and look up gay sex sites, always making sure to clear the history before going to sleep myself.

I was walking through the woods by myself, wearing a sleeveless Roll Tide shirt and a pair of matching crimson nylon shorts with two white stripes down each side. I was horny and hadn't had a chance to relieve myself in the three days since I'd gotten to church camp. All the boys bunked in a barracks, and it was too dangerous. Even the bathroom wasn't possible—it always stank in there. This was my first chance to be alone, and I wanted to wander down the path and get as far from the camp as I could. My dick was hard in my shorts already, and I couldn't stop thinking about Keith Kennedy.

I looked back over my shoulder. The camp was well behind me; I couldn't even hear it anymore. But to be on the safe side, I left the path and went down the hillside. About twenty yards down, there was a creek, and I climbed down the bank beside it. Once I was down next to the running water, I looked back over my shoulder. I couldn't see the path anymore. I smiled to myself and pulled my shirt up over my head. I leaned back against the bank as I slid my shorts and underwear down to my ankles. I closed my eyes and started pulling on my dick.

In my imagination, I was back in the locker room, drying myself off with a towel after taking a shower. There was no one else there; Coach had kept me after practice for some reason that didn't matter to the fantasy. I heard a cough, and I looked up. Keith Kennedy stood there, smiling at me, stark naked. His dick was hard and he was holding it in his hand. His curls were damp, and there were spots of water on his chest. "I was waiting for you, Cord," he said, walking toward me. I dropped the towel as he took me into his big strong arms and kissed me on the mouth with his thick, sensual lips, and I shot my load into the fast-moving creek water. I moaned and kept pulling, making sure I got every last drop out, my whole body shuddering with the pleasure. I stood there for a few moments before finally pulling my shorts up and putting my shirt back on. I climbed up the bank and headed back for the trail.

"I was there, watching you," Nico whispered, his smile not faltering. The look in his eyes, I'd seen that look before in other people—when they were looking at the person they were in love with.

I felt nauseated.

He got up and walked over to the wingback chair where the clothes he'd selected for me were draped. "I was in the woods—my parents always thought it was rather amusing to take Lorenzo and me out into the woods where church camps were being held, to teach us our craft, how to use our powers." His eyebrows went up. "We used to practice casting spells on the church kids." His grin turned into a smirk. "My personal favorite spell was to make the kids horny, make them want to have sex." He laughed. "I always wondered how many babies were conceived at church camps."

I would have laughed were I not so disgusted by him. I walked across to the chair and picked up the pants. The velvet felt sensual against my skin. I stepped into them.

"Those are going to look so hot on you," he purred.

"Where were you? I didn't see you," I asked, pulling on the pants. The velvet excited my skin as the material slid up my legs, and I could feel myself getting aroused again. I shook my head and tried to remain focused. I put my arms into the shirt sleeves, pulled it up, and started buttoning the shirt.

"I was actually in the trees, up above your head. You didn't need a spell, though—you were quite horny enough on your own with no help needed from me. Did you ever get a chance to be with Keith Kennedy?" Nico asked. He cocked his head to one side and grimaced. "Lorenzo's coming. Your entertainment must be ready."

I could hear the footsteps on the staircase as clearly as if it were me making them. When had my hearing become so much more intense? Everything was more intense, I realized. I remembered the way my veins had burned after drinking Nico's blood. Was I actually becoming a god?

I could see into Nico's mind, through his eyes, but was that his power or mine?

I closed my eyes.

I sensed . . . something familiar. Something familiar was coming, but it wasn't from inside the house. It was outside—on the other side of the woods. I could feel it in my bones, in my mind, and I tried to grasp hold of the sensation, make it take shape in my mind.

But then the doorknob began to turn and that sensation was gone, overpowered by Lorenzo. I could smell him—he still smelled of sex and sweat and to a lesser degree, tobacco. In spite of myself, his scent was intoxicating. I wanted to shove my face into his armpit and breathe deeply. My asshole twinged from the memory of the pounding he'd given it, but I didn't want a replay of what had gone before.

No, I wanted to hold Lorenzo down and force myself into him as he struggled and resisted me, as I slapped his face and bit his nipples until they bled . . .

Blood.

A cramp ripped through me, almost causing me to double over in agony. I saw Nico look at me, concern in his eyes, just as the door opened and Lorenzo stood there, that nasty, cruel smirk on his face.

I could see the vein pulsing in his neck.

I curled my hands into fists.

"No, you cannot. You must wait, fight the need," Nico's voice whispered into my brain. *"Hold out for a little while longer—after the entertainment, you can drink your fill. Resist your hatred of him. I've done it as long as I can remember."*

I pushed the animal, that primal urge, back down inside of me.

"You're dressed, good," Lorenzo growled in that voice that made my anger rise. "Because all is in readiness. Nico, are you ready for tonight's entertainment?"

I could feel the hatred radiating off Nico, and I looked over to Lorenzo, confused for a moment. How could Lorenzo not be aware of it?

Nico had done this to me. He'd turned me into a vampire, had broken all the rules by giving me his blood to drink, turning me into a god. He'd destroyed Jared's life. And with a pang, I remembered what I'd learned, which hadn't really made sense to me until that moment. Jared had been on his way to meet his fiancée for dinner. He was in love, had even been thinking this was the girl he was going to marry. He'd never shown up, because Nico had arranged it so that I would encounter him, when my own need was so strong I couldn't resist the nearest available artery—

And with a jolt I asked myself, *And just why had I waited so long to feed? Why had I let it go so long? It was an insane thing for a vampire to do. Jean-Paul hadn't taught me much about being a vampire—but he had taught me that much.*

I glanced out of the corner of my eye at Nico. Maybe he had been behind that as well.

I felt anger begin to bubble up inside of me again. I'd been used, treated as nothing so much as a pawn in whatever game he was playing. Why? What would he gain for me to be so powerful?

"Come along, then, vampire." Lorenzo mockingly bowed

to me. "I know you need to feed—you were looking for food when we took you last night in New Orleans, and you haven't fed, so you must be famished." He gave me that nasty smirk again, the one I longed to wipe off his face with my fists. "Soon enough, you will have someone to feed from. But the honor of who you will drink from has yet to be ascertained. That's our entertainment for the evening."

I glanced at Nico, who was also smiling. "I . . . I am hungry," I said, and it was true. Another cramp consumed me, pushing everything else out of my mind until it passed. And that didn't make sense, either. I'd drank from Nico just hours earlier. I shouldn't be hungry again so soon. But I'd also gotten the hunger much more quickly the night before after feeding from the stripper at Oz. Why? *He'd said "last night"; my God, I've been here that long? Why hasn't Nigel or Rachel come looking for me?*

It didn't make any sense.

Nothing made any sense.

I followed Lorenzo out of the room, again feeling like I might drift off into the air with every step that I took. Outside of the room, he went down the staircase. When I reached the top of the stairs, another cramp ripped through me, and I grabbed on to the railing to keep from falling. The railing shattered into splinters in my hand.

I stared at it, unbelieving.

Lorenzo was still going down the stairs, and Nico waved his hand and the railing reassembled itself.

"You're much stronger now. I told you, you're becoming a god," Nico's voice said in my head, sounding absolutely delighted. *"You must be careful. If Lorenzo even suspects . . ."*

"What can he do to a god?" I responded without even stopping to think. I kept walking down the stairs, and in my head I saw myself with my hands around Lorenzo's neck,

squeezing, as his face turned purple, his tongue coming out and turning black as I kept up the pressure, determined to wipe that nasty smirk off his face for all eternity.

"Don't. He might be able to read your mind," Nico cautioned as we reached the bottom of the staircase. *"His seed is inside of you. He might be able—"*

"Come along!" Lorenzo was standing beside a door. It was open, and I could see it led out to the veranda. I could see torches burning, cowled figures standing around the lawn. Lorenzo clapped his hands with an almost childish delight. "We don't want to keep them waiting any longer!"

I will show you who is the master here, my pretty dark one, I thought with a sneer of my own as I walked out onto the veranda. I paused to get my bearings. There was a long lawn that sloped gradually down to the riverbank. I could see the moon's reflection in the little waves and dimples on the surface of the river. Enormous, ancient live oaks and their long twisted branches dripping with long strands of thick Spanish moss cast shadows across the lushness of the thick grass. I could smell the river in the cool breeze lazily drifting up the slope to the house. The air was heavy and damp, yet cool. Despite the cloudlessness of the indigo night sky, it felt like rain was coming. I looked up and saw the stars scattered across the dark blue, and there was a haze around the full moon's glow. There was power radiating from that moon, and I closed my eyes and turned my head up to it, absorbing and drinking it all in thirstily. The night seemed alive to my heightened senses, and I could have stood there on the veranda for hours, experiencing it all.

I sensed Lorenzo move across to the stairs and opened my eyes. Nico nudged me, indicating I should follow him. My head felt light, my skin sensitive, and again I felt like I could simply float up into the sky if I just willed myself to do so. There was another power surge from inside me, a wave of heat blasting through me, and I rode that wave as I walked down the steps. The grass felt damp and cool beneath my bare feet, and I could feel its energy, its life force caressing the soles of my feet as I walked across it. There was a well-trod path leading down to where a circle of people stood in the flickering light cast by torches mounted on tall rods. They were in the approximate center of the back lawn, halfway between the back veranda of the house and the banks of the river. Their circle was also centered between two enormous live oaks, their long gnarled roots almost reaching the spot where the circle of witches stood.

As I followed Lorenzo, I became aware of colors swirling around each of the people, who were all wearing cowls that concealed their faces. I stared at the colors in wonder.

"You're seeing their energy, their auras." Nico's voice sounded delighted inside my head. *"And you can actually control their auras if you want. You can send them different energy and affect their moods."*

I didn't respond, merely nodding as I kept walking. I focused on keeping my thoughts shielded from him. Out of the corner of my eye, I could see his own energy, which was a pale red, so pale it was almost nonexistent, and somehow I knew he was drained, that somehow whenever we touched, I drained energy from him, storing it inside of me, like a weird vampiric battery.

And it was making me even stronger.

The colors I could see around the witches deepened as we drew nearer, and I closed my eyes, willing the colors to go away. When I opened my eyes again, the colors were gone.

I smiled to myself.

They parted to let us through, and I saw they were standing around a pit.

There were two men in the pit, and I recognized one as

the stripper from Oz. The other I didn't know, but he was equally as beautiful as the stripper.

"What is the meaning of this?" I asked.

"One of them will be your dinner," Lorenzo replied with a nasty smile. "But first he has to earn that right. They will fight to the death, and the winner will be your dinner."

CHAPTER 15

I wanted nothing more than to wipe the smile from Lorenzo's face. I felt the power within me surge, anxious to be released. *"It would be so easy to destroy him,"* a voice whispered in my brain. I glanced over at Nico, but it wasn't his voice, and he wasn't even looking at me. He was staring down into the pit, his eyes alight with excitement, his mouth open. He licked his lips, and I was repulsed.

I stared down at the stripper and saw details about him I hadn't noticed in the poorly lit bar. His eyes seemed a little glassy, as though he were disoriented and didn't know where he was, but they were a beautiful, vibrant blue. His skin almost glowed in the torchlight, like it was lightly oiled. I could see veins in his arms and in his lower abdomen leading down into the white jockstrap, which was all he was wearing. It was bright in the light and emphasized the big bulge it contained. His cock was semihard, pulling the fabric away from his skin. His legs were just as thickly muscled as I remembered, and his skin was shaved smooth, though I could make out stubble forming on his strong pecs and on his legs.

He looked up, and our eyes met, and I went inside his head.

His name was Blaine and he was in his early twenties, from a little town in the part of Louisiana called Acadiana. He wasn't pure Cajun—his mother was from Texas, but his father's family went all the way back to the time when the French were driven out of what is now called Nova Scotia by the English. He was proud of his Cajun heritage, even if his parents had kicked him out of their house when he was seventeen because they caught him with another boy. With no money or food or anywhere to live, he had made his way to Baton Rouge, where he got a job working as a dancer in gay bars, living in a homeless shelter until he managed to befriend some other dancers and moved into their house. He got his GED and then met a nice older man one night named Tom who practically adopted him and took care of him. It was this man who got him to become a personal trainer to make more money, gave him a home and love, introduced the boy to his friends, and Blaine's body began to grow bigger and stronger as he flourished with his new-found family. Pictures of him on a muscle Web site led to an offer to make gay porn, and with his daddy's permission, he flew out to Palm Springs to do his first shoot, and he became extremely popular. But even as he kept building his body, doing more porn shoots and posing for photographers, building up his personal training business, he wanted more out of life. He wanted to go to college, like he had always wanted to, and become a medical technician. With his daddy's support, he got into LSU and now was very close to completing his degree. He was happy, he had a good life, and he had worked very hard for it. He still danced every once in a while because the money was good, but he was looking forward to the day when he could finally just work in a hospital and leave the porn and the money from his body behind. Daddy was still Daddy, but their sexual relationship was over—but he would always love Tom.

He wasn't too aware of where he was; all he knew was there were people watching—there were always people watching him. That didn't bother him; he was used to it. There was a man eight feet away from him in a black jockstrap who wanted to kill him, so he had to kill him first.

And looking up into my eyes, he knew that I would be his reward, and that was making his dick get even harder.

I looked away and hated Lorenzo with a passion I'd never felt before. I felt the power surging down inside of me, but it wasn't time, not yet—somehow I knew that.

But I also knew I wasn't going to let this end in death.

I looked back down into the pit, at the other side from where Blaine stood.

The other man was also beautiful but not as ruggedly masculine as Blaine. He was taller—Blaine was maybe five seven at most; this man was easily around six feet tall. His hair was thick and dark, and he, too, had beautiful blue eyes. And while he was muscular and defined, his muscles weren't nearly as thick as Blaine's. His legs were long, and I knew he had a beautiful ass at the top of them. He was wearing a black jockstrap, and his bulge wasn't nearly as big as Blaine's, but there was also a stirring there. He didn't look up at me. His eyes were focused on Blaine across the pit from him.

Look at me!

His head turned upward, and he found me. His face was model pretty, with thick black brows over deeply chiseled cheekbones, a strong square jaw, and a wide mouth that seemed ready to curve into a smile as he looked up at me.

I lost myself in the blue of his eyes.

His name was Robert, and he was twenty-two years old. He wasn't from Louisiana; he was actually from up north—Pennsylvania or Pittsburgh? Somewhere like that, and he was going to Tulane, where he was almost finished with his own degree. He, too, was gay, but his parents were actually fine with it. He was a good student, a good person, and had lots of friends and a good life. He liked wrestling—it was arousing for him—and he often wrestled with his boyfriend, who was named Chip, who was also a student at Tulane. Robert wasn't sure what he was doing here, either, or how he got here. The last thing he remembered was going into Good Friends Bar in the French Quarter with a group of his friends, and everything somehow went green, and the next thing he knew he was in this pit, staring at a man with a godlike body, both of them wearing jockstraps, and he was excited. He loved Chip, but this other guy was a fantasy for him. He'd always dreamed of wrestling with someone with that kind of thickly muscled body, and he wanted to be dominated by him, and—

I looked away, unable to take any more.

The boy had no idea he was in a fight to the death—but Blaine knew.

The unfairness of it all filled me with a righteous fury.

My fingers itched to go around Lorenzo's throat.

The idea of a fight to the death, and that it would be for *my* entertainment, my pleasure, was sickening to me. The idea that this pretty young boy was just tossed into the pit as nothing more than *meat* for Blaine, something for him to destroy—and this was supposed to *entertain* me—infuriated me, and the fury was making that power, that *thing*, inside of me stir, wanting to be let out. It made me want to give Lorenzo a taste of his own medicine. Blaine was a good person, who'd worked hard and overcome difficulties that would have destroyed most people to make something out of himself. He was better than this, didn't deserve to be treated like this. I wanted Lorenzo to suffer. I wanted to feel his bones crack in my hands, crush them into powder while he screamed in agony. I wanted to leap down into the pit, toss Robert over my shoulder, and fly up into the night and away from this place. He had friends, people who loved him, who were probably even at this moment wondering what had happened to him, worried about him—

"How is he different from Jared?" that horrible voice jeered inside of my head again. *"How is what they are doing to this kid—and to Blaine—any different from what you did to Jared? You didn't kill him, but you took his life away from him. He can never go back to his life, now, can he? Remember Tori, his fiancée? Right now she is sitting by her phone, waiting for it to ring, hoping against hope that Jared is going to turn up alive, that he isn't lying in a shallow grave somewhere. Tori has a very vivid imagination."*

"Maybe that's true, but that doesn't make this right."

I closed my eyes and struggled to get the power to settle and subside. Somehow I knew that it wasn't yet time.

But I hoped that it would be before either of them were hurt in any way.

"Aren't you happy?" Nico's voice danced with delight, and I turned to look at him, forcing a smile onto my lips so he would think I was pleased, hiding my utter revulsion. "I got him for you," Nico went on as I turned back to stare down into the pit. "I know you were attracted to him, but you never got a chance to do anything about it. Now, once he is finished with that boy, you can drink from him and his body is yours for the taking." He licked his lips, his eyes glittering. "He is quite a specimen, isn't he? Maybe you'll share him with me before you completely drain him?"

I wanted to kill him, grab him and pull him into my arms, sink my teeth into his neck and drink his oh-so-sweet blood until his body was nothing more than an empty husk in my hands.

Instead, I managed to push that urgent desire aside and say, in a low, lusty whisper, "Of course I will. After you've given me so much, Nico? How could I not share him with you, my love?"

I somehow managed not to choke on the words, and his

reaction to them only deepened my contempt. He practically danced in place, licking his lips as he looked down at Blaine's masculine beauty.

I didn't look back down at the two humans. Instead, I looked around at all the witches standing around the lip of the pit and wondered how many times some kind of similar competition had taken place for their entertainment. I closed my eyes and could almost hear the death screams of dozens of men and some women echoing out of the pit. It was a place of evil, haunted by death, drenched in the blood of so many.

This had been Sebastian's coven, and these had been his witches. I wondered if they had been evil to begin with, or had he infected them?

Regardless, they were all evil now, and they had to be destroyed.

As much as I despised Lorenzo, hated sharing the very same air he breathed, his angelic-looking twin was far worse, even more twisted and dark in his soul. Lorenzo wore his evil proudly like a badge, but Nico? He pretended to be something other than what he truly was, while he sat in the shadows moving pieces on his dark chessboard.

Sebastian had never truly been the witchmaster; he had merely thought himself to be their leader all the while dancing as Nico pulled his strings.

As Lorenzo danced even now, not knowing his twin was planning his death.

There was no sound other than the wind in the trees and the crackling of the burning torches.

And again, I sensed something terribly familiar, getting closer. I somehow knew that it was neither Nigel nor Rachel, but the familiarity . . . I sniffed the air again. There was a faint scent in the air, a scent that I knew all too well.

Jean-Paul and Clint were near, certainly near enough for me to catch their scent in the air.

I tried not to smile as I realized just how close to death these evil witches actually were.

"They're going to fight to the death?" I said, wondering if they, too, could smell the approach of two powerful vampires. "For my benefit?" I allowed my voice to take on a timbre of pleasure. Let these monsters believe their barbarity pleased me, aroused me, made me happy! "The blood of the victor will be full of adrenaline," I went on. "Adrenaline is so delicious."

"It's all for you, darling Cord." Nico turned his eyes back to me, and even in the dark I could see that he looked faded, weak. His body was beginning to feel the effects of the power I'd drained from him. I was tempted to reach out and place my arm around him, to take the rest of his power and let him die, but I knew it wasn't time yet.

I wondered if I could leech Lorenzo's power as well.

I allowed my hand to brush against his arm, and he turned to smile at me. The same electrical surge I'd felt touching his brother rushed through me again. My veins felt briefly aflame, and I let my hand drop.

So, I can leech power from witches.

They had wanted to create a god. They just didn't know I was going to be the god of their destruction.

I looked across the pit and smiled at an older woman. Only the bottom of her face was visible to me beneath her cowl, but her wrinkled lips formed a smile in answer to mine.

I closed my eyes and focused, thinking that my skin was coming into contact with hers, imagining how it felt, and I felt a surge.

I opened my eyes and smiled to myself as she staggered a bit before righting herself. She shook her head, confused.

So physical contact wasn't needed.

Excellent.

Lorenzo cleared his throat and stepped forward almost to the very lip of the pit. He spread his arms and began to speak in a loud voice that carried.

"Members of my coven, my brothers and my sisters," Lorenzo announced, "as you all know, when we lost our master Sebastian, we struggled without leadership, until my brother and I"—he waved his hand at his brother, and Nico inclined his head forward slightly—"decided to take our rightful place at the head of our coven, accepting the mantle of responsibility for all of our well-being. There were those who felt Sebastian's plans were wrong, over-reached, and could not possibly come to fruition, that the powers that would be ranged against us would be too powerful to overcome."

There were murmurs, some of the others nodding agreement.

"Sebastian believed that, after millennia of their rule, the time of the Councils and their rules had passed, that they were nothing more than anachronisms, vestiges of a long-dead past that had no bearing on modern times. Sebastian looked at the world and saw that the humans we had been sworn to protect from destruction were now on a path that would lead to their self-immolation and were determined to take this world with them in the mad rush to Armageddon, and he knew that the time of human ascendancy was past. They were given a birthright and they squandered it, with their pettiness and greed and selfishness and arrogance. As such, my brother and I decided that the best way to move forward was to follow Sebastian's plan, come what may, and that it was better to die for a great cause than to continue to sit on the sidelines. There is a war coming, and we are prepared for it. Some of us may die, but what better way to die than as a martyr for the greater good?"

More witches were nodding, some saying, "Here, here" as he continued to speak.

"And here and now, I would like to share with you the news that we have accomplished our first step to achieving our ultimate goal." He pulled me forward. "Behold our vampire, Cord."

Is he completely insane? I wondered as the coven oohed and aahed over me as if I were some kind of show dog. I smiled at them all, looking around the pit. *A coming war? The complete destruction of humanity?*

And I knew they all had to die—there was no question.

And I would take great pleasure in destroying them.

Inside of me, the power tried to surge again, but I kept it under control. I could smell Jean-Paul and Clint even stronger than before. They would be here soon, but somehow I knew I wouldn't have to wait for them, wouldn't need their help.

I was becoming a god.

"He is under our control—my brother's and mine. With him at our side as our enforcer, we cannot be stopped!" The triumph in Lorenzo's voice was unmistakable.

I glanced at Nico out of the corner of my eye, and he was smiling slyly at his brother. His eyes met mine.

"He has no idea what I have planned for him, Cord. Together we will destroy him."

I nodded and lowered my eyes, lest he read something in them I didn't want him to see just yet.

At first, there was no reaction from the coven to Lorenzo's words. But then, one of them began clapping, and soon all of them were clapping and cheering me.

I was their destroyer, not their enforcer.

Nico took my hand and squeezed it. His hand felt warm and dry, desiccated and weak. The pressure he tried to put on my hand with the squeeze was nothing. I smiled back at him as he winked at me, and I took a deep breath.

More power flowed into me through his hand, and his eyes . . . I almost laughed at the look in them.

Finally, so close to the end, he realized what he had done.

I looked into his eyes and went into his mind.

"You will do and say nothing, Nico. You will merely stand here next to me and not warn anyone. I am your creation, and if they knew, they would kill you anyway. This is why it was forbidden so long ago for a vampire to drink the blood of a witch, to mess with godhood. I am draining your power. I am taking your life force and adding it to my own. My power grows with every second we stand here. Can you feel death's grip on you?"

And the last of his power drained into me, and he stood there, and I saw death in his eyes.

But I kept him animated.

It was too soon for anyone else to know.

I let go of his hand and he stood there, the living dead, an empty shell.

"And now, for our entertainment, these two men will battle for the right to feed our vampire!" Lorenzo clapped his hands, and down in the pit, the two began circling each other.

I didn't want to watch but couldn't look away.

"Not yet," the voice whispered in my brain. *"Almost."*

There was glee in that voice now, and somewhere in my mind I knew that it didn't matter whether I waited to destroy them or did it now.

But it would somehow be more pleasing to wait, to let them have their pleasures in viewing the struggle beneath us in the pit.

And so I watched, knowing I wouldn't permit either of them to die.

With a predatory smile on his handsome face, Blaine launched himself at Robert. Robert's cock was hard inside his jock, and so was Blaine's. Robert took a few steps backward until he could go back no farther, his back against the wall, and there was a smack as their bodies came into contact. Blaine's nipples were erect, and his ass flexed and clenched inside the straps of his white jock as he began driving his fists into Robert's beautifully defined abs.

I glanced around the pit, and all of the witches were mesmerized by the contest.

The fools, I thought, and looked back into the pit.

Blaine still had Robert backed up against the wall, still punching, his back muscles flexing. Robert's face went quickly from confused to pained to scared. His eyes came up as his breath blasted out of his body from yet another connected punch, and I looked deep into his terrified eyes.

"This isn't what I'd thought it would be, like when me and Chip wrestle around in bed as foreplay. This isn't foreplay. This hot muscle guy is fighting for real, and he wants to hurt me. I can see it in his eyes and his face and what's worse is he's actually getting turned on by hurting me. He's punching me so fucking hard my abs hurt. I don't know how much more of this I can take but I don't think he's going to stop I don't even know if I can fight back oh my God this isn't hot at all this is scary I thought we were just going to wrestle around in jocks and the loser was going to get fucked and I was fine with that this guy has a hot ass I'd love to fuck but I wouldn't care if he fucked me either for that matter he's so hot but he's going to hurt me—"

"Relax, my pretty Robert, just go with what is happening. I won't let anything hurt you."

He nodded almost imperceptibly, gasping as Blaine drove another brutal punch into his stomach.

"Don't hurt him, Blaine. Pull your punches. You know how to do that, don't you? Put on a show for the good people."

And I felt Blaine come back into himself. He paused for a moment and stepped back from Robert, whose legs were a little wobbly. Blaine shook his head and looked up at me. I nodded down at him, and he turned back to Robert. He stepped forward and punched him again in the stomach. But it was more loud than painful, and I could see the terror in Robert's eyes lessen as Blaine reached down and grabbed hold of the black jock. He twisted it into his fist until it snapped, and Blaine tossed it back over his shoulder before stepping back. Robert's dick flopped up, and I glanced over at Lorenzo. He was watching them, his eyes aflame, his mouth open and practically drooling. The notion that a few hours earlier he'd been inside of me, driving me almost insane with desire, nauseated me now.

Another hunger pang tore through me. This one felt like a jagged knife was being shoved into my intestines and twisted. My vision swam in and out of focus, and it took all of my willpower not to scream from the agony.

Nico's hand squeezed mine reassuringly.

The only thing keeping him alive was my will. His life force was gone, but his heart was still beating, his blood was still flowing.

I stared at him for a moment and saw the blue vein in his neck, pulsing with each beat of his heart, and remembered the sweet taste of his blood, how nourishing and refreshing it had been—and how I'd felt after.

Stronger.

More powerful.

I have made you a god.

The power was addicting.

I had taken his life, but would more of his delicious blood make me even stronger?

Control. Keep control. You'll be able to feed soon enough. Both the blood and the power.

I swallowed and turned my attention back to what was happening below me. Robert had collapsed and lay panting, facedown, in the dirt. His ass was up in the air, and Blaine was stepping out of his own jock, his swollen cock angry and red, anxious for release. He got down on his knees and forced Robert's legs apart. He pulled Robert up until he was on his knees and spread Robert's ass cheeks and spat into his hole. He shoved his cock in and Robert's mouth opened in a howl that echoed off the house and the trees. Blaine flexed his ass as he drove deeper inside of Robert as the howl died off into a growl of pure animal pleasure.

"Isn't this a beautiful thing?" Lorenzo whispered to me. "This is the true natural order of things for humans—to be our sport, entertainment for us to watch and appreciate. This world was never meant for them to rule over; this is how it should be." His eyes glittered with bloodlust, and he reached down, letting his hand brush against my crotch.

Again, I felt some of his power flow into me through my cock, and I shuddered.

It was so intense.

And I wanted more.

Robert howled again, and I turned to look back as the two of them fucked. The other witches were enrapt, unable to stop watching.

"I'll let them both come before he kills the other," Lorenzo said, winking at me.

"Let him live," I said.

Lorenzo turned to me, a strange look on his face. "What?"

I looked him square in the eye, focusing deeply on the words. "Let the loser live, Lorenzo. I don't want to see him die before me. I don't need the sacrifice."

The power begged to be released.

Lorenzo's will collapsed before mine, and he nodded.

We watched in silence as Blaine pounded away at Robert's ass, his face glistening with sweat.

If Nico hadn't given me his blood to drink, Robert would most definitely have died in the pit, and Blaine, who just a few days earlier had nothing more on his mind than upcoming finals and having to dance on the bar at Oz in his white briefs, would have been a murderer.

These witches were evil, and destroying them was going to be a pleasure.

I could smell Jean-Paul and Clint. They were at the head of the driveway, on the other side of the forest. They would be here soon.

"*Now,*" the voice whispered in my head.

I let go of Nico's hand and he collapsed, dead.

"What..." Lorenzo stared at me. "What have you done—"

In one step I put my arms around him and sank my teeth into his neck. I was so hungry, and his blood was even sweeter, more rich, more satisfying, than Nico's had been. His magic power flowed into me as well as I pressed my crotch against his, and he trembled in my arms, and the power continued growing inside of me, and then I was finished with him and tossed his body aside.

The rest of the coven wasn't even aware of what had just happened to their leaders, so intent were they on watching Blaine and Robert finding pleasure in each other's bodies.

So ridiculously easy.

I sensed the big SUV Clint was driving coming up the driveway through the oak forest. If I wasn't finished before they got here, I'd not be able to take what I wanted.

I closed my eyes and focused.

And the power began to flow out of the coven and into me.

My body began to tremble, and for a brief moment I resisted the current, every hair on my body standing on end, but then I gave in to it and it began filling me up. I could feel my erection straining against the velvet pants. I was so aroused; this was better than sex, this was better than sex on drugs, this was better than sex on drugs while drinking the blood of a beautiful boy, and I was becoming powerful, oh so fucking powerful, that no one, no one was ever going to be able to contain me again.

For a split second I worried that I might overload, that my brain circuits would fry—*this was forbidden for a reason*—but then I realized I could not only contain all of this but also there was room for even more, and I felt myself rising in the air, floating.

I opened my eyes and saw that some of the witches had already collapsed, their dead bodies sprawled on the lawn, while the others who still lived, who I was still draining, were standing but their bodies were twitching, and I felt myself float back down to the grass as, one after another, their lifeless shells fell to the grass.

And I looked down as both Blaine and Robert came at the same time, both of their sweaty bodies convulsing, their voices mingling in a howl.

Again, I felt the hunger convulsing me. The power needed to be fed.

And below me were two humans.

I stepped over the lip of the pit and landed beside the two former combatants as gently as a feather.

Blaine looked up at me and smiled. "You were in the bar the other night," he said. "I waited for you to come back, but you didn't. Didn't you like me?" He pulled his dripping dick out of Robert and stood up, watching me.

"Of course I liked you," I replied, beckoning him to come toward me. He did, and turned his head, exposing his neck and the juicy jugular vein.

"Feed from me, my master," he whispered.

So, the spell he'd been under hadn't been completely broken.

Nico said I was a god, and I certainly felt like one. I felt like I had the power to destroy worlds, that if I wanted to I could split the world in half and send the two pieces spinning off into the great void.

And again, I felt the hunger.

I bent down and bit into his neck, and his body quivered as his blood began flooding my mouth.

And I heard the unmistakable sound of a car pulling up to the front of the house. The engine shut off and doors slammed.

They were here.

I licked Blaine's wounds and they closed. He smiled back at me, his eyes partly closed from the feeding pleasure.

As I watched him, his eyes seemed to clear as he came back into himself. He shook his head and said, "Where . . . what . . . where am I?" He looked down at himself and over at me. "What the hell—"

"It's a long story, Blaine," I said wearily. "But we need to get out of here." I gestured to Robert, who had gotten to his feet and was staring at him, his mouth open.

"Are you—"

I put one arm around Blaine and the other around Robert. I coiled my legs and gave a little hop. We rose out of the pit effortlessly and landed next to where Lorenzo's body lay. I looked down and felt a little sick. Lorenzo's body was dried and desiccated, like a mummy lying in its tomb for thousands of years.

"My God," Robert whispered, looking around at the corpses, "what happened here?"

I closed my eyes and imagined the bodies disintegrating, turning to ash, and the ash being caught up in a breeze that carried it all down to the river, where it would wash out to Lake Pontchartrain and eventually the Gulf of Mexico.

I felt incredibly tired.

"Cord! Cord, are you all right?"

It was Jean-Paul.

I took them both by the hand and walked with them up to the veranda. Their eyes were wide open, and I knew they were close to going into shock. All of this was too much for their brains to handle. When we reached the veranda, Blaine whispered, "What the hell are you?"

I'm a god, you foolish mortal.

I sat down on a chair, exhausted. I felt like I could sleep for a thousand years. But they needed clothes, so I focused what little energy I had left and wiped the memory of almost everything that had happened from their minds and sent them up to the room where I'd been with both of the twin witches to get some clothes. *"And hurry."*

Obediently, they went into the house.

The door had just shut behind them when Jean-Paul and Clint came around the corner. As little as two days ago, I would have been glad to see them. Now I was just tired and didn't care.

I didn't care that Jean-Paul didn't love me the way I wanted him to. I didn't care about anything anymore.

"Cord?" Jean-Paul knelt next to me, his brown eyes full of concern. "Are you okay?"

I nodded. "I destroyed them all," I said, the effort almost more than I could handle. I tried to summon the power inside, but it didn't respond. I was a god, but even a god had limits, apparently.

Just minutes before, I had felt like I could destroy the world.

Now I was so tired I could barely keep my head upright.

"There are two humans inside the house who have to go back with us," I managed to say. "You are going to take us back to New Orleans?"

They exchanged a glance, and Clint said hesitantly, "Humans?"

"It's fine," I replied, and heard them coming down the stairs. "They'll be here in a second." My eyes closed as I heard the back door open.

Jean-Paul picked me up in his arms, and I was aware he was carrying me around the house. I could hear Clint talking to Blaine and Robert.

I heard Jean-Paul saying, "It's okay, baby. I'm here now."

The last thing I heard before losing consciousness was him telling Clint to burn the house down.

And then everything was blessed darkness.

CHAPTER 16

I do not know how long I slept, but I woke to the sound of rain on the roof of the SUV and windshield wipers going back and forth in their monotonous rhythm. I could also hear the even breathing of Blaine and Robert. I opened my eyes.

I was stretched across the second seat of the vehicle. Jean-Paul was driving, and Clint was sitting in the passenger seat, looking out the rain-spattered window. I sat up a bit and could see that we were on the causeway bridge, somewhere in the middle of Lake Pontchartrain. I turned my head, and in the far backseat the two shirtless humans slept, cuddled comfortably together.

I felt recharged, revitalized—everything within me in balance. The power was still there, but it also rested, dormant until it was needed again. I swallowed. As much as I would like to believe the entire thing had been a dream, it wasn't.

I now had the power of a god.

I closed my eyes and gently probed inside Jean-Paul's and Clint's minds. They had no idea what had happened to me, no clue what I'd done to the coven of witches. I saw the entire thing again through their eyes—finding me on the back veranda of the house, no witches anywhere in sight. The torches still burned around the pit, and when Robert and Blaine had joined us, Jean-Paul had scooped me up and carried me because I was too tired, too drained to stand, let alone walk.

And Clint had set the mansion of the twins ablaze before we drove off into the night.

I was more than a little afraid. I remembered the intoxication of absorbing the witches' power, sucking their essence dry and killing them. I didn't understand the power I now possessed, but one thing I was certain of: The witches had made it clear that it was forbidden and had been for millennia. I didn't quite understand everything they had said or that I had gleaned from their minds, but I knew that the Nightwatchers wouldn't approve of my new power—and neither would the ruling Councils.

It would make no difference to them that I'd destroyed a coven of rebellious witches who'd wanted to create a new world order, no matter who or what had to be destroyed in the process. It wouldn't matter to them that I'd had no choice in any of it—from becoming a vampire to being Sebastian's victim and the twin witches' to being fed Nico's blood.

I was an abomination and would have to be destroyed.

"I won't go down without a fight," the voice whispered inside my head again, *"and the cost of destroying me might just be too high for them to pay."*

I shuddered.

I wasn't sure I wanted to be a god, wasn't sure that returning to New Orleans was a smart move. I might be able to keep all of this a secret—the powers, the blood of the witches, the ability to drain power from witches—but somehow, I had a feeling Nigel would be able to tell.

I would not be the kind of god Nico and Lorenzo had wanted me to be, the kind Sebastian would have been had he succeeded in his plan.

I'm kind of like Superman, only I need to drink blood.

I laughed out loud before I could stop myself.

"Oh, you're awake now, are you?" Clint turned and looked between the two front seats at me. "How are you feeling?"

"Better," I said carefully.

"We were worried about you," Jean-Paul said without taking his eyes off the bridge. The rain was coming down in almost continual sheets, and he'd slowed down. I didn't see any taillights ahead of us, and there were no headlights behind us. "You can't trust witches."

No shit, Sherlock, I thought, irritated, and looked back out the window. "How did you know where to find me?"

"As your maker, I can always find you," Jean-Paul said with more than a little arrogance. "As soon as Nigel called me and let me know you'd disappeared, Clint and I were on the next plane to New Orleans." He reached over and patted Clint on the leg.

I knew that tone, and I took a deep breath as I kept the anger down. It was that same patronizing you're-just-a-child tone that used to drive me crazy when I was with him. I was tempted to read him the riot act—*you didn't teach me anything, why did you deliberately keep me ignorant about everything, I could have been killed, and you let me go off on my own, knowing full well I was easy prey for witches or rogue vampires*—but knew it would accomplish nothing. It would only further convince him he was right, and I would be damned before I would give him that satisfaction.

"Besides, it's all settled, now that we've found you," he went on, his smug tone making it clear he thought they'd rescued me. "There won't be any more of this 'on your

own' nonsense. You belong with us." He glanced at Clint.
"We'll be leaving from here to head to Ibiza for a few
weeks. Remember how you always wanted to go to Ibiza?"

I closed my eyes. The old me would have jumped at the
prize and everything would be forgotten, everything forgiven like nothing had ever happened in the first place. It
was embarrassing to remember how easy I'd been. No wonder he thinks I'm a child—all he had to do was dangle a present or a surprise in front of me and I'd be happy all over
again.

"Doesn't that sound good?" Clint said in a wheedling
voice similar to the one my mother had used when I was a
child to get me to eat spinach. "Ibiza! All those beautiful
European men, and you know they have the best dance
music on the planet. Won't that be fun? We'll dance all
night and sleep all day, just like old times."

I could feel him looking at me, and I opened my eyes. He
was frowning, and I knew he was trying to read my thoughts
and couldn't. He was confused.

"I've changed a lot since I last saw you."

He looked startled, and I smiled back at him.

"When did you learn to hide your thoughts?" Jean-Paul
asked, and I knew Clint had ratted me out telepathically.
"You shouldn't be able to hide your thoughts yet; you're too
young. And you . . . you can't hide them from me." I could
hear the doubt in his voice. "You shouldn't be able to do
that."

"I shouldn't be able to do a lot of things," I replied,
slouching down into my seat again and closing my eyes.
"Wake me when we get into the city."

I didn't sleep, though. I didn't need any more rest. I just
didn't really want to talk to them anymore. I didn't want to
talk to anyone—besides Nigel, that is. I would be frank

with him, would tell him the truth about what had happened, what I had become. Somehow, I knew I could trust
him. He might be a Nightwatcher, he might be as old as the
earth itself, but I knew I could tell him everything, and it
would be fine.

As the SUV clicked off more miles, I thought about Jean-
Paul. Seeing him again had been nothing like I'd imagined.
I had hoped he would come after me when I left Palm
Springs and had really been disappointed when he hadn't.
A part of me had known he wouldn't—I was merely a toy
whose luster had dimmed for him, and I would never be
anything more than that. There would always be a link between us, because he had made me, and he had shown me
a world I'd have never dreamed of back when I was human,
beating off at night in the empty showers at Beta Kappa.
Even had I come out of the closet, told my parents, dealt
with all that bullshit, I would have never gone to all of those
gay party weekends all over the world. I would have never
lived on South Beach, looking at all the beautiful men,
shopping at the exclusive shops, doing the designer drugs,
and having the time of my life. I wouldn't trade that time
for anything, and I wasn't going to rule out never going to
the White Party or the Winter Ball or Black and Blue ever
again—but for now, those things held no interest for me.
Jean-Paul had shown me what it was like to be gay, all the
possibilities the world held for gay men.

But I wasn't just gay. I was also a vampire, and it was past
time for me to know what that meant as well.

I was actually more than a vampire. I possessed more
power than any other vampire—maybe. There was so much
I didn't know, that I hadn't even been aware I didn't know,
for so long.

As for Jean-Paul, it didn't hurt anymore that he didn't

love me the way I wanted him to. He would never love anyone that way. It had nothing to do with me. And that had really been the core of everything, hadn't it? I thought the problem was me. It wasn't and never had been. I'd been too young, too new to life and love and relationships to understand that.

But now I did. Sure, Jean-Paul would always be able to get to me, get under my skin, but wasn't that the way it worked with family?

"We're almost there," Clint said as the SUV turned down St. Ann Street. It was still raining, and Jean-Paul pulled over to the curb just across the street from the Rawhide.

"Why are we stopping here?" I asked.

"This is where our friends in the back get out," Jean-Paul said.

I felt a pang of disappointment, but I knew it made sense. I'd developed a soft spot for both of them, but it was best I never see either of them again. Their friends and loved ones were no doubt terrified and worried about them. I heard them stirring, and I looked back over the seat.

They were both such attractive men, and both had bright futures—as long as they never knew anything that had happened to them. I focused on them and commanded them to get out of the SUV. I added another command that once the SUV pulled away from the curb, they would forget everything.

"Okay, guys." I smiled at them. "Time to go."

They climbed out onto the street, and I waved good-bye to them before the door closed. As we drove down St. Ann, I looked back at them on the sidewalk. It was raining, and they had no shirts, no shoes, nothing. They looked disoriented, but I knew they'd be okay.

At least they'd be able to return to their friends and family.

"How's Jared doing?" I asked when we rounded the corner at Royal and Orleans.

"The mess you created?" Jean-Paul replied in the voice that always got under my skin. I fought the urge to smack him on the back of the head.

"I didn't create that mess," I replied. I could feel the anger building, and sure enough, there it was, the power, wanting to get out, unleashed. "Jared and I both were being manipulated by witches, so no, it's not my mess. I was involved, yes, but I didn't 'create' the mess." I struggled to not lose my temper, to keep everything under control.

"It wouldn't have happened if you hadn't left Palm Springs."

"It wouldn't have happened if you hadn't turned me into a vampire."

"ENOUGH ALREADY!" Clint roared. "You two sound like a couple of bitchy schoolgirls, and I'm tired of listening to all this bullshit, okay?"

Neither of us answered. He was right, of course.

The old me, the person I'd been before leaving Palm Springs, would have argued with him, turned it into something more than it was.

Really, it was a wonder Jean-Paul hadn't killed me.

He found a place to park just past the house, and when he was finished parking, I got out and stood on the wet sidewalk. I hugged Clint when he got out, long and hard, and whispered in his ear, "You're right, and I'm sorry. I was always kind of a brat, wasn't I?"

He looked startled at first and hugged me back. "I never minded, really. I loved having you around, and I've missed you."

I looked into his eyes and knew he was telling the truth.

I felt a pang. Clint had loved me, truly loved me, from the moment he had first seen me on the street during Mardi Gras. I might have shared Jean-Paul's bed (most of the time), but I was just a passing thing for him and would never be more to him than that. He felt a responsibility to me as his maker, and I was sure he did want me to come to Ibiza with the rest of them.

But Clint had always loved me, and I'd never seen it. He'd never said anything to me about it, all that time. And even now, I wouldn't have known, or seen it, if I hadn't become something else.

I kissed him gently on the mouth. "Thank you for everything, Clint," I whispered as Jean-Paul came around the corner of the car. "You were always there for me, and I'm sorry I never realized until now that—" I broke off.

Sometimes it's better not to say the words.

I hugged Jean-Paul, which startled him. He froze for a moment before relaxing and actually hugging me back. "I've missed you," I said, and I meant it. I was done with the games, done with childish things. "And I'm sorry I left the way I did. It was wrong, and I'm sorry."

He kissed me on the cheek. "I've missed you, too, boy." He pushed my head to one side teasingly.

But I won't be going to Ibiza with you.

I climbed the steps and unlocked the front door of the house.

Rachel was seated at the piano, and Nigel was on the couch, reading a magazine. They both looked up when I walked in, and Nigel smiled, clearly delighted to see me. He got up and gave me a hug. "I knew you'd be okay," he said in my ear, and then put his hands on my shoulders and examined my face. A smile played at the corners of his lips. "We have a lot to discuss, don't we?" One of his eyebrows went up.

Damn, he was good.

Rachel narrowed her eyes as she looked at me. She was trying to get inside my head, I could tell, and smiled to myself. *She can't do it anymore, and it's driving her crazy.* I struggled not to laugh out loud. She looked confused, and I winked at her.

"He's learned how to shield his mind."

I could hear her thought as clearly as if she'd spoken the words aloud.

Oh, yes, things were going to be a lot different from here on out.

"How's Jared?" I asked as the door shut behind Clint and Jean-Paul.

"Why don't you ask him yourself?" She gestured toward the bedroom door with her head. I crossed the room, slid open the pockets doors, and shut them behind me.

Jared was sitting up in the bed, wearing a white tank top that was a size too small for him. It was obviously one of mine, and his nipples were poking through the thin fabric. He put down the book he'd been reading and folded his arms. "Cord." He said it flatly, without emotion.

I resisted the urge to listen to his thoughts and sat down on the edge of the bed. "How are you?"

He shrugged, his muscled shoulders going up and down an inch or so. "Better." He gave me a humorless smile. "When I woke up and found out I'm a vampire, let's just say I wasn't in a really good place. I'm better with it now, though."

"Jared, I'm really sorry—"

"No need to apologize." He waved his hand. "What's done is done. And apparently it wasn't really your fault." He looked at me, his beautiful brown eyes sad. "I guess we were both kind of under some sort of spell. I don't understand what it's all about, but Nigel and Rachel have promised to explain it all to me."

"I don't think I understand it all myself," I replied, "but I'm beginning to." *Best to leave the explanations to them. I don't want him to know what kind of danger he'd been in.* "For what it's worth, I'm so sorry about everything. I'd never do anything to hurt you or your family."

He just nodded and didn't say anything.

I could hear the others murmuring in the other room, and I heard the front door open and close and knew Clint had gone.

To get Quentin, that's where he's going. He's all a part of this somehow too.

But I didn't want to listen in on their conversation just yet. I knew they'd tell me everything, and if they didn't, I could listen into their thoughts.

I'd certainly know if they were lying.

It no longer bothered me that Jean-Paul didn't love me. I'd listened to his thoughts in the car—it was easy, and getting easier every time I did it. I could even narrow the focus to what I wanted to know—the brain was an amazing thing. Even though we—most people, most *humans*, I kept forgetting I wasn't human anymore—think we are only thinking one thing at a time, our minds are thinking many things we aren't even aware of. We focus on what's important at that moment and think that's it. But there are thousands, maybe even millions, of thoughts racing through our brains at any given moment, and it's just a matter of focusing on one strand of thought and shutting the others out. It's something we don't even have to concentrate on within ourselves; it's second nature, like breathing or walking or whatever. So, I had focused my eyes on Jean-Paul's head and listened for my name.

It didn't hurt as much as I would have thought it would, but I *was* changing. It hadn't been a mistake to leave him and the others, to come back to New Orleans. Others may think it had been, but I didn't agree with that assessment. All of it, everything, had been set in motion by forces beyond my control long before that final explosion between Jean-Paul and me in Palm Springs. Hell, my even being with Jean-Paul in the first place hadn't been in my control; the witches had done even that. Not even Sebastian, for that matter—the one I had cursed whenever I felt frustration and anger with what I had become—had been to blame for anything. Sebastian had been nothing more than a pawn for the twin witches, for all that he had been the witchmaster.

Nico had even been playing his own brother.

Everything had happened according to Nico's design. He had moved us all around like pawns on his chessboard, and all because he had seen me in the woods when I was little more than a child and had wanted me. Nico had led me to Jean-Paul, and thus to Sebastian, and eventually away from Jean-Paul and back to New Orleans.

And I had destroyed him, and his brother, and his entire coven.

He had wanted to make me a god so that we could rule the world together.

It never occurred to him that I would have the power, the ability to destroy him.

In the end, he'd been as big a fool as the rest of us.

"It's going to take some getting used to, this whatever it is." Jared looked away from me, and I knew he was thinking about his fiancée—*Tori, her name was Tori, Tori Crawford*—and how she and his family would never know what happened to him. He would have simply disappeared while walking from his car to the restaurant, just another weird unexplained disappearance in the French Quarter. It happened all the time, and his family and loved ones would never know peace. Every time the phone rang, every time someone knocked on their front door, they would hope—and every time, their hearts would break a little more.

At least my family thought I was dead.

"When you were"—I paused to clear my throat, to think of a less offensive way to say it—"transitioning, several times you said to me you never believed I'd died in the fire. Is that true?"

He didn't look at me, just sucked his lips in and nodded. "I didn't want to believe it," he whispered. "I couldn't believe it."

I nodded and walked over. I touched the side of his face, and he leaned into my hand. "I don't understand," he went on. "I mean, back before"—he swallowed—"when I was *human*, I never thought about you in that way, you know, but now . . ."

I kissed the top of his head. "Things are different when you're a vampire," I replied. "Don't worry about it, okay? You've got a lot to learn—we both do." I patted his shoulder and walked back into the living room.

"So, what now?" I asked, crossing my arms and leaning against the wall.

Nigel stared at me, his eyes narrowed. I met his gaze evenly, and after a few moments his eyes widened. *"Oh, yes,"* I heard his voice inside my head, and knew that no one else could hear it. *"I suspected this was going to happen to you. Are you okay with this, Cord? I hope you are—because there's no turning back for you now."*

"It is what it is, Nigel. Apparently it was my destiny."

He was ancient, I knew, even more ancient than Rachel knew or suspected. He went back further than Egypt; he not only was there when the pyramids were built but also he was there when the plain at Gaza was empty of monuments. He was there when the Egyptians were little more than animals.

He went back further, and I saw the world he was from—a civilization even more advanced than the one we knew and lived in every day. For a brief moment, I saw a city of marble and sandstone, where magic and science worked together in harmony to create a world of ease and comfort no one in our time could even begin to understand or conceive of, except as—

"Heaven," I said aloud. "That's where the concept came from."

Nigel stood up and walked over to me slowly. When he got close to me, he put one hand on either side of my face and stared deep into my eyes.

And I let him in, wanted him to know.

But once he was inside, all he said was, *"You are the one."*

And he was gone.

The front door to the house opened and Quentin burst through, pushed by Clint. His face was twisted with anger, his body tense. I was tempted to send him soothing, calming energy but resisted. I was pretty sure I didn't want anyone besides Nigel to know what I had become.

What I now was.

At least, I didn't want anyone to know for now.

Quentin looked around the room, his eyes flashing angry fire no one but I could see. When his eyes came to rest on me, they widened and color drained from his face. *He knows.*

"You lied," I said, "when you told me you turned your back on your powers."

"Powers?" Jean-Paul looked at me and back at Quentin.

"He's a witch, and a powerful one," I answered, never taking my gaze from Quentin. "You didn't turn your back on your powers. You turned your back on your twin."

Quentin's jaw set and he tilted his head up defiantly. "Sebastian wanted to use his powers for darkness," he replied. "The powers are a gift from God, to be used for good, not evil. I had no desire to become a demon."

"You knew," I went on, turning to look at Nigel. "He knew all along what Sebastian and his coven were up to, even if he didn't want to be a part of it."

"What are you talking about?" Clint asked.

I laughed. "Do you want to tell them, Nigel, or should I?" Rachel started to say something, but I cut her off. "No, Rachel, Nigel hasn't been completely honest with you, either. He hasn't told you everything." I couldn't help myself from letting a taunting tone creep into my voice. Good enough for her—she was enough of a bitch to me, I reasoned. "Were you, Nigel?"

Nigel didn't answer me, and instead asked Quentin, "Who are your people, Quentin Narcisse? I can find no record of your family, and that's not possible. It is impossible that such a powerful bloodline of witches could exist without the Nightwatchers knowing."

"Did you know about Nico and Lorenzo?" I asked, not bothering to drop the mocking tone. "And their entire coven? How did you not know about Sebastian? And what they were up to?"

He turned slowly to look at me but didn't answer.

"I would suspect there's a traitor in your group, Nigel, someone who's been working with them all along." I shrugged. "All evidence of the Narcisse family has been erased from the records—because they don't want to be known, and who knows how long ago it was done? How long has the Narcisse family been pursuing their agenda with their coven, an agenda that is contrary to everything the Nightwatchers stand for?"

"You didn't even know three days ago what a Night-watcher was." Rachel didn't bother to mask the contempt in her voice. "And now you—"

"Haven't you noticed the change in him?" Nigel asked softly. "You've noticed, haven't you, Jean-Paul? Clint?" They both shook their heads. "You can't access his thoughts, can you, Rachel?" She shook her head. "He isn't masking them from us, you know. We don't have the ability to read them any longer, unless he chooses to let us in."

"But only witches—" Rachel's voice died in her throat and her eyes widened. "Oh, dear God."

"There were two branches of our family," Quentin said into the shocked silence. "The white branch and the mixed branch. The white branch—my *grandmere* always said they were evil, dedicated to evil. Our side of the family fled this area, went up north to hide in the bayous so they wouldn't know we were alive, so they couldn't use us. One of my ancestors cast a protective spell—she was a very powerful witch—so that the branch from St. Tammany Parish believed we were dead, extinct." He sat down next to me and took my hand. "I didn't want to lie to you, but I had to. Sebastian had found the other branch of the family, made contact with them, put me and my grandmother in danger. I didn't know what you knew and what you didn't know." He turned to Rachel and smiled. "I didn't even know you were vampires. But that wouldn't have made any difference. I had to be sure that my cousins didn't know I existed, otherwise they would have killed me, tried to take my power. That's what they were all about, the power."

"They used your brother," I said to him softly. "I don't

know if that's any comfort, but Sebastian wasn't dark until they turned him, you know. They were using him. They even used you, Jean-Paul."

Jean-Paul looked startled.

"Yes," Nigel replied. "They knew about this house. They knew about you and your fraternity. Jean-Paul, you hardly hid your existence. It was Nico, wasn't it? He was the more powerful, the more cunning of the two." He began explaining to them the whole plan—the plan that resulted in me being what I was now.

But he stopped short of telling them what I was, and it surprised me that none of them asked.

Nigel explained the whole sordid story of how I became a vampire.

But again he stopped short of saying what the twin witches wanted from me—and what they had made me.

When Nigel finished, silence descended upon the room.

"So," Jean-Paul said into the silence. "Gather your things, Cord. Our flight to Ibiza is early in the morning."

"I think," Nigel said slowly, "that Cord will be staying here with us for now."

Clint looked at me, his eyes confused, pleading.

I nodded. "That's right." I got up and walked over to where the two of them were standing. "Thank you for everything," I said in a soft voice. "I wish I could go with you, take up my old life again, but I'm on a different path now." As I spoke the words, I felt the power surging within me.

Jean-Paul nodded and hugged me. He walked out of the room and down the hall. Clint looked at me, his lower lip trembling. I put my arms around him and whispered, "I do love you, Clint, please know that. I'm so sorry I was so blind for so long. But now . . . now I can't be with you."

He nodded, and I felt the wetness on his cheeks when he

whispered back, "It's okay, Cord. We have eternity to be together." He kissed my cheek and followed Jean-Paul down
the hallway.

I turned back to face the three left in the room.

Nigel cleared his throat. "Jared has agreed to come with
us, Cord, to train to be a Nightwatcher. I hope you'll join
us—and you, too, Quentin."

I was startled when Quentin nodded and said it would be
an honor. *Of course, he knows all about the Nightwatchers. He
knows about everything,* I realized, shaking my head.

"I'll go get my things," Quentin said, and went out the
front door.

Rachel looked at me sourly and also got up and walked
out of the room. I heard her walking down the hallway, and
then a door opened and closed.

"Well?" Nigel asked, leaning forward with his hands on
his knees.

"Of course," I replied. "What choice do I have? I either
become a Nightwatcher, or they will try to destroy me. Isn't
that correct?"

He didn't answer me. "There may be a war coming,
Cord, one that has been long in developing. We're going to
need you—and your powers. We can train you in how to use
them, control them. You're going to have to be vigilant."

"Because power corrupts," I replied, closing my eyes.

It was there. I could feel it and took a deep breath.

I need to always be able to control it.

Because if I couldn't—

I didn't want to think about that.

"We leave at sunset tomorrow," Nigel said, getting to his
feet. "I have some research to do, if you'll excuse me." And
he left me alone in the room.

Three years earlier, I mused, I'd been a closeted frat boy

coming to Mardi Gras to get laid. For the next three years, I was a baby vampire, going from one party to another and having a good time.

And now I was something no one had ever seen before, no one had ever dealt with before.

A chill went down my spine, but I shook it off.

I could handle it—I didn't have a choice.

I went down the hall to my room to pack.